'A truly original literary mystery, and a bold meditation on care, judgement and exploitation. *Clinical Intimacy* drew me in immediately, then had me reading more urgently as its formally innovative story deepened. You gradually piece things together, never completely certain, and aware of yourself as another voice, another consciousness with its own preconceptions, in the cast of characters. Among many other qualities, Gass is able to puncture the bromides and platitudes of contemporary life – the ways some of these were thrown into sharp relief by the pandemic, and the ways in which we persist in them obliviously still. Despite this sharpness and discernment, it's a humane work that really seeks to understand. One of the human and social qualities it really wrestles with is *charm*, or even compassion and its multiple distortions. Like the best really serious novels, it's profoundly uncomfortable, avoids easy dramatic answers and forces you to really think and question – yourself as much as its own narrative. An unmissable debut.'

Luke Kennard, author of *The Transition*

'*Clinical Intimacy* is a fascinating exercise in understanding a life through the shadows it casts in other people's lives. It asks us whether great kindness can be a pathology, or if it is just pathologized by people to whom it is alien. Beautifully conceived and written, psychologically and politically acute, this is a debut of great breadth and power.'

Sandra Newman, author of *The Heavens*

CLINICAL INTIMACY

Ewan Gass

doubleday

TRANSWORLD PUBLISHERS

Penguin Random House, One Embassy Gardens, 8 Viaduct Gardens, London SW11 7BW
www.penguin.co.uk

Transworld is part of the Penguin Random House group of companies
whose addresses can be found at global.penguinrandomhouse.com

First published in Great Britain in 2024 by Doubleday
an imprint of Transworld Publishers

A CIP catalogue record for this book
is available from the British Library.

ISBNs
9780857529602 (hb)
9780857529619 (tpb)

Typeset in 13.5/19pt Perpetua MT Pro by Jouve (UK), Milton Keynes
Printed and bound in Great Britain by Clays Ltd, Elcograf S.p.A.

The authorized representative in the EEA is Penguin Random House Ireland,
Morrison Chambers, 32 Nassau Street, Dublin D02 YH68.

Penguin Random House is committed to a sustainable
future for our business, our readers and our planet. This book
is made from Forest Stewardship Council® certified paper.

Contents

Declaration

The following manuscript is submitted as supporting document 3.2 ('Audio Transcript') towards the degree of Master of Letters. The document consists of 79,330 words. I declare that the work is my own, and that I have followed the formatting guidelines throughout.

The interviews were in the first instance recorded in person. Each of these interviews was strictly time-limited, with discretionary exceptions that I explain in more detail in the 'Methodology' section of supporting document 2.2. In all other respects, I adhere to the FAR framework developed in Harris, Jackiewitz *et al.*, 'Towards a New Phenomenology of Listening: Implementing the FAR Framework', *New Frontiers in Psychology*, 73:3 (June 2004), 1045–78. This approach seeks to minimize interviewee Fatigue, to facilitate a controlled yet spontaneous Association of ideas, and to enable frequent opportunities for Reflection between recordings. Subjects were initially interviewed in their own home or residence – for reasons again expanded upon in the 'Methodology' section.

Following the outbreak of the COVID-19 pandemic, and the announcement in the UK on 23 March 2020 of a mandatory nationwide lockdown, I was forced to have recourse to voice memos, which interviewees would record remotely and then send on to me in encrypted form. (Details of these security measures can be found in the 'Ethical Considerations' subsection of supporting document 4.3.) For ease of reference, I have divided the audio transcript into three sections: 7 January–23 March 2020 ('Outbreak'); 23 March–28 May 2020 ('Distancing'); 28 May–30 July 2020 ('Easing'). Three appendices provide relevant supporting documents.

Other than the removal of redundancy or very occasional irrelevance, I have not sought to emend the recordings in any way in my transcript of them. My punctuation attempts to recreate the natural rhythms of spoken English; italics denote emphasis, or the direct rendering of another's thought or speech; and asterisks indicate where an interviewee recorded separate voice memos in one sitting. I reproduce the interviews in the order in which they were conducted; the numbering of interviewees, by contrast (see below), reflects the order in which I first made contact with each of them. While I encouraged each speaker to recollect the relevant events in chronological order, this was – for understandable reasons – not always possible. The reader should therefore anticipate some redundancy and recursion.

Several individuals with whom I would like to have spoken did not feel comfortable putting their thoughts on record. This therefore remains only a partial account.

The anonymity of those prepared to go on record is of paramount importance. In the following, I therefore employ a crude series of abbreviations, which indicate the nature of the relation of the person in question to the principal Subject (S). Persons are divided into 'family' (A), 'significant friends and acquaintances' (B) and 'clients' (C). S comes from a small family of direct kinship, as the table below indicates. The distinction between significant acquaintance (B) and client (C) proves somewhat porous; I nevertheless retain it for reasons of expediency.

	I	2	3	4	5	6	7
A (*family*)	mother	father	sister	wife	uncle		
B (*friends*)	→	→	→	→			
C (*clients*)	→	→	→	→	→	→	→

I would like to extend my thanks to the Arts and Humanities Research Council for having funded this research in the first instance; and for having offered further discretionary funding so as to provide smartphones. I am grateful for the support and resources of my host institution; I am even grateful for their refusal of my application for an extension to the submission deadline – which forced me to produce this dissertation with an undue haste whose benefits I was ultimately able to perceive. In the context of the present circumstances, many of us fall prey to feeling our work holds little or no significance. But I have come to believe we owe it to those who have suffered – in ways most can barely imagine – to try to keep working, and to find meaning or common feeling where we can. Perhaps we can also attune ourselves to the longstanding suffering of others – which we might previously have overlooked.

This work is dedicated to my parents, who always encouraged me to keep both an open mind and an open heart.

I

7 JANUARY–23 MARCH 2020

('Outbreak')

DIRECTIONS TO INTERVIEWEES

In the week before our session, try to think about the history of your interactions with S. Do not do so in a structured manner – I am interested in the personal nature of your reminiscences, rather than comprehensiveness or analysis. Try to focus on sensations and details, rather than logical connections. Do not over-prepare in the form of notes, scripts, etc. Before our sessions begin, I will invite you to close your eyes for a period of twenty minutes. This time may involve some further recollection of S – although there is no obligation for it to consist of anything whatsoever. Do not seek to banish seemingly extraneous ideas or associational trains of thought – these may prove useful to your recollections. Following this period, you will speak about your reminiscences for a further twenty minutes. Do not concern yourself with specific phrasings, or the correction of perceived mistakes. During this period I will not seek to prompt you in any way, or to respond to any questions or appeals to involve me. Do not let silences disconcert you.

A I

I was thinking – just now, when I had my eyes closed. I know you told me to try to think about nothing, but I was thinking back to when I first learned I was pregnant with S. I felt calm, numb. I think partly because of the way I lost my first. Spina bifida – they try to cover up the truth with a Latin word, but the sound of it, *bifida*, only brings out the awfulness. The child would've been born with a curved spine. Even now I can't bring myself to use a pronoun. We learned midway through the first trimester. You can't see much on the ultrasound at that stage – it's a mercy. We wanted to keep the sex a surprise – then we kept wanting not to know, only for different reasons. Knowing would have stopped the spina bifida being unreal. Stopped it being a foreign term. Maybe I speak for myself. I was never fully sure what he was thinking. In the corridors, at the clinic, A2 walked a little behind me, which was strange, when, as a rule, he went ahead. Car keys jangling from his fingers. Everything was clear when I was sitting in the dark – but now I'm talking, I'm losing the thread.

I miscarried soon after – just as the doctors said I probably would – which took the decision out of our hands. Though we both knew we'd already made it. We knew it without saying anything, by the way we looked at one another when I started bleeding. It was tangible. Relief. You'll cut out everything you don't need, I suppose. You'll cut out this?

We didn't go back to trying in an organized way, like before. When I saw the line on the pregnancy kit, I just told myself, *That doesn't belong to me, that red line doesn't mean what it meant the first time round.* You had to wait two hours, in the late seventies – the kits often gave false results. I remember unlocking the toilet door – we always kept it not just shut but locked, I suppose we'd missed the window in our married life where we could've started to open up – going downstairs and putting the positive test on the newspaper in front of him, just to the left of the plate of toast he didn't stop eating, thinking to myself, *You have time while his back's turned to prepare the right face, the face you know from the women in the films. Let him carry you in his slipstream.* And he did. He carried me all the way.

But the numbness lasted. You said to just describe it all without worrying how or whether it fits in, so that's what I'm doing. It was honestly hard to know anything was happening in there. Everything felt lighter than the first time. I barely even chucked up. *Your body is prepared*, they all said. *The piping is laid down.* Because a woman equals plumbing. Ha. I felt nothing until the panic hit at the twelve-week check. *I can't do this I can't do this I can't do this.* Sitting in the waiting room, I could only breathe by saying those four words, over and over, until I remembered what they meant, and couldn't breathe again. Funny how lucid you are at moments like that. Moments when you're losing your mind. Like your car keys – you see them so clearly when you've lost them. I remember thinking, *Would I be shaking like this, talking uncontrollably like this, if there was even one other person in the room? Probably not. Probably you'd be smiling and pretending to read* House and Home *or whichever magazine's at the top of that pile on the table. So, you can't be really and truly going mad, when you think about it – no, not if you can control it in front of other people. So it would be fair to say that if in a moment you're wriggling on the floor, having a fit, it's because you'll have willed it, you silly cow, you'd even be enjoying the attention.* That was how I reasoned with myself, how I punished myself, while my body was shaking. A2 was holding me by the shoulders. Telling me the second time always goes more smoothly. I stopped shaking – but not because he'd reassured me that it was going to go smoothly. Because I didn't want him to know how little my fear had to do with it going smoothly.

I can admit it now. It wasn't losing another one I was worried about. It was having it. Having *him*. By this stage we used the pronoun. I was terrified of him making me a mother. When I wasn't cut out for it. That was how my mother used to phrase it. *Some people just aren't cut out for it.* Like we have little dashed lines – for the scissors – to show our limits. And I knew motherhood was my dashed line. *You'll learn, every new mother starts from scratch, you tap unsuspected reserves.* I'm talking as they did – but they didn't understand what was wrong with me. Nor did I – but I knew it was wrong with me. I had fantasies about shutting my swollen body down through sheer force of will. Dragging it around the streets like over-ripe fruit that never falls from the tree, while it – while he – finished his whole infancy inside me, carried on growing. Those dreams I had, grotesque. Changing the food I ate to suit his adolescent hunger – burgers, chips and Coca-Cola. I slept so badly that when the dreams did come, in the hour before dawn, they were vivid. We'd taped the pale curtains with brown cellophane to block the light. Maybe all sorts of women feel like this – but it certainly never came up at those antenatal groups where the fertile

women I remembered from before were already back for
their second or third. I tried to tell A2 – *I won't be able to
do this, I won't know what to do.* He told me statistics
showed how common it was to have doubts. They'd given
us piles of literature. He made a show of reading it. *You
don't know how caring you are*, he said. He was right. I didn't
know how caring I was.

Then I suddenly felt calm again – the calm of
resignation. My God, do you know, I had no idea how
much I needed to say this, until I started saying it. Even
though it's not what you need. Resigned that I couldn't
prevent the child from being born. Resigned to be unable
to mother him. At first it would hurt – but only at
first. Soon the routine visit would come – perhaps an
anonymous tip-off. The social worker would quickly grasp
the gravity of the situation. I saw it so clearly. Maybe the
visions came from the hormones. The social worker came
dressed nicely in a blue skirt. She could see I was tired, so
tired, she might say something about this not being
uncommon. She'd bend down and with great professional
competence scoop up my child, who stopped crying
instantaneously. She'd allow me to walk to the front step
and wave them off. Sometimes as a consolation I'd let
myself write a little coda – where I could see him, all

grown up, with a foster-mother who looked like one of the experienced women from the antenatal classes. She'd taught him the names of all the flowers that grew in the front gardens, which I always forgot. She'd let me visit him briefly three times a year.

I was about to burst with more than a baby when my waters broke, two weeks late – too early even so. *Now it's happening*, I thought, over and over and over, in the passenger seat. *Now they're going to take him from me*. A2 could probably hear me repeating this through gritted teeth – presuming I meant the midwives, meant 'take away' in a positive sense. Listen to me rattle on. It's been so long since I talked. I mean *really* talked. I kept waiting for the traffic jam. It happened in the movies, the frantic dash – you know the part, where the husband carries the wife for the final stretch, shouting like a madman when he reaches the hospital gates. But the streets were empty. He held my hand – strange, he used to hold it more when driving than anywhere else. Sometimes I thought he only held it as an excuse to steer with just one hand, which he liked to do. I was in awe of the way he could steer and signal and work the clutch all with his free hand, the weaker of the two. He stroked me tenderly, like he meant it, with his other hand – all the way until he killed the engine.

Then I was slowly travelling back to myself in the delivery room, realizing, as the numbness faded, that I was the body that had just done that. I'd needed the epidural – having stupidly held off until I'd had to beg. The child was the first thing I saw – all these bits of what used to be me still stuck to him. The nurse was about to wipe him down, but I shocked myself by making this animal sound, gesturing I needed him to be brought to me, without delay. I don't know if you know the sort of sound I mean – the sort of need I mean. I don't want to presume anything about you – I know how it feels for people to presume things about you. A friend of mine had just had a seriously premature baby. I remember her telling me how he was small enough to fit into a large freezer bag – how he had so little fat he seemed nearly transparent, how his early skin bruised so easily she had to touch him with special gloves for the first two weeks. I was thinking of her and of how lucky I was as I tried and failed to smooth out all the red crinkles on this small shrivelled and shivering thing, realizing that in the end it would be fine – that time would smooth out the crinkles all by itself. I was starting to say to him, *S, my S*, because I knew right then which of the names we'd been considering was his name, as he bawled in my arms and then stopped bawling. The alarm means we need to stop. I get it – just

9

let me finish. I realized as I stroked his bare scalp that I understood how to stroke him. I didn't know where the knowledge came from – but there it was, fully formed. Sometimes those idiotic things people say turn out to be true. I knew or thought I knew that only this stroking could keep him alive. I knew I'd never truly felt my body until this moment. Not by myself, not with anyone else – not even when I used to go riding as a young girl. The realization might have depressed me, except the happiness was flooding through my body, as the sensation returned, the irrelevant pain, as I stroked him. I knew. I knew he wasn't going to be taken from me.

We're going to help one another, I said to my baby, stupidly, as if he could understand. *We're going to help one another grow.* I could read the nurse's indulgent face. It said, *In this state you just have to let them get away with everything.* It's time to stop.

B I

I've remembered our first meeting so often, I'm less and less sure whether it actually happened. There's a name for them – false memories. I suppose false memories reveal something. Might even show more than the truth – show what I wanted S to be. You're recording? Our classes merged in primary school. Late eighties, class sizes ballooning – not that we had much to complain about, in our affluent-catchment-area, Church of England school. Mumbling hymns in the morning assembly. *I am the Lord of the Dance, said He.* We sang 'dance settee' instead of 'said he'. Inaudible rebellions. Screen memories. That's what they're called.

They had us pray in the afternoons. That's actually my first memory of S. *Say thank you for all the things you should be grateful for. Thank you, God, for Mummy, for Grandpa, for Grandma, for each of my collection of stick insects.* I always got stuck after pizza, for what to thank God for. We had to close our eyes – just like you had me do, a minute ago. They dimmed the room. Some children would fall asleep – drool, pick their noses. By that age you haven't forgotten you're an animal. One day I opened my eyes – to prove God didn't exist. Just a crack at first. I still remember the terror – that the light flooding my vision was a thunderbolt, sent by the Creator, to punish a little boy for not believing. That was when I saw S. His eyes were open wide. He was pulling faces. He had a big smile. Then he scrunched up his face and looked angry. Then he stuck his tongue out and waggled it – like a crazy person. Then he looked so sad I thought he'd cry. When our eyes met, his face froze. The first and only time I ever saw him blush.

I plucked up the courage to approach him –
afterwards, in the concrete playground where the boys
played football and the girls did hopscotch. I asked him
what he'd been doing at prayer-time. He told me he was
practising his emotions, while nobody was looking. Then
wondered – as if there were some logical connection –
what I thought would happen if we suddenly screamed in
the midst of the school assembly. I had a strange feeling in
my stomach at the question. As if somewhere I'd already
wondered it myself, in those exact same words, only then
forgotten. I couldn't stop fantasizing about it. Screaming
abruptly, when the whole school stood up to greet the
headmaster – the thought made me dizzy, the feeling you
get at the top of a high building. Sometimes I covered my
mouth with my hand, to toy with the idea I was about to
do it – playing with it, like a child plays with a wobbly
tooth, hanging by a thread, with its tongue. *They'd expel us*,
S said confidently. *If we ever did.* I imagine my mother was
anxious that evening, when I asked her what the word
meant. I dreamed about it. S and me – expelled, for
revealing ourselves.

But it properly began with the photographs. That
memory *is* clear. A group of children were having a heated
discussion about the afterlife. The way kids talk – with
absolute conviction, when they have no idea. Drugs,

making babies, why Freddie Mercury was ill. What happens when you die. Everyone had a theory. A Jehovah's Witness had to fight back the tears when he explained we wouldn't be able to play together in heaven. S kept quiet – I followed suit. Later, when it was just the two of us, he whispered he knew the truth. About the afterlife. I was burning to know – cared less about the secret than I did about its revelation – the privacy of its revelation. Right from the start, intimacy means conspiracy. Against the world. S asked me what I thought happened when we blink our eyes. It seemed obvious – but when I thought about it, I realized I had no idea. I stood there, stupidly. Waiting for S to enlighten me. *Every time we blink our eyes*, he said, *our mind takes a photograph. The photos develop from the moment you die. Heaven's a darkroom. So think before you blink!*

From that point on, we were undercover spies, with hidden cameras, only better – they were always at just the right level. When I saw something I liked, I blinked. My best marble. My toy cars, frozen at high speed, racing down the carpeted stairs – I took a photo. My mother never had to complain again about nearly breaking her neck. My mother's hands. I held my eyes until they watered, to avoid taking photographs I didn't want. The woman with several chins who came when the usual babysitter was busy. Got stupidly angry when I let my guard slip and took a snapshot by mistake. Cropped my stepdad from each family portrait – every three months, standing at the exact same spot, by Grandma's mulberry tree. Little Stalin. I started actually to see the world – now I knew I'd have to live with it for eternity. The day the rougher boys were kicking that puny kid around. *Odd Bod*, they used to call him. He had a speech defect. I did nothing. I took photos – for some higher authority to act on them.

Sometimes I tried to work out what S saw in the world. A field trip to the coal-fired power station – our school's idea of a nice day out. Trying to work out what he could see that I couldn't, in the curve of the smokestack against the horizon – rain drizzling, smoke billowing. The homeless man who used to lie on the ground near the school gates. Today's parents would have had him removed. His long, yellow, curving fingernails. The older children used to torment him by laughing hysterically in his face – laughing until they turned red. I forced myself to do the same – until S told me about the photographs he'd taken of his sleeping bag, moving up and down as the homeless man breathed in and out.

Maybe they're already developing – even before we get to the darkroom. I've kept the negatives, if nothing else. At times I felt almost convinced S only pretended not to notice – when I couldn't fight the urge to blink straight at him.

A3

Tell us the story, they all used to say. *Tell us the story how you came into the world.* Expectant faces, the whole family. So right from the start it was really all about S. We learned it by heart. Performed our little pantomime. The story of how my brother tried to kill me before I knew my own name. Me, lying on the ground, squirming like a newborn, *wah wah wah*, while he leaned over me, squirting imaginary hair conditioner in my eyes, for the thousandth time – just like he had for real, when he'd wanted to get rid of this new thing that had come into the world just to spoil his fun. To steal his attention. As if. As if I ever stole the slightest fraction of his attention. He danced while I lay on the floor.

They laughed. They always laughed, even Grandma, Grandad, who never did – laughter being the original sin. I'm starting to get resentful. Can feel it building up in me. Very clever of you – to put a tape recorder in front of people, get them to start talking. Mum'll love it. I'm only doing this for her sake. She always was a great talker. She'll

talk and talk, analyse it all by herself – do your job
for you. She'll use all the right words. That was always
one of the things they had in common. Very articulate.
You might need to polish me up a bit, I'm afraid. They
could always explain to me, using just the right words,
why it was I was wrong. *A3, do you know you have a very
articulate brother? – Yes, I know, thank you for the useful
information.*

I don't want to sound like this. Mum's got it into her
head that somehow you can help. As if you're going to put
in a kind word for S. Get some glowing testimonials
about what a nice chap he really is – drop off your audio
tapes for the police, or for the journalists, or for the
judge, or for the prime minister. Make us all anonymous
whistle-blowers – for what, I don't know. Cut my part,
when you do. I've never liked the sound of my own voice,
particularly when it comes out sarcastic. Of course I'm
worried about my brother. If I thought there was
something I could do, say, I'd do it – say it. But talking
won't help. Mum's always been naive that way. The power
of words! She'll analyse it, turn it into a story. Then one of
the details will change – she'll give you another story, just
as pretty, that has nothing in common with the first.

You know what I thought about in those twenty
minutes? I'll tell you. *Where are the thuds?* Sorry not to give

you something more profound. *Where are the thuds?* I
thought. *Because pretty soon there'll be thuds, and if they're
not kicking lumps out of one another, left to their own devices,
it's probably a sign of something worse.* With two young boys,
that's what troubles you most. Silence.

Imagine filling the tape with my little stories. My daily
routines. Great entertainment that'd make! Harassed
mother worries whether she can take her two boys back
to the café where last week her youngest dragged a
woman's bag across the floor until she prised it off his
hand, peeling each finger back, one by one, until he burst
into tears, and me, hating this woman, not being able to
say it out loud – not with everyone sitting there, looking
over the tops of their laptops, judging the indulgent
mother.

Don't worry, I'll get back to S. I'll get back to S, so you
don't have to listen to me. But this will be the first and the
last time. I told Mum I'd do this, but I'm realizing as I talk,
I can't. I don't want to feel that old resentment – even if I
had the time. I'll talk until the tape runs out, but that's it,
I'm afraid. Not that I'd have been of much use in any case.
I have no idea when it started, how it started, how he
ended up in such a mess, how he ended up so *interesting* –
interesting enough that you turn up. You asked for early
memories. Only our little pantomimes came to mind, and

then I was nearly half asleep. It's become my one talent. Give me five free minutes, I'll fall asleep on the spot, standing on my feet.

There was only one thing, when I came to, at the thud that never came, one small memory. I'll tell you, because I promised I would. It was one of those endless car journeys. Family holidays to Grandad's chalet. It was really a caravan, but we called it a chalet. Guess we had aspirations. I hated being strapped in. *Are we nearly there yet, are we nearly there yet?* I must have been a right pain. S behaved himself well – of course he did. The way he sat there, colouring in with crayons, reading, absorbed, made you need to misbehave. Then I saw it. Crawling slowly across his bare arm, green-purple, flickering legs. Flies brought dirt – we learned that at school. It must have got trapped. Dad liked the windows open but would shut them in the tunnels, because of the exhaust fumes. The fly crawled slowly over my brother's skin. My brother sat there, perfectly still. I saw his gooseflesh, as if in close-up, and a shiver went down my spine. It still does today. For once I stopped thrashing around, stopped kicking the back of the driver's seat, frozen, watching him, while he let a fly crawl along his arm. I couldn't look away. Why was he doing it, I wanted to know, why was he doing nothing. Maybe he enjoyed it. Maybe he couldn't stop it. Couldn't stop a fly. I've given you the little I have. I don't want to kick you out. Finish your tea, it's getting cold.

C5

I remember that guy so well! You say his name is S? Kind of funny how I never did think to ask. Kind of funny how I couldn't draw you a picture of the man – what with how observant I normally am. The teachers all did tell me how observant I was. *C5, they told me, you notice things.* And I did. Like details of a person's attire, or what have you. Or when something is moved just a little bit from where it was. Not that noticing gets you very far. It doesn't get you very far in this world. Sometimes I think to myself, *C5, if you're so damn good at noticing, you must be able to use that for something in the world.* I don't mean being no security guard. No looking at people on grainy videos. One of them teachers – the one that told me how I was observant and all, I liked her – she said maybe I could be a drawer, illustrator. I figured she was joking – till I saw from her eyes she was for real! Nope – that ain't my thing. Sitting still, looking at some apple all the way over across the room. Bit more red. Bit more yellow. Dab dab dab, dib dib dib. Ain't my thing. I need to get up close to things – feel them push back at you.

How you get to know what that thing is where you can excel – when you never get the chance to do it? Woodwork. Maybe I could have been good at the woodwork – with those machines that hold the blocks in place. Hell, I don't know what I'm talking about – woodwork probably isn't even the proper name. *Carpentry*. Well, where I came from there was no *carpentry*. Go work for chump change in the dime store, or pull in real money hustling. Motherfucking carpentry. How you get to know if you can do it if you don't get the chance to do it? Guess I'm getting old enough now that I never will know. You need money even to start. Like everything.

Yeah, I'm taking the long road around, I know it. They say to me, *C5, how you gonna stick to a job if you can't stick to a track of thought?* Maybe I go the long way round. But I find my own way to where I need to get. S let me tell my story. At first I took him for just one more of those guys who try to explain in fancy words how to eat asparagus. How to be an integrated person in society. The centre used to give us asparagus guy after asparagus guy – only now the money's gone. Go ask the men in suits where – then translate it back out of gobbledegook for the rest of us. But when S sits down near to me, I can see he's different. Firstly – he looks at me. Sounds simple, but it's not. Secondly, he comes up with none of that bullshit about how difficult I must have had it. Let me be the judge of how difficult I must have had it.

So he gets me talking. I couldn't begin to tell you the things I say to him. We only had half an hour. He sits down – real close to me, which normally makes me uncomfortable. Only this time before I know it, I'm telling him about all the things that happen to me, like I've been storing them up – well, I *have* been storing them up. Shit, the things I told him. About never having felt at home. Not when I was a kid and I actually had a home – 125th and Lexington. About how the choice when you're eight isn't whether or not to run shit, but whether the shit you run is dope or weed – and I count myself lucky crack still wasn't on the scene.

Told him how my dad called me back down to live with him in Georgia – he could see the way that neighbourhood was going. He was already a big fancy doctor, with an airbrushed photo on his webpage, one of the few to make it. Now he even has letters after his name and a building named after him – not that he gave much of what he got to the woman who brought me into this world.

Told him how at school the Southern kids talk in this way I'm not used to – I'm one of three black kids, the others don't need to be told to tuck their shirts in. Then when after four years I'm finally used to being cooked in that summer heat, I get called back to the city – Dad having gotten tired of me or cured me – only now it's not my city no more. At the block parties, when everyone is doing the robot or the pop 'n' lock, they all say, *Dawg, what happened to you, you be dancin' like a Southern boy, for real, hoedown style.* When I open my mouth, they say to me, *Dawg, what done happened to you, you be talkin' like a white boy, you a regular Uncle Tom, tap dancer.* And I tell S how I keep my head down enough to get through college, so I can follow the one who back then was the love of my life, all the way to this island, where I can barely keep the food down. No more at home here than I was off Lexington, or in Georgia – only now I've come to like the feeling of not being at home – don't know what it would *be* to feel at home. Along the way I lost my language and picked up other ways to talk, bit from here, bit from there – so I speak like nobody, speak like everybody. And I realize too late she really *was* the love of my life, so I decide to stay in this island to win her back, though I don't – win her back – but I do like the work. I'm starting to work with young offenders, delinquents. They respect me because of where I'm from – sure, I play up my accent from time to time. And I have so many ideas for how to take this shit further, setting up my own centre, but this was back when all the money ran out and so they started to shut down or scale back. A new guy took over and suddenly there were complaints about me – I never learned the details or who was behind them. I let myself be persuaded I had prospects. It was a bad time, bad investments. Each time I tell myself, *C5, you trust too easy* – like even now, telling you the ins and outs of my life, when I don't even know you. And I'm getting to thinking, *I need a way out, there's no way out. I need a way out, there's no way out.* I'm walking, to nowhere, telling myself, *Each fork in the road, choose the bigger road – you might finally end up somewhere.* Till I'm out on the big roads, and then I'm walking on Spaghetti Junction. There's no place for no pedestrians on the side – I can feel the cars as they whizz past – and I see on this green traffic board, in big letters, WALES 150 MILES, and I think to myself, *Wales, maybe that's where I'm supposed to go. Never been there – it sure can't be worse than here – plus one-fifty is a nice round number.* So off I set. Those cars still are whizzing past. From time to time I get to thinking one or another be slowing down, only I can't make out what anyone shouts, supposing they wind down the window. My head is swimming from the exhaust fumes – *there's just a little further to go*, I tell myself, *till I get to Wales* – when I see the cars all move inside to let an ambulance past. *Must have been a crash*, I tell myself, because those lights are flashing like with the emergencies – only then the ambulance slows down. *It's coming for me*, I tell myself. It pulls over into the hard shoulder – you see I learned all the words – and this guy climbs down from the ambulance, not even wearing a white coat like he's supposed to, and from nowhere I'm falling on to him, and these tears are streaming down my face, and I'm asking him, over and over, *Are you here to take me to Wales? – We're going to take you where you're safe*, he says, and I try to explain everything about how I'm only trying to get to Wales because of how the system has messed me around. But he injects this liquid into me, and it makes it so that even though I can form the words real clear in my head, my mouth can't get to saying them out loud – and he's reading from a script about being sectioned under Section 37 of the Mental Health Act, telling me I'm lucky to be going where I'm going, this centre has contacts with outside providers who can make me well. So here I still am, and apparently they can't say whether I'm well yet – feels like I've been waiting for ever for the letter that tells me I can go. *But the one thing*, I tell S, *the one thing that keeps me going is my story, the story of my life – I have it so clear in my head, all I need is the one person who can write it down for me. The last time I was out for a long stretch, I got in touch with Jeffrey Archer, because I thought he was the man to do it.*

When it came out of my mouth, my story sounded so different to how it sounds now. Like how I wanted it to sound. It had details I've clean forgot. S sits there and somehow I know he hears me. The only thing he says is, *Jeffrey Archer, explain it to me, why Jeffrey Archer?* So I explain how Jeffrey Archer has done time inside. I read about it in the newspaper. *If he's done time, he knows about the kind of places I come from – but then he's educated, being a writer, so he can make my story sound like I should.* Now S is starting to smile. Don't remember much about his face – but I sure remember that smile. Now all of a sudden we're both laughing. You know the way you laugh with someone – one of you manages to stop but then the other one starts again. It hurts to laugh so hard. I don't know what I'm laughing at – but it feels good.

So what did Jeffrey Archer say? S wants to know. I tell him about the appointment I made with his secretary, after Jeffrey Archer asks how on earth I got his number – he sounds just like I imagined. How I travel on this train and then this village bus, to his village – all the straw roofs and beautiful blossom and don't ask me what – and how Jeffrey Archer's assistant greets me. How uptight I get, pretending to like the tea, feeling all tight in this suit – I'd filled out since the last time I wore it – then finally the big man himself comes down – only stays for five minutes, so I have to tell it too quickly. After a while he cuts me off and tells me how the early years have promise, Lexington and 125th – he seems more interested in the hustling than everything else, even though I tell him that never really was my world. Tells me there might be something there. You can tell a white person from the way they say *ghetto*. He gives me his card – which I only went and lost in the rush of the move.

Don't do it, S said – now he's not smiling – *don't write your story that way. Set it down just like you told me, from beginning to end*. I ask him the thought that's been dawning on me. Was this why he came – to help me write my story? S goes quiet. I keep thinking he's going to say, *Yes, I'm here to help you write your story* – but then this look of confusion comes on his face. *Why do you* think *I'm here?* he asks. And I tell him I don't know – the centre sends these people, the asparagus people, the people that make you hit the carpet when you imagine it's your mother. Then comes the familiar knock at the door – only for once I don't want to hear it. Time to finish off. *So will you come back?* I ask. But by now I know the real answer. I know it by the way he's talking to the attendant in the hallway – hushed tones – then S leaves. He's smiling, but the smile is different to before. Like the smile you smile when you're sad, or when a thing is beautiful. Who the fuck am I kidding? Like he finds my story beautiful. When he's gone, it hits me – no way to make contact with the guy. No Jeffrey Archer business card. Don't even know the man's name.

I forced myself to forget it, these past two years, until you showed up. Otherwise it was too painful. Now it's all coming back. I asked the administrator if I could see him again. He said something about how regretfully there'd been a clerical error. Which I took to mean no – not the slightest chance of him coming back. I tried to scratch out some of the things I said to S – with this old ballpoint pen of mine – but my wrist starts to cramp in this room. My bones must be getting old. Maybe you can even put me back in touch – with S. I'm learning to use his name, sitting here with you now. You think you can give him a nudge – remind him about my story? I just nodded when the administrator replied. Though who knows what the word *clerical* even means.

B1

Thanks for rearranging at such short notice. Like just about every care home, we're down by a third of our staff over the last two years. When the agency can't provide cover, which happens more and more, it falls to yours truly. Because I'm so caring. Because I can't say no. You choose which. It's probably the relevant question – now I think about it – if you want to figure out S.

The care home. Don't get me started on work. If I start, I won't ever stop. I've been doing an even worse job than usual – pretending to pay attention to them when they tell me their stories. Since you first came, I've been remembering little details for the first time in decades. It came to me, the name of the parallel world that S and I created. Hole of Ice. HOI, we used to scribble, in the margins of our schoolbooks, sketching glaciers and frozen lakes. I spent half my adolescence trying to erase, in my mind, what we wrote, with coloured pens. That's a good way to define growing up – learning to feel ashamed. Learning shame, to cope with what you can't get back.

Our parallel world mirrored everything that mattered in real life. Parents, schoolmates, celebrities became, in no particular order, princes, tyrants, peasants. At first we used to replay whatever had happened that day, controlling it by reliving it, in our frozen country. Then the order was reversed. From one day to the next, without warning or explanation, we stopped talking to a boy in our class, all because of something his alter ego had said. I learned how to cope with the real world, by forgetting it was real. I'd always been scared in the swimming lessons to dive down to retrieve the black brick at the bottom of the pool, until it suddenly became a precious treasure.

Now that they no longer sprang from reality, I had no idea how to keep up with S's plot twists. To come up with some of my own. I became terrified that S would grow bored and leave the world we'd drawn in such loving detail. Leave me. To go and play football, or tag, or just play 'rough' – as Mum called it – with the other boys. For a whole fortnight he did play football. He insisted it was an undercover mission. To understand how the other side thought. I'd written him off, was amazed when he walked back to me in the playground, a big smile on his face.

S hid our parallel life. He incorporated it in the real world – where he'd started to excel. Much more than me, who only had a black brick to show. He won a prize at school for a story, which he read out loud, winking at me when he got to the hidden references. He swore he was only racing through his maths exercises in order to spend more time on our stories, which by now stretched to hundreds of pages. It never stopped him getting top marks. One day our world suffered a cataclysmic change. From then on we wrote HOA in the margins. Hole of Acid. The frozen lands melted, everything was bathed in a yellow glow with the aid of the sketching set he'd got for Christmas in our final year at primary school. Perhaps it was our way of acknowledging that we couldn't stop the world we'd made from coming to an end, of its own accord.

At night I fantasized about dilemmas. I had to put to death one of two people close to me. Tell me other children do this? In fact, don't. S or my stepdad was easy. I got a sick thrill from rehearsing my speech for when he climbed the scaffold. I was going to be magnanimous at the last, you see. S or Mum? More difficult. I enjoyed the difficulty, lying in bed. S or me? Easier. How noble, to be the martyr, for the sake of him, for the sake of us, which he'd carry in him, in all the marvellous things he'd go on to achieve. S or God? No hesitation. He wasn't real, anyhow. That was the first night I ever failed to fall asleep. I couldn't work out why, if He didn't exist, I was feeling so guilty. Hold on. It's the care home. I felt the phone vibrating in my pocket the whole while. I was speaking to try and ignore it – but I'm going to have to go in.

A 1

Your body forgets. Your mind has nothing to do with it. My body was forgetting S, even when he was still young. I kept a journal, to try to record the sensations from those first weeks. Glued in the wristband I had on when they discharged me, next to S's own tiny bracelet. They snipped his off, like another umbilical cord. I kept mine on, until A2 told me it was unhygienic. The journal was an old wedding present that had lain empty all that time. It must be at the bottom of one of those boxes upstairs. The stitching on the spine has come loose. I'll know it as soon as I see it.

I started writing when A2 finished his paternity leave. The company gave him ten days. He buckled on the eighth, said he had some things to sort through in the office, and a couple of hours turned into the whole afternoon, and then the next day too, and from then on business as usual – worse than usual, because they were going through a restructuring. I wondered whether I had the right to say *I* was going through a restructuring. I hadn't realized how much newborns sleep. At first I fussed over him. Woke him, in my anxiety. Then I learned to trust his heart would keep beating, that his little mouth would keep taking breaths. And I surprised myself at how alone I felt. If I'd ever been that alone before, I'd never felt it. There had been my family, then A2. I didn't know what to do with myself. I needed to put my love somewhere. So I started to write.

I addressed it to S. I wanted to tell him, the person he'd become, that I was watching him sleep, wanted to embarrass him by telling him how beautiful he'd been. But pretty soon I was writing to no one. For no one. Which explains how I could be so honest. I couldn't even tell you, today, what I wrote in that journal. I was so tired I could barely hold the pen – but knew that if I let it slide for even a second, I'd fall asleep for hours and forget what I needed to say. The handwriting must be illegible.

Then one day A2 found it. I didn't think I was hiding it – the journal – just putting it in its appointed spot. He'd gone up into the attic looking for a blanket. The bed got cold, he complained, when I got up to feed S, and I was never back for long enough to warm it. *What's this*, he said, *what's this you're hiding?* – *Read it*, I said. *There are only good things inside.* I could already only barely remember what I'd written. *I've read the first pages*, he said. *I can tell you I have no desire to carry on.*

S used to point his finger at something and say *duh-duh.* Meaning, *What's that?* And I realized I had no idea. Even if I knew the word. And so I made myself look at it properly, for the first time, and he and I could explain the world to ourselves. Those lift-the-flap books. I used to hear my voice, and think, *You've never sounded so fluent, but deep down you don't know the meaning of any of these things you're pointing at.* So we learned them together. We learned the words for things and those things started to pop up everywhere. I remember stroking the raggedy edges of the books, which he'd chewed before he could read, because I didn't want to overwhelm him with my love. Then he was reading for himself. Lying there snug in the crook of my arm, so that his voice reverberated through my body. When he stumbled over a word, I blamed myself. When he mastered the pronunciation, I pulled him close, so that his voice could keep echoing in me.

I knew almost from the start that our bond unsettled A2. *You can only really interact with them*, he told me, time and time again, *once they learn to speak.* I didn't contradict him. I didn't tell him they speak to you most of all before they babble. When S began to speak in full sentences, A2 started on about all the perils of only children. They grew up spoiled or needy or insecure. Or 'too much in their own heads'. You can tell whoever listens to this tape that I'm making scare quotes with my hands. He was trying somewhat unsubtly to tell me that S would grow up to be just like me. That we'd be two peas in a pod, thoughtful and isolated. So then, not isolated. No, he'd be isolated. We had to keep moving, he insisted. I think it was around now I started noticing how he drummed his fingers on the table. Strange how you can be with someone for a decade and suddenly notice such things. Moving, keep moving. Before the kids, each year we had to travel a little further in France, because what was the point in sticking to what you knew, however nice it was? We got nearly as far as the Spanish border – then the holidays stopped.

I don't know what to tell you about how it was when A3 came into our lives. I think I'm apprehensive, after what she said to me the other day. After you recorded her. She told me some very hurtful things – even though I kept telling her it doesn't matter whether she does or doesn't speak to you. In any case, that time was all such a daze. The journal was already in the box. I'd told myself it would be easier, because this time I knew what to do, but none of the things that worked with S worked with A3. She wouldn't keep still. I knew it was unfair, but I couldn't stop myself seeing his drumming fingers in her – putting all my frustration at the south of France into this squirming little thing who wouldn't stay still, when it's just they don't, newborns, most of them at least.

I don't know what you're talking about, A2 said. *She's placid as can be.* And it was true – when he dandled her on his knee, she immediately started to gurgle with pleasure. He was there less than ever, to dandle, despite what he'd said about the IT retraining making his hours more flexible. I tried it, to jiggle her up and down, on my knee, just like he did. It never worked, though – she screamed her head off.

And S, sitting quietly by himself. By then he'd become a confident reader.

That time's a blank. A jumble of images. Feeling guilty about trivial things. Giving in when they screamed at me from the back seat to roll down the window at the service station – they liked the smell of petrol. Letting them lick the batter off the spoon. Good mothers were supposed to worry about salmonella. If I rattle on, it's only because I've never talked about this. Not even with the other mothers. Particularly not the other mothers. That was all we talked about, endlessly – our children – but we somehow managed to say nothing.

I wanted other people to notice him – then felt stupidly possessive whenever they did. The hairdresser. She used to do all the kids on the street, give them identical bowl-cuts – boys and girls alike. Afterwards, she blew smoke rings in my kitchen, though I don't remember once offering her a cup of tea. She told me in her loud voice how almost all the children fidgeted, squirmed, even tried to snatch the scissors from her hands. But S did none of these things. He knew, as soon as her hands were on his head, which way to turn. I smiled. I didn't know how else to respond. Then comes the bit I can't tell you –

which is why my brother will have to take over, just like I explained.

C7

My dear, please sit a little closer. I do not wish to make you feel uncomfortable, but my hearing is not what it once was, even with this plastic contraption that the new carer affixes to my ears, and my voice does not carry as it used to. That is the primary consideration, since I gather that the bulk of the talking will fall squarely on my shoulders. I have half a mind to tell you all, dear girl, down to the most compromising details. Yes, make yourself comfortable, as comfortable as this hard-backed furniture allows. You will see that I make no concessions to modernity.

Speaking to you this way brings it all back to me. *Dear Boy* was what I called him. He stopped being S after the first couple of sessions. Then the pet names sprouted. Oh, the pet names. They will make my soul ache to recollect them – but I cannot resist. Dear Boy sometimes was *Dear Boy*. On other days he was *Darling Cherub*. At weekends he was *Inamorato*. When he had misbehaved, he was *Naughty One*. For a whole fortnight he was *Kyle Walker*, the association footballer – a silly whim of mine. It made him giggle. It made us both giggle. There we were, giggling along, a pair of schoolgirls. *Come on, S*, I would say, my face suddenly serious, *we have work to get down to.* His smile vanished. Down to it we most certainly did get.

You must forgive an old man his caprices. I will try to communicate to you the information you require, concerning the subject of your investigation, only let me please embellish the path as we go, make it primrose. I have so few opportunities to speak to others these days, and even the loveliest words wither when spoken to no one. Each morning I sit alone and ingest my battalion of bright-coloured pills. There are the blue capsules to keep me *buoyant*, as my uncultivated doctor likes to put it, of which I now take three a day since S's sudden dis-appearance. The mustard-yellow vials supposedly arrest the erosion of my hemispheres. For I suffer from what I like to call Ravel syndrome. My doctor does not understand the reference, and you are almost certainly of the wrong generation. Maurice Ravel. *Boléro. Dum* da-da-da *dum* da-da-da dum dum. Torvill and Dean. They twirled on the ice and the judges all raised score cards that showed perfect marks. Well, *Boléro* was the piece to which they twirled. Perhaps you can look it up on one of your electronic contraptions. When *Boléro* was first performed, nearly a century ago, the critics were taken aback. That single melodic line, brilliant in its idiocy. *Dum* da-da-da *dum* da-da-da dum dum. You see Maurice, old Mo, had previously always been so rococo. Well, they examined the corpse that soon thereafter he became. Half of his brain hemispheres had been worn smooth. So this was the secret of *Boléro*. Ravel's neurological degeneration had banished the extraneous. *You are in the early stages*, the doctor told me, jabbing at the scan with a pen that seemed to do no writing. In time the same fate shall befall me. Only I have no melody. I have only my lovely useless words, and my memories of S.

Dear Boy, I would say, *speed me in my chariot* – and he would lift me into the latest version of the motorized glider. Off we went! The new one goes really rather fast – I can surpass even those fetching lads in tight bright shorts with the swoosh above the thigh. I was large and encased in reinforced metal. I easily outpaced the other seniors with their inferior models. I frequently left S in my wake, as I shifted through the gears – not that there are literal gears, although those frisky engineers will surely integrate them into the forthcoming model – and gratified myself by imagining first, second, third, fourth, take-off! Abraded hemispheres gives one carte blanche to think what one likes. My chariot possesses all the advantages of a regular automobile, without the irritating requirement to stick to a particular lane. *In vitro* mothers pushing oversized buggies of octuplets squawk as I swish by.

I barely required poor S at all, except on the rare occasions when my thick tyres encountered a gradient too steep even for their rubber traction, whereupon, puffing hard, S would catch up in order to steady, pivot and propel the car that I had become. We sped at top speed under a bridge, past a metal ledge on which were squatting a long row of white seagulls – in their midst a single pigeon, pretending to be a white seagull. I was overtaken by animal spirits, as the wind whipped, depriving me of my cap. *Leave it, do not turn back, leave the cap!* I cried, madly, rashly – a remote-control car steered erratically by a village yokel with fine cheekbones.

No, the words have not failed me. The words have not failed me, not yet. I will put a stop to it, as soon as I can feel they are going. My silly, little, useless words. They are all that I have. I never learned to do anything useful. I never learned to string together the pretty words usefully. When young I would sit on mother's lap and pore over the dictionary. She had already had her dentures fitted, although her teeth had been perfectly sound. At the time, the National Health Service recommended wholesale extraction from the age of thirty-five on hygiene grounds.

I sat upon the lap of my toothless mother and read the lovely words. Oh, how I wished to use them! How I wished to have an occasion to use them! Some of them were so lovely that I knew I would be lucky to have a single moment in my life when I could employ them. I will not blush in telling you that I used these words with S. I cannot possibly tell you what they were.

Look at me, my dear. I understand that you would really rather not – but please look at my ruined face, if you can bear it. I am afraid that it is essential if you wish to learn anything about S. You see, he would look at me. He would humour me, looking at me. He would pretend that I was a person who could be looked at, so that I could pretend the same. So that I could remember that handsome man I once was. I promise you that I once was – so handsome that I would catch my profile in the tinted glass of each car parked on the street, slowing down as I walked past, when I thought my legs would never fail. But I see you cannot look at me. Very well, gaze off into the corner of the room, pretending that it is in compliance with your associational procedure or whatever you like to dress this up as – whatever 'this' is. But I saw what flickered in your face when for that briefest second you obeyed my dictates. It was disgust. It was the attempt to correct disgust. Disgust that a vile old man should have laid claim to pleasure. Disgust, because you do not wish to hear the one thing that you came here to hear me say. Well, perhaps I will not say it. Perhaps I will keep it all a secret, under lock and key, between S and me. Yes, I have half a mind to say nothing. My silence will bring him back to me, in shadow form.

But here I go again, pretending to be strong. Pretending to withhold from you what I cannot even give you. For the finest words in the world cannot convey the pleasure I took with S. Please understand me, this is not a matter of modesty. I am far too gone for prudishness, shame. I am tired of pretending to be the perfect *pro forma* of a person. I never did feel comfortable in this country, not even when as a child I was brought here because its populace was prepared not to massacre my family on account of its name. The English must bury a pleasure that they are terrified to experience in its unadulterated form. That is why their favourite food is sandwiches. No, if I do not tell you what S and I did together, it is because I cannot. Because no words would suffice. Certainly not the words of that awful article you sent me. That article may use S's name, but it does not know the first thing about him.

In any case, the news article that you sent me appears to have disappeared from the face of the earth. This, I take it, is why you had to access the Wayback Machine to find it. Oh yes, I know all about the Wayback Machine. An old colleague who is versed in these contentious matters told me all about it. He has had his own brush with scandal. He was trying to mend a student's egregious comma splice – proffered a semicolon in track changes, only for said student to interpret said semicolon as a wink, file a formal complaint. Naturally he was cleared, but by then the damage was done. Open letters and suchlike. Yet all worked out for the best. My colleague recorded his disciplinary meeting with the powers that be, leaked it to the press, became a pin-up for the alt-right. Permanent gardening leave – crowd-sourced donations fetch more than his pitiful academic salary ever did. He's come to enjoy the students who wave placards at his talks. They feed one another. I told him all about S – one shameless man to another. Showed him the article. *This story disappeared for a reason*, he said.

S had come to me highly recommended, from a retired colleague who counts as one of the few brilliant men whom I have encountered, most certainly the only brilliant man in that pleasure dome that advertised itself as a temple of learning. He was one of the first to rediscover Boolean logic, whatever that means, demonstrating long before it was fashionable to say so that the human mind is a computer. It may certainly be true, as was nearly everything that he said, although I refuse to believe it, preferring other explanations when I complete my cryptic crossword. He never took a sabbatical, least of all when forced to retire. Now he has progressive MS and can move but a lone muscle in his chin, to which he attaches a long stick with an adhesive cotton pad, with the aid of which he turns the pages of the latest scholarship, printed out from the World Wide Web. His eyes blink in a binary code that he takes to confirm his earliest hypotheses. His internal computer is unaffected. He remains abreast of all manner of cutting-edge developments, somehow plugged into all manner of fora, flora, fungal thought that I can barely fathom, and it was on one of these webbed spaces that he hit upon S, whom he hired to do more than turn his pages – if you catch my drift – and whom he highly recommended through the medium of blinks, in his old digs, which came with the sinecure, and which he never left.

S was handsome enough that I resolved on our first meeting to behave as if he were quite the imbecile. He humoured me in this, shaking his head sadly when I asked him, for the third time, *Have you yet read the eminent Andrei Platonov, Dear Boy, have you yet read 'Soul' or 'The River Potudan', as I instructed? You* perhaps do not place the allusion. Platonov is one of the last great examples of a pan-European humanism that today's supposed critics would not recognize if it stared them in the face with its serpentine eyes. I am teaching myself Russian to learn what remains untranslatable. Oh, there is life in the old dog yet, brain or half a brain! I am trying to talk over this cursed egg-timer, which leads me to presume that our session must draw to a close. *For Whom the Egg-Timer Tolls*. That can be the title of my memoir, published posthumously. Still forcing a smile at it all, when rigor mortis long since set in. Still dancing with lovely words around what I cannot bring myself to say. Let me give you a hint. The words that I most liked from those dictionaries were actually very short and simple. Perhaps we can speak again. My decline is not so very rapid. If we meet again, we can pretend, just like before, and I will tell you all. All that is in my power to tell.

A5

Look, I'm a man who likes to get down to brass tacks — no flowery stuff — so let me make myself clear from the start. I'll do this, for my sister's sake — because it means something to her — but I'm not going to do the whole shut-eye malarkey, and I'm certainly not going to spend a lot of time dwelling on my feelings. I'll fill in the gap that needs filling in – Aɪ doesn't feel like she can, at this junction. Is it junction or juncture? You've gone and got me all self-conscious about small differences. I dread to think how many hours my sister spends – dredging it up, analysing. Not that I'm against all that, if you're that way inclined. I just don't see the point. What's past is past. At the end of the day, there are the people who like to analyse and the people who prefer to get on with life. I have a head on my shoulders. You have a head on your shoulders – quite a nice head if you don't mind my saying. We all have heads on our shoulders, but what's the good in thinking for thinking's sake? Maybe she thinks you can put a good word in for S. I don't know about that – these things are complicated, it all goes on behind closed doors. Quite why S would go and get himself mixed up in that sort of thing – it goes over my head.

But let's start at the start. Which was back when Mum phoned me out of the blue, Tuesday afternoon, which wasn't our appointed time – *that* set alarm bells ringing – saying something garbled about how Aɪ was so upset she'd thrown a vase at the conservatory wall because her life was over, so what did it matter? I remember the conservatory because I helped with the plastering. *Slow down, Mum*, I said, *slow down* – thinking, *This is finally it, the*

moment she goes crackers. That was always the fear, what
with the isolation and the simple fact of being old. When
she finally did slow down, she kept on repeating the same
thing. About the squash clothes. A2 had been playing a lot
of squash. I remember him being keen. Punishing game,
squash – dominate the centre, whack the wotsit about –
get your opponent to do all the running, wear them
down. Bit like life, really. Get the centre – get control.
Anyway, he'd been playing even more squash than usual,
three matches a week, until the day when A1 asked him, all
casual-like, how did the match go, and he said, just as
casual, *Fine, good, lost – but narrowly, strong competitor*, blah
blah blah – so A1 asked him in that case why were his
squash clothes as clean as when she took them out of the
wash, and to that he had no answer but the truth. *His
fancy woman* – that's what Mum called her – even when
she could barely string a sentence together, she kept on
saying it, *fancy woman.* The vase hadn't even smashed, A1
had told her on the phone. She couldn't even make it
smash.

It put me in a bit of a bind, to be honest – this coming
at a difficult time when my second marriage was hitting
the rocks. You know, for two whole days last week I
couldn't even remember the name – of the woman I was
having a bit of hanky-panky with. In the end I had to go

on Facebook – like I do to remember birthdays. She's taken pretty good care of herself, to judge by the photos. Never say never. But I did feel a sense of duty. *A5*, I thought to myself, *you owe your sister this*. She'd never really asked for anything and we all knew she got the short end of the stick – or is it the long end of the stick? – anyway, the bit of the stick you don't want to get. When really she should have taken up the university place she was offered, not let herself get talked into vocational college just because she was the girl. She always was the clever one. Only too sensitive. That was exactly what worried me. With sensitive people you can never be a hundred per cent sure whether a crisis is a real crisis – or just something they've blown up out of all proportion. So I got in my – you know, for the life of me, I can't remember whether back then it was the Ford Fiesta or the Nissan Micra! They did list cognitive fog as a possible side effect of the blood-thinning stuff they get you on. Whatever 'cognitive fog' means. Whichever one it was, I got in the bloody car, telling myself, *A5, your sister needs you*.

The long and the short of it was I stayed six months. I think it must have been the Micra, because I got it when the Berlin Wall came down. Step one was getting her to eat. Now I've never been much of a cook, but I got to grips with the basics – those little things, microwavable, you know the ones I mean, cheese puffs, that kind of thing. *A1*, I told her, *you've got to eat — and anyway, even if you don't, it'll make you feel better to have a nice full stomach.* She used to have these little flare-ups, where she lost her car keys or her glasses, which by the way were normally hanging around her neck on that cord! *I'm going mad*, she used to say. *I'm going mad.* I knew this was my moment to intervene — there was no reasoning with her once the shaking set in. I think she picked that up from Mum, but with Mum it got better with time. *You're not going mad, A1,* I used to say to her — this seemed to calm her down a bit. After a while I could see it did her good to cook for me — so we did a switcheroo and I took over vacuuming the stairs, though I can't claim to be a natural in that department.

Break down the day into manageable tasks. That's what I tried to get her to do. *Come on, A1,* I said. *Now lunch is over, we can start planning dinner.* There was the TV licence to renew — regardless whether or not we think the government can justify it. Going to the tip — that took up another twenty minutes, half an hour if you timed it for when the roads were busy. And it wasn't like there was a shortage of useless junk to chuck out. I had to bite my tongue. She never wanted anything changing, even if I offered her mates' rates or my old cast-offs. It's funny —

she's analysed and analysed that marriage till the cows come home, but even now she's barely changed any of the furniture. What this place really needs is a front-to-back refit. Rip those skirting boards out, sort the damp. Fresh lick of paint. In the end, all I got to do was dibs and dabs. That threadbare sofa your arse – excuse my French – is sinking into right now. That dates back till then. Funny. Like she's made a whatchamacallit – shrine – to the man who left her.

But anyhow the bit I was building up to was how we broke the news to S and A3. She kept pushing it back and pushing it back, like she wanted to keep pretending, for their sake, and for hers. At least that's my read on the situation – seeing how she only went to pieces once they left the room. But in the end, I planned it all and even prepared the juice and biscuits I remembered they liked. Well, I'll be blown! I was sure I'd get through this in one sitting. But there we are, you get gabbing – before you know it it's over. You know what, next time I'll make notes. It's amazing what these new gadgets can do. I find myself making notes more and more these days. We can do it over a couple of days, like you suggested – next time I'm pretty sure I can get it done and dusted. I'm just off the ring road, so the traffic should be fine. Amazing, these devices. Every song ever written – all there, at the touch of a button. I'm guessing you're not recording now, so I can tell you how nice you look in that top.

B1

I'm not exactly proud of what I first thought, when S told me his parents were separating. But I'm not going to pretend that I'm ashamed, either. *Now we're more together than ever.* That's what I thought. Where 'more together' meant *against the rest.* Against authority. Which, more than anything, meant male authority. We hated the fathers and the stepfathers. This time I know I can speak for S. We hated their stupidity. Their clumsy feet. We hated the way they jogged up the stairs. Their lack of peripheral vision. We hated the way they ate without chewing, their fat necks. We hated the Top Trump cards they collected, the way they fought for marbles, the suits they wore, how they pinched you under the table, the weird groans of satisfaction, the way they couldn't dance, the way they looked at anyone that dared to dance, their Nike trainers, their beige cords, their pot bellies, their bald spot, the sandy hair that had started to sprout on their arms, the magazines passed around on the bus to the leisure centre, the way they lied their way right to the top, the way they told you, *Look, I'm not going to pretend to be your father,* before pretending to be your father. We hated the sweat patches, the whistling when *Sports Report* came on at 5 p.m. on a Saturday, we hated the way they all looked up to the teacher, Mr Thompson. *Call me Mr T*, he used to say, because he was cool. We hated the way he looked at the eleven-year-old girls, the way they learned from him how to look at the eleven-year-old girls.

You can probably tell – it's been a long day.

S hated it every bit as much as me, I knew he did. Only he was cleverer about it. I showed a little too much what I thought, got pushed around, learned to shut up. S turned it all into a joke. Made them feel they were in on it. Because blokes like jokes. They never saw he was laughing at them. He did it so silently. Started calling his dad by his first name. Just like pals. He was telling him not to be a father. His father being only too glad to agree, I'm sure. He'd got S a computer, which at the time was still rare, cobbled together, a motherboard, extra RAM – all cast-offs from his new IT job. The games took an eternity to load. We were waiting, one day, for *Zelda* or whatever to begin, when I noticed a stack of magazines tucked away under his bed. S, I said, *what's that? – Nothing*, he replied, but I'd already reached for one, instinctively, which wasn't like me. S, I said, *I thought you didn't like football*. He was weirdly rigid, the controller in his hand. I flicked through the pages. Men running around in bright shirts and shin pads, jumping, embracing. I stared at him, expectantly. Comical, now I come to think about it. Like a housewife confronting her husband over the stash of pornography she's just found. It felt like this was how adults argued – petulantly, just like children, over nothing, only with something under the surface that couldn't be said.

It means nothing, S said, in a tiny voice I'd never heard. *It doesn't matter*, I told him, but before I could finish, he'd grabbed the magazine, torn it into shreds, then started on the rest of the pile, grabbing several at a time, trying to rip through them. *Means nothing*, he kept repeating, *means nothing.* I moved without thinking, pinning him, under the wooden bedframe, until he went limp in my arms. First point of physical contact I can remember between us. There must have been countless others, only they didn't matter. He went limp, but I didn't know how to relax my hold. Then he tried to hit himself a couple of times with his fists, until I covered his face, wrapped my arms around his head, to stop him hitting the wooden bedframe. I was dizzy with happiness, having him back with me, having the proof, scattered on the floor, that all this male stuff meant nothing. But then I thought something terrible. Didn't think it, saw it – saw him, with his father, tearing up all our maps and stories, telling him, *It means nothing.*

It seemed completely plausible. He was breathing steadily. I couldn't relax my hold on him – not because I didn't want to.

Why don't you two hang around any more? my mum said, once secondary school had started. *You used to be such good friends – he only lives down the road.* Our mothers even conspired to arrange a meal in McDonald's. We sat in near silence, while they tried to push the conversation on our behalf, and the clown danced in make-up for a group of children. I was learning to be strong, impervious. I told myself I'd out-S S. Once I asked him if I could go with his father to a football match. A2 brought a milk crate for me to stand on, this being before all-seater stadia. It got confiscated at the turnstiles, potential hooligan weapon. I stood there, standing on tiptoe to try to see past the men's shoulders, squinting at other distant men kicking a pig's bladder around. In the end I gave up, let my eyes drift to the programme A2 had bought us. Rows of statistics, matches played, goals for, goals against. My eyes ran down the row of numbers, till I'd memorized them all, without any sense of what they might correspond to in the real world.

Next week, the boys at my school asked me who was the season's top scorer, a malicious smile on their faces – I answered in a flash. From then on, I was protected, never part of the in-crowd, but spared the worst. I'd always thought men lived and acted in the real world. Now I saw the real world existed only to make the numbers change – the numbers, into which you could always escape. I used to invent some excuse to leave the conversation, when people were getting too much, lock myself away in the bathroom, gazing at the tables of figures, the rows of digits. So I learned to be a man. By mistake. Just look at me now. Receding hairline. True, no beige cords yet. Can even – get this – make small talk with the one other male care worker in our department. He and his wife have just had a baby. He takes longer than he needs in the bathroom. I know he's looking at numbers.

There I go, making this all about me. I'm going to come right out and say it. Can you give me a copy of these recordings? Each time the tape ends, I find it hard to believe any of this ever happened.

A5

Righty-ho. I've done my notes – just let me bring them up. That's the thing with these doodahs, you get all these pop-ups you can't switch off. This Chinese flu is spreading – not that I should probably say that. Anyway it's in Spain now. Three cases in the Canaries, it says here.

Is that Marbella? There was a time when my first wife and me looked into going, to Marbella, when we were still trying to patch things up. Maybe deckchairs under the sun would have done the trick. Paths not taken. Sorry, these devices suck you in. Where was I? Juice and biscuits, is what I wrote. Do you know the Spanish influenza killed more than the First World War? Not a lot of people know that.

I'm scratching my head at what I might have meant by juice and biscuits. Oh, right, the children. We sat them down with the juice and biscuits. I've found the thread again. Now, people are people, children are people too, and with people it always pays in the long run to get straight to the point – perhaps with some juice and biscuits on the side. That's what I told my sister. Not to beat around the bush, just come out with it. Easier said than done, I can see that. It was tough on Ai, having to do it with her husband still away in his honeymoon phase with that fancy woman. I saw her once in passing – she wasn't all that fancy. Well, they do say beauty's in the eye of the beer holder. That was a little joke.

We'd gone over the script beforehand – I even made notes of the main points, on lined paper, in case she wanted to refer to them once we got going. But when Ai started speaking, her voice came out all quivery – I could see it would only be a matter of time – so we went straight ahead to plan B, which was for me to take over the lion's share of the talking. *A3, S*, I said – it's good to call people by their first names – *your mum and your uncle have something to tell you.Your parents are getting separated.* I gave A1 a chance to pitch in, but I could see she was still struggling – so I listed all the most important points. How Mum and Dad both still loved them. How this happened to more and more families nowadays – so they wouldn't stick out like a sore thumb. How normal service would resume soon – maybe something better than normal service – once their dad came back into the picture. They might see more of him than before – he'd said something about joint custody, before the squabbling over maintenance payments got really bad.

They took it pretty well, all things considered. A3 burst into tears, but they say that can be a good thing – like when they fall from a height. Babies, I mean – it's when they don't cry you need to worry. S was quiet, but I took that to be a good sign too – he was growing up. He was going to need to do quite a bit of that, now he was the man of the house. Everyone remarked on how mature he was, and so I addressed him – man to man – explained how he'd need to learn to take care of his sister. But he just carried on staring at something past my shoulder, not moving his head or even blinking. To tell you the truth, he used to make me a bit uncomfortable at times. He always was like his mum – on the sensitive side, only he didn't seem so anxious or underconfident. I ended up looking back over my shoulder to see what had captured his attention – only I couldn't see anything special. He was looking at nothing, just like you are now all these years on – funny coincidence, now that I think about it. *S*, I said – all this staring was starting to bother me – *you know grown-ups should really make eye contact with other grown-ups.* Then he stared straight at me – kept looking at me like he was making a point of it, but somehow not in an aggressive way, just curious, or maybe perplexed, though it wasn't like he didn't know who I was. I put it down to the shock.

From then on in, it was all about getting a routine hammered out. A1 still made a nice roast every Sunday – force of habit, it had been her husband's weekly treat. It was good to get back into the swing of things, only she sometimes set a place for A2 by mistake or drifted off at the end of meals, remembering out loud to no one in particular how this was when he would lick his plate. I say let a man lick his plate – if he must. A1 was probably right, we could have handled it better – the way we told the children – but hindsight is a wonderful thing. We were all doing our best, in the circumstances – it wasn't like I had had much by way of training. I don't remember signing up to having a young child thrusting her hand in my face – all red and covered with bite marks – saying, *He bit me*, with the other hot in pursuit – *Don't listen to her, she bit herself.* What are you going to do – get them to open their mouths so you can compare teeth? The marks were already starting to fade in any case, so that wouldn't have worked.

The fights were actually easier than when they got on. They made me feel like a right idiot, parroting their made-up language with one another – I never did find out whether the words really did have meanings, or were just designed to irritate me. I can tell when someone's making a fool of me – so after a while I learned to keep myself to myself. I don't need much to keep me going – beyond a steady flow of cups of tea. Ai has always been good at taking care of that sort of thing, ever since she was a child.

One day I do remember – towards the end of my stay, when Ai seemed recovered enough for us to have Mum round for dinner. Almost like we were a proper family again. I helped out with the dishes and whatnot. Made my special coleslaw, which I'd become good at – not that nowadays I can remember the details. The children both made an effort to get the table set. Plates and cutlery and wine glasses – one each for the adults and one for S too, because Mum and Dad always said it was good to introduce children to alcohol in controlled doses. Apparently this was a thing the French did. Oh yes, Mum and Dad were both very into the French – the tip-top of culture. Hang on, there's a better word way to say that – it's on the tip of my tongue. Epitome. Can you cross out 'tip-top' and put down 'epitome' instead? I'm getting into this now – I'd like to get my part sounding as good as I can. It was all quite jolly, really – talking, like the old days, about this and that. Out of the corner of my eye, I saw S bringing the glass of wine to his mouth, but then I got distracted – until the shattering noise and the glass falling in pieces on to the table. For a while I didn't know whether it was wine or blood, soaking into those napkins we'd taken so much trouble over. Mum was shrieking her head off – like I say, she's sensitive – and A1 sprang up to help S. He didn't seem to have cut himself – there was only one big shard of glass, which I scooped up with the dustpan and brush.

After all the agitation we settled back down to the dinner – poured S a replacement glass of wine. Only he didn't drink it, didn't touch a bit of the food – not even my fancy coleslaw – just sort of waved his cutlery over it. *There must have been a flaw in the glass*, everyone kept saying, whenever there was a gap in the conversation. *There must have been a flaw in the glass.* Our plates were polished clean by this stage – we were waiting for S to finish, when he suddenly got up, without a word, and left the room. *He's gone to the toilet,* I said – more to break the silence than anything. The truth was I had no idea. *I'll go and find him,* I said – when it was clear he hadn't gone to the toilet.

I'd gone round and round in circles – when finally I saw him right at the bottom of the garden, in the shade, on one of those fold-up chairs, you know the sort I mean. *I brought you your lunch, S,* I said – putting down the unfinished plate near him but not too close. He wasn't moving a muscle, but his body was giving off this strange kind of energy. All straight and tense. Don't ask me why, but I was suddenly sure, seeing him hold his body like that – I really had seen him biting down on the wine glass. I hadn't believed it – because why would someone do a thing like that? I suppose children like to test limits. Whatever it was, it felt good to report back that he was just taking a bit of time out but would be back for dessert.

Half an hour later, there I was – back at the bottom of the garden. By now it was completely covered in shade. Flies buzzing around the food. Boys at that age should have a healthy appetite. *Look*, I said to S, *I know right now it feels things are difficult – what with your dad having upped and left.* S told me without turning round that his dad leaving didn't make things difficult. At least I'd got him talking, I thought – even if he put big spaces between the words, as if I was an idiot, or a foreigner. *S*, I said, *your dad isn't—* but he cut me off. *I know he isn't a bad person*, he said. Don't ask me how he knew what I was going to say. He said 'bad person' in this sarcastic tone of voice – as if his dad wasn't even capable of that. He was beginning to get on my nerves, to be perfectly honest with you – I hadn't reckoned with being out there for so long. *Sports Report* was already halfway through the classifieds, and back then you couldn't catch up at the touch of a button – you needed to use teletext, which was a faff in itself.

So I tried a different tack. *S*, I said, *at some point you're going to need to be a big boy – to take care of your mum. She needs support.* He turned round at that. That's good, I thought, now we were making progress at last. *Don't tell me how to take care of my mother*, he said. *I know exactly how to take care of my mother.* It was exactly what I wanted him to say – so I don't know why he had to say it like it was a threat. Still, it was a good sign, he was back in the world of the living – after the wine glass incident. Perhaps he needed to break something. It didn't seem there was much more to say, so I went back in to tell them he'd be back in soon for his dessert – and this time I was proved right.

I left my sister's house not long after that – I came to feel I'd done what I could. Let me just scroll back over my notes – nope, I think that's all. All of the important bits. Would you look at the time! Two minutes over. You let me go over a bit. Not quite bang on schedule – but near enough. Strange – remembering those times. You tell yourself you'd do things differently – but I've learned over the years, you probably wouldn't, even if you had your time over again. Well, if you ever need me again, you have my details. If I'm still allowed to say so nowadays, I must say I find you very pleasant company.

A I

Thanks for being patient with my brother. I'm presuming you had to be, given the way he is – given the two or three things he said to me about you. Don't think I've ever known him to notice a woman's earrings before, for what it's worth. *His heart's in the right place. Just a shame about his hands.* S said that once. Now I can't unthink it, whenever I see him.

A5 told me not to get my hopes up about recordings no one was listening to. *As if that's why I'm doing this*, I told him, *because someone's listening!* It's a good job he's so uncurious, else otherwise he'd have asked me the obvious question – *Well, then, why are you doing this?* Why am I? I think about it, between our sessions. To make myself feel better, maybe? Hardly. Because S won't? That's more likely. *But tell them*, I said to him, *tell them the whole story*. I said that to S just the other day. I know you asked me not to talk about the present situation, but there it is. *So where do I begin?* he asked. *Begin at the beginning*, I said. He snorted. The poor-old-mother snort. *You think the specific people who are interviewing me right now will care about a little sob story*, he said, *when everyone in here has their own little sob story – much that it helps them? – But it might help them see*, I said, *that you're not . . .* I trailed off. Because whatever I'd have said would have been stupid. He didn't even dignify that with a snort. I knew that I was going to lose him soon. Story of my life right now – conversation by stopwatch. I heard the beeping.

So maybe this is why I'm talking to you. To feel close to him, even now. Mildly pathetic. To be interviewed, like him – say all the things he won't.

It was like waking from a dream, the morning when I saw A5 doing the washing-up, badly, and knew I had to get him out of the house. Knew I'd have to care for the children on my own. Sometimes it's like that — extra weight makes it easier to carry. You spend hours waiting for someone to help you with a suitcase — then you see your child struggling, you pick up their rucksack and don't feel the burden.

Those years went fast. S was struggling at the new school I'd let my parents talk me into sending him to. *Such a shame to waste that government scholarship. Of course, in a perfect world, the public sector* — on they went, and on. He nearly disappeared in the uniform I'd bought two sizes too big, anticipating a growth spurt. Waving him off at the bus stop, I could barely see him under the knotted tie and blazer. That first winter, his lips got chapped. I had to run down the hill with the balm he'd forgotten. He never cried when he came back, but I knew. The little porch where you come in — you've passed through it — I could tell how his day had gone, by how long he lingered in that porch, between the two doors, before coming inside.

Then things changed. Not that he came to like the school. I think in retrospect he was learning to master it, his dislike, from somewhere deep within himself. His psoriasis went away. He'd shrug me off, if I ever asked questions, about his day, about his friends. He seemed to have friends. Got invited round. They never came to ours.

I convinced myself it was because he was the only child to live in a house that was falling apart at the seams. So it suited both of us not to talk about his friends.

It was about at this point – fourteen, fifteen – that we started talking about me instead. Said like that, it sounds so stupid – single mother confides in adolescent son. But it wasn't like that. It developed so gradually, it was there – before I could find it strange. We each had a glass of wine, now he was a little older, and I talked to him about what was on my mind. I was doing a lot of thinking back then. For the first time in my life. About A2. Now the reality had sunk in. Then less and less about him – I realized how uninteresting he was, how uninteresting we'd been. I went back to the very early years. I couldn't afford therapy. My first years, when I felt almost certain my parents hadn't brought me up – but then the scene always dissolved when I tried to fix the faces of whichever adults owned the house I could see so clearly.

S was interested. Not putting-it-on interested – because why would a teenage boy bother to put it on? He had a way of asking the right questions. Despite his lack of life experience. Or maybe he instinctively knew not to ask questions – maybe he just signalled for me to go on. Much like you. He wanted to know about the miscarriage. About his older sister, as he insisted on calling her.

Once I asked him, S, *where does it all come from, all this curiosity? — From you*, he replied, quietly and simply. I flushed. I'm not used to receiving compliments. I'm not so sure – now – whether I should have taken it as a compliment. Maybe it was wrong of me, to open up as I did. Maybe I should have tried to remember he was a child. Maybe that's what I want him to tell them. The interviewers. *It's all her fault. Mum's fault. Let her stand up in public and take the blame.*

Catwalk was almost always on his lap, when we spoke. The children came up with the name when she was still a kitten. Stroke with the fur, not against it, I remember teaching them. She used to arch her back in pleasure while he stroked her, gently. Beads of saliva on her chin. I saw his hands, soft, hovering just above her spine, arched, anticipating his touch. I remember the wine tasting metallic all of a sudden. Then it finally hit me – what it reminded me of. It reminded me of the way I used to stroke S, all those years ago.

c6

It is such a treat to see a new face inside this small room whose walls I know like the back of my hand. I imagine it must have been difficult to gain entry. That is the one possible explanation for why S has not yet managed to pay me a visit. It was on his account I had to be brought here, because when he left me in the lurch, I suffered the third and till now worst crisis of my life. Now I am better but I am unable to contact S as, in the hurry to leave, I did not have the wherewithal to bring my address book. I do not want to get my hopes up, but perhaps you could pass on my contact details.

Here it is quiet most days, apart from the carers, who are not much fun. They change so often it becomes difficult to keep track, even if they shorten their foreign names into proper English ones. There was a time when things were very lively in this small room, before they forbade visitors. We were a rum old bunch! There were afternoons when Susan was here and Mavis was here and Christine was here and Agnes was here and Carmel was here and Teresa was here and I don't know who else was here. Honestly, it was hard to keep track, with all the coming and going. Gabble, gabble, gabble! We were like a gaggle of geese. Perhaps that is why they forbade visitors – you may wish to keep your voice down.

Come here and sit beside me so we can turn the pages of my scrapbook together. It will all make more sense with my illustrations.

I should tell you about each one of these ladies and of their relation to S. They all wished to hog him. They all liked to think they knew him best. They could get competitive – at times I had to put a stop to all the argy-bargy. *He can't be here at everyone's beck and call*, I tried to tell them. *We're not even the only ones! The poor man needs a rest from time to time.*

Turn the page, please. Oh, that! That is my scribble of a strange creature that is a cross between a badger and a rat. Well, you must find all of this very silly indeed.

Susan is a nice girl with a soft voice and wavy strawberry-blonde hair that I could not possibly draw even with the felt-tip pens that the carers provide for me. She looks more than a little as I looked, at her age, before my troubles truly began. I try not to let on how life might turn. It is important to safeguard innocence. She is dreadfully shy around boys, having heard from Mother dearest of their bad ways. Of all men she talks to S alone. This I suspected from the glint in her eye. She blushed, but was happy to spill all, about what they got up to, walking through the fields or writing silly private notes in public. S wrote things that made Susan cover her mouth to trap the giggles in. I would have loved an S in my life, because I also had to walk through fields when young – but I had to walk through them alone.

Mavis – an entirely different kind of person, very severe with the religion. Oh, she is always recounting stories from the Bible, quoting bits of scripture off by heart. Yours truly never paid attention in church services! It is from Mavis that I have taken the words you can see, written in red felt-tip. *For, lo, the winter is past, the rain is over and gone. The flowers appear on the earth, the time of the singing of birds is come.* That comes from the Song of Solomon, which sounds so nice even if people get into awful heated rows about the naughty bits. Mavis could recite it better. She tells a lovely fable – walking with Lord God in the snow, looking down and seeing only one pair of footsteps. He carried her the whole way, you see.

Mavis's hardships have only fortified her faith. She has had a great many hardships – therefore her faith is entirely fortified. But this does not prevent her from appearing on the balcony, like a vision. *Mavis!* we shout, those of us who have gathered in the room, knowing she has only gone and done it again, gone and locked herself out of her sheltered apartment and hurled the key deep into the courtyard. But the thick glass impedes our concerned voices. Those plastic screens on the balconies are there to prevent people from jumping to their oblivion. The caretaker has to call the fire brigade, so the firemen can carry Mavis down. Two weeks later, there she is – back out on her balcony. Key dropped in the dark courtyard.

Mavis tells me S sits with her for hours considering the sacred texts, which he takes so seriously that she aspires to convert him to the faith. If you want my opinion, that seems very unlikely, since other information contradicts Mavis's assessment. Nevertheless it is nice to hear her recite from memory. The part about the flowers always puts such a spring in my step. I love birds, apart from robins, which are considered by many to be friendly, cheerful and chirpy, but in truth are highly aggressive, fighting to the death over their territory. I've met people like that.

In the mornings the caretaker comes to clean my windows. My windows are already spotlessly clean, which is how I know he is really there to eavesdrop.

Christine. Now she's a one, I tell you. Christine finds it hard to walk straight because of this thick belt they tie around her when she has misbehaved again, which prevents her from touching her secret parts. After one such episode of misbehaviour she stopped getting her regulars, which is how the supervisors knew – they note down all our vital measurements. Christine told me this in great detail. She wasn't abashed in the slightest. She in fact appeared to be savouring her revelations. Despite the lack of abnormal measurements, she was apparently big with child by the time the carers cottoned on, which angered them – it being too late to rectify the situation. Christine only got to hold her bawling little one for a matter of minutes.

Sometimes Christine tries to tell me about the things she claims she and S get up to. I try to shush her or drown her out by putting my hands over my ears, shouting *lalalalalalalalala*, like when you are a child, but for some reason her voice keeps ringing crystal-clear. The other terrible thing Christine does is to scribble down all of her dirty thoughts into my scrapbooks, which despite my best efforts she is somehow always able to locate. Well, there is not much hiding room in here. Then I have to scribble over all those lurid words – till I have nearly pierced the paper.

Christine tells me she was doing naughty things with S when she told him to take off his precaution so she could feel again what it felt to be a mother for another four minutes, but S had said 'no' – he had said 'no' for the first and the last time. I find this story very unbelievable. Sometimes people put a little bit of truth into a made-up story, and if you want my opinion, this is what Christine has done. Perhaps S only told her 'no' once – but in relation to a different thing at a different time.

I was grateful for all this company, even Christine's company, after Daddy and Auntie died in such quick succession.

I learned it is not fair to have favourites back when I had a large collection of stuffed teddies, when all the others would look sad. Nonetheless, if I were to have a favourite among the ladies, it would probably be Agnes. Agnes is a very quiet sort – dreamy and contemplative. Agnes is not one for this world as we presently know it. That is probably the way she would put it, being so good as she is with words. Not that so much as a peep comes from her pretty little mouth. But when she puts pen to paper – then it all simply pours out! Agnes is the only one I permit to write in my scrapbook. The others only mess up my neat arrangement without permission.

Agnes sits for hours gazing out of the window for inspiration. Outside are few inspirations aside from the trees whose branches are bare in winter and the car park where the man who runs this establishment drives away, every day, at the exact same time, in that stupid big jeep with the fifth tyre stuck to the boot – not even touching the ground – and so Agnes has to create poetry from her imagination. S assists with the rhymes. Never the first word, but what completes it. *Just like 'he' rhymes with 'me'*, Agnes says. Silly girl! I know she's getting into a poetic frame of mind when those fingers start a-tapping – one, two, three, four! You see, Agnes writes traditional poetry, where you count syllables. She'd put this all much better than me. It's a shame she isn't here.

Agnes wrote a series of poems about S. If we keep turning the pages we might reach them. But we will have to skip a good part of the middle portion, because Christine found one of these poems about S, and changed some of the content into vulgar expressions that did not even rhyme. It is a constant running battle – to keep those two apart. I prefer not to think about Christine and to think instead about Agnes, holding hands with S, as the two of them write their poem, squeezing one another's hands to count syllables.

When I was a younger woman, at the previous institution, before I was let out into the community to be cared for by S and by other people, they would always put a wet sponge on my head before they applied the electrodes. Now water always evokes electricity, which proves most problematical for the carers who must soap me daily. But I am getting ahead of myself, putting myself first, when I should take my turn after all the others.

Carmel is quite a tough nut to crack. She doesn't say much – but when you do get her to talk, out it comes. She's in an institution for her own good and for the good of other people. She needs careful supervision on account of her history of violence. Her face turns vacant telling you about what she did – as if she was talking about someone else. In her youth she had a lot of unchannelled frustration. Daddy was out of the picture, teaching Middle Easterners how to extract oil, so her mother became the outlet, all the more so when it became apparent she wouldn't fight back. Some people are good at accepting what's done to them.

Carmel said she hadn't hurt S but had thought of hurting him. She knew or claimed to know he'd let her, if she asked, or she wouldn't even have to ask, because he'd somehow already agreed. During these parts of the conversation, I went quiet. I didn't like to think about poor S being hurt. It would break Agnes's heart – even Christine's heart, too.

Carmel grew up very quickly as a young girl and so she was able to overpower her mother. The only thing her mother would say, when she was being pinned down on the ground, was *Be careful, Car, you don't know your own strength*. It was true. She didn't know her own strength. Anyhow, after that she didn't whack her mother any more, but she did take to locking her up. For one whole week she locked up her mother in the basement with only a few crusts of bread and barely any tap water. She only turned the key when she heard Daddy's car in the drive and her mother, thinner than ever, but otherwise still the same mother as before, said nothing. By this point, Carmel was talking and talking. I saw the scene so vividly she didn't even have to describe it. The stacks of chopped logs in Carmel's basement that got brought up to feed the chimney. The saws and drills. The little bit of light through the grimy window. It was like a dream I once had.

Teresa is just like me. We met walking on some street one day. There was a thin layer of reddish-brown stuff on all the cars and on the tops of the walls. *What's that reddish-brown stuff?* I asked Teresa. I know it's not normally the done thing – to speak to a total stranger in the street – but it somehow felt natural. *It's desert sand*, Teresa said. *Blown all the way from Africa, in the night, before settling down here.* Teresa certainly seemed to be an expert on the subject. It turned out she had spent some time as a young child moving around the Middle East, because her father was extracting oil. Just like mine! Her father also had a long white beard with whiskers. He also used to touch her thigh like mine did. The parallels are extraordinary when you think about it. There are times when I think we're going to get to talking about our naughty daddies, but then one or another of us always nips the conversation in the bud. Nowadays Teresa and I rarely speak. It's funny, how sometimes you avoid the people most like you. They end up reminding you of you.

S is a kind man, Teresa said to me once, and I got a bit uppity, because it was such a simple and true thing to say, and because I felt it too, but she'd said it first. I should try to say what I feel more often, because then people speak back to you in return. That is what had happened to Teresa. Apparently S had told her how she was very intelligent and how she reminded him of his mother, who according to him was one of the smartest people he had ever known, only she never found out what to do with her smartness.

Well, and who am *I*, you must be wondering. Well, there is not very much to be said on that account. I am C6. I am the host. I invite them in and make them cups of tea. Not that Susan ever touches hers. She tries to put something stronger in, behind my back, which she's smuggled in. I really just provide the space. I try to make sure they all have what they need, just like I did with my teddies all those years ago. *Stop being such a fusspot!* Carmel tells me. The others laugh at that. I have to, too.

I don't really know why I'm telling you about all my friends, when they come so seldom to visit. Most days I have to content myself with sitting in here on my own, remembering details about S, even if our relationship was not so special, even if he only helped me in a practical manner, fetching the groceries and offering me his arm when I was having a shaky moment, and so on and so forth. In the spring when the branches turn green with leaves, Mister Squirrel comes to visit. He moves up and down on the small branches that shake with the wind, and even when it is very blustery he always keeps his grip with those lovely little paws. I look at him, in his tree, and he looks at me, in my room, through the thick clear glass. It always cheers me up.

Sometimes I tell the carers or the caretakers whose faces change about my friends. There are some who sit there in silence before saying, *Yes, dearie*, and then try to pin me down firmly so they can get to work on the scrubbing. Then there are others less kindly disposed. I have learned not to share details with one of the more regular carers, after she told me not to start speaking about the other people. Because we all knew where that would lead – speaking *as* the other people, putting on silly voices so I could avoid personal responsibility for all the bad things that committed me to this institution.

I cannot fathom why this regular carer is so unsparing – it is not as if my friends have come to visit, since the new medication. Sometimes I contemplate stuffing the tablet in my cheek, but I know it is for my own good. There has been not a squeak from Susan or Mavis or Christine or Agnes or Carmel or Teresa for a good two months now.

When I asked S whether it was a bad thing, to keep letting my friends visit me, he was quiet for some time – then explained that different persons and voices sat inside every one of us, that all we could try to do was let them come to an arrangement. He told me he would quite like to have names for what lived in his head. He explained how another of the people he cared for had made the bad impulses inside her into a person – and then that person disappeared.

I told S my reservations. *We don't need to make them go away*, said S to me, and he squeezed my hand. I believe Agnes later wrote a poem about it.

The day before they had to take me in, they were all pounding on my skull telling me to find S. I went on the computer and tried to find his webpage that Auntie had shown me all those months before, but now it just said Bad Gateway. Well, we have got to the end of the book and this is how I imagine it – that lowered portcullis blocking the lousy darkened tunnel with slimy cobblestones, leading to nowhere. Bad Gateway.

I'm getting used to the click of that tape recorder now. To
the realization I'll never be able to say all the things I want
to say. One evening in adolescence, the doorbell rang. I
opened to nobody, but then S jumped out of one of the
bushes in the front garden, giggling, with a group of
people I didn't recognize. They had streamers in their hair,
some of the boys were wearing bras over their clothes,
the girls were cupping their breasts, even though they
were still wearing tops. I could hear my mother traipsing
down the stairs, so I stepped out into the cold, shutting
the door behind me. When S stood there grinning at me
that way, long-time-no-see, I couldn't control any of my
emotions. Couldn't control the fact I'd had emotions.
After shutting down completely, I'd been learning to feel
again – the way teenage boys do – in controlled doses.
Sitting in the dark listening to the music I bought with
my lunch money, which I left at home each morning,
because I knew I'd otherwise give in to hunger. Press a
button. Switch the emotions on. Press another button.
Switch them off.

But I couldn't control the dose of feeling I got from
S. He'd let his hair grow out, I saw a silver stud glitter in
one lobe when he tucked a strand behind his ear. I was

intimidated by his friends. Their clothes, their haircuts, the easy assurance – all that cost serious money. S was swaying, for a moment I thought he was drunk, but then he told me, lucid as ever, how they'd been walking around the neighbourhood, when he'd remembered this was my street. I shouted to my mother I was going out, suddenly ashamed of the clothes I'd carried on letting her pick for me. They were swigging from a Still Tango bottle. I nearly spat out what I'd expected to be Still Tango. The bottles are dark, see, one of them said – that way you can smuggle gin into biology class.

The rest of the night's a blur. They were all called things like Clarence and Alexander. Relaxed parents with drinks cabinets, holidays abroad, cleaners to tidy up the trashed house. Class resentment, it never fades. We wandered aimlessly. S hadn't changed the way he walked. From the hips. We ground to a halt in a car park, at which point one of the Clarences or Alexanders approached S from behind, with a cigarette lighter. The strand they'd lit fizzled to the root, leaving this awful stench of burning. S didn't move. They did it four or five times. He stood there, motionless, letting them set his hair on fire. They handed me the lighter. I set fire to a strand of my old friend's hair. I didn't think to ask questions.

You knew him when he was young, one of them said. *Was he always like this?* I didn't know what 'like this' meant. I forced myself to drink from the Still Tango bottle – first time I'd ever drunk more than the half pint of shandy my dad allowed. I felt sure that if I could just carve out a little space, a bubble, a cocoon, I could make S remember – the photographs, our parallel world – but his new friends always formed a protective scrum around him. We were on the move again. I recall being suddenly terrified by the little wood, by the embankment – not because it was dark, or ominous, but just because it was there. I couldn't minimize or maximize it. I remember vowing to myself to give up all the video games, give up all the numbers. Pinching myself, hard, for having lost the world. *Our* world. *B1*, S said to me at one point, *you've gone quiet*. But his voice came and went – now he was standing close to one of the bra-less girls, while someone wound a spool of red string around them, wrapping them up tight, like butterflies reverting to chrysalises. They kissed – I felt a twinge in my stomach. I stood around, waiting for it to be over. They couldn't break free. *There's nothing for it*, S said, *we'll have to get married*. I felt the twinge again.

The rest of the night came back to me in waves – waking late the next morning, hot, flushed. I'll spare you the grisly details. I put my hand on the wall, which was spinning, winced, and saw my lacerated fingers – remembered the mound of newspapers, delivered early that morning, fastened with plastic cable ties, which we'd dragged from the newsagent up the hill in a fit of 5 a.m. inspiration. The *Sunday Sport*. Old-fashioned tits and ass, innocent by today's standards. I looked at the cover girl, inviting me to look back at her – and then it came to me. That boy, who must have had a name, must have had a face, who at some stage puked in my mother's rose bushes – that boy's tongue, churning in my mouth. *Well, here's one who won't be needing the* Sunday Sport *any time soon*, somebody had said – and another voice, snickering. I ran myself a shower. The water hit me and I thought of the football scores. It took a while to realize the water was scalding.

I barely moved from the computer monitor for the next two days, until my mother pulled out the adaptor cord, to put a stop to it, and I set my alarm clock for 2 a.m., crept down the stairs, shut the door to muffle the crackling of the modem, which I still sometimes hear in my dreams. I played, died, played, completed the levels, started over again, my body frozen except for my hand, which held the mouse, flinching from time to time when I thought I could hear S in the bushes, behind the curtains

I'd drawn tight. It was getting light and I could picture him then, clear as the day about to dawn, willed myself to see him, staring at me, staring straight through me. And I pressed eject, crashing the game, frozen on the screen – because I knew if I didn't do this right this second, I never would – grabbed the CD-ROM, bent it back upon itself until it snapped, rainbow light streaming over the jagged edge. I crept back up to my bedroom and slept through most of the Sunday. When I awoke, I announced I was going for a walk. Mum couldn't believe her ears. I needed to get back to the woods. I was having strange thoughts about lying down and letting creepers and vines cover me. I looked at the blue sky, trying to work out what was missing. Then I saw it – that there was no cursor to control, with my hand, moving mechanically in my pocket. Windows 95 – you're probably too young to remember – the desktop was a perfect blue sky. Listen to me – I'm starting to lose my voice.

A I

I suppose I was getting to the end of what I had to say – even before this pandemic came along. No point dragging it out. You'll move on to the other people, all sorts of people I know nothing about – people I'm sure I couldn't understand, even if I tried. We grew up in a suburb, S went out into the world. I'm not trying to sound self-pitying. I was prepared, for him leaving, for both of them leaving. You spend half your life, as a woman, preparing. Preparing for the day *your petals fade* – how my mother put it – before you've even bled. While my brother and all the other men lived in an eternal present. They still do. I remember overhearing S talking on the landline. *Oh*, he said, *she's playing the piano a lot, having a menopause*. I felt certain he was talking about me. Though I never played the piano.

What could I tell you, anyhow, from that point on? That he took care to call me weekly, as soon as he'd left university? He still does. I can't complain. I pressed a button on my phone by mistake the other day, and it gave me this list of all my recent calls scrolling back weeks. There they were, S, A3, once a week, twenty minutes, twenty-two minutes, twenty minutes, twenty minutes. Like clockwork. I listen for the echo now, to know I've been put on loudspeaker. So that their hands are free. To cook or wash or do whatever they need to do.

I tell myself, each time the phone lights up with his number, *This time I'll tell him, tell him what I've been thinking, tell him about the little things I've seen*. Then when I hear his voice, I forget what they even are. Maybe they don't bear remembering. Even now he phones each week. Even now I tell myself – mention this, mention that. As if it might distract him. Divert him. Then I hear his voice, and it all seems so trivial. I hear his voice, and I know it should be broken, know it is broken, in reality, but he's putting in a great effort, to keep it together. So that's how I try to help him. We both try hard to keep it together. And talk about the weather. When he hangs up, I ask myself why I couldn't just have told him the one thing I needed to say. *S, you never set out to hurt anyone.* I've been long enough with this thought to know I'll never say it. Which is why I need to tell you, before the tape stops for the last time.

Listen to her going on, you must be thinking. *The old mother defending her son from things she hasn't the faintest clue about.* And maybe you'd be right. I'm not saying any of this to persuade you. I'm only talking to keep you in the room with me. There, I can say it. For some reason – to you I can say it. I don't know the next person I'll be able to look in the face, and I just want you to stay with me, even though I know nothing about you. I'm realizing – only now – how little I know about you. What'll you do? Will this whole project have to stop? Can you get an extension? S says that's what will happen to him. He doesn't put it that way. *Limbo*, he says. *They're just going to leave me in limbo.*

I'm going to ask you something that might sound crazy. Only – do you think we could somehow find a way to carry on with these meetings? Not face to face. There must be a way, even if I've run out of things to tell you. Even if you don't listen to the little I have to say. It's just that – this will sound stupid – I've come to rely on these sessions. I understand if you're busy. You must be busy. You can stay for the address, at least. He's addressing the nation in ten minutes. We all know what he's going to say. I don't think I can stomach it alone. That grinning face. Even the people that criticize him, they call him by his first name. And then he's won – he's won, by getting you to use his first name. As far as I'm concerned, that man has no name. Now he's going to tell us how to live our lives. I've got just enough time to fetch a stiff drink from the back of the cupboard. I don't know about you, but I need it.

C7

So we find ourselves here, once again, in one another's company. You may have noticed the addition of a cushion since the last time you slouched in that hard-backed chair. I thought about you from time to time, looking uncomfortable, trying to hide it. At my advanced age, I try to resist the sentimental urge to succumb to charity. But I have never been able to resist a chiselled jawline. You must tell me if you happen to have a younger brother. Drat, out with it – perhaps I came to like you. As a person, I mean. Not that you gave me overmuch to like. Perhaps that was it. I appreciated your quality of reserve. It is a rare commodity in your generation. So let us take another scoop of peach sorbet. Artificial sweetener will give us a rush of energy, even if it cannot sustain us. This morning I took an extra blue pill, as the doctor stated I may. Otherwise you may have found me crying, and even telling you the unvarnished truth.

But we must press on. I must try to tell you what I can about S, and about cuddles, as I used to call them. We have precious little time before they shut society down. These absurd restrictions will give the imperial states liberty to do what they have long wished. The Chinese can perfect perma-surveillance. The British – they will prohibit tactile contact once and for all.

Yet for all my bold talk, I am far from an epicure. Pleasures of the flesh dawned in the twilight of my years, through those sessions with S. I can pinpoint the time and place. A Thursday, our usual slot, mid-afternoon, some three years hence, when I entered my spacious newly reupholstered bedchamber to see Dear Boy sprawled on the divan in the silk pyjamas that were his on a generously long-term loan from a generous patron – the identity of whom I could not possibly divulge – a strip of pure sunlight pouring as if through a garden hose down upon his exposed veal-white breast. Danaë, it finally occurred to me – Dear Boy resembles Danaë, inundated by the golden shower that the god Zeus had become. An idea gestated. I dolled up indolent and lolling *Inamorato*, so far as his physiognomy and my shaking hand would permit, in conformity to what I recalled of the Titian painting. I mean the version hung in the Prado – all others remain trivially inferior. My hand was not shaking from infirmity alone. I daubed Dear Boy with rouge plundered from the make-up kit of my deceased wife – may God rest her soul. The make-up kit was as undisturbed as the room in which it sat – the cleaners dust but otherwise leave her room untouched. I do not believe she would have grudged me her blusher. Downstairs I plodded, so fast as withered limbs allowed, to arrange Dear Boy back into the posture he had so naturally assumed. He was reading the newspaper as he sometimes liked to do. I suppose he wished to stay abreast of current affairs.

By the time I had finished, he was a very passable Danaë, reclining on the divan with the loaned pyjamas suggestively arranged, assuming unbidden the vacant stare that quattrocento painters discovered in the harlots who formed models for divine subjects. I dreamed of burying Dear Boy in an underground bunker, like Acrisius – you may need to look up the reference – transmuting myself into Zeus, himself transmuted in a golden shower, although this final phase defeated even my plastic capacities.

Well, converting Dear Boy into a statue got the blood pumping – and so, over a single mad afternoon I forced him into a series of poses, caking him until the make-up kit ran dry. Dear Boy, patient, uncomplaining Dear Boy, reclined, while I made him into a Saint Sebastian, pierced with rubber arrows I refused to return to the naughty children from next door. He became a passable Saint Jerome, as painted by Caravaggio – suffering me to trim his bouffant into something approaching a tonsure, to affix a velvet beard to his chops – as he nods off over his manuscript while the quill remains erect and a *momento mori* surveys all through unseeing sockets. Then I got him to recreate some of the monochrome Mapplethorpe photographs, towards which I confess a sneaking regard. The less said about those scenes the better.

Dear Boy had the most amazingly blank face. It suggested nothing so much as – nothing. It permitted the beholder what aubergines or snails permit the chef – he absorbed whichever flavour he was soaked or brined in. Once, in a fit of inspiration, I decided to violate the norms of perspective that I, like everyone, had learned from Giotto. With savage strokes I refashioned Dear Boy into the sombre abstract work that hangs in the Rothko Chapel — a sanctum that brings unutterable relief, largely because stepping inside invites brief respite from the United States of America, whose expanse you have had to traverse to get there. It did not work, my brief experimental abstract phase, did not work at all, and so I returned to my realist idiom — naturalistic, with a gossamer touch of the supramundane. I daubed him with foundation, decked him in scarlet breeches, and hoopla! — he was Rembrandt's Polish Rider. For a fleeting antic moment, I thought about sullying myself by climbing upon all fours — assuming the passive equine role — but aching joints and revenant self-consciousness intervened. In any case, the brushwork on the horse is so inferior that art critics generally impute it to Rembrandt's studio assistants.

It is abysmal how happy it makes me to recall this time. Do slap me in the face if I go on much longer.

I was recovering from all this exertion, when I remembered all of a sudden the eyeliner upon which I had leaned so heavily, literally and metaphorically. Back I turned – the door swung open to disclose a strange spectacle. Dear Boy was dressing back into his standard clothes, make-up scrubbed from his face. His appointed departure hovered – this was when I would grow maudlin. Clearly he had not anticipated my sudden return. For a second I caught his face, before it registered my presence. Perhaps this, I reflected, was S's true expression. Smiling at me, he quickly adopted the mask that until now I had mistaken for the man himself. I decided to make inquiries – inquiries not, perhaps, unlike those that you are presently conducting.

S, I announced, *you will soon leave.* He smiled sadly, obviously expecting to have to smooth out another maudlin phase, or tell me in that sweet voice that overtime was an option. With my hand I waved away the words that he had not yet formulated. I asked him but to answer one question, in the little time that remained. S, I said, *do you think of me, once you have one foot out the door?* He conveyed vague platitudes concerning how fond of me he had grown. *Very nice, very nice*, I interrupted, impatiently. Dear Boy was starting to fascinate me. I wished to learn how he was put together. I wanted to know how he was connected from one moment to the next. If indeed he *was* connected from one moment to the next. I was paying him good money and could do what I liked.

I tried another tack. *How about others*, I asked, *significant or otherwise — do you think of them, while you are with me?* Under his tranquil unmade-up face, a little twitch suggested he was starting to catch my drift. *When I am with you*, he said, *I am with you*. Nice words! Nice to say and nice to hear — but I was resolved not to let him off the hook. *S*, I replied, reverting to his proper name, *I fish for no compliments with my puny tackle. I simply wish to understand. I presume you have wife, husband, some other legal fiction*. I nodded to the little band of pale skin that exposed a recently removed wedding ring. At this there was a flinch — barely perceptible, but even my late age permits fine discriminations. I was warming to my theme. It really was all so interesting. I know you agree, or else you would not be here.

I do not judge, I continued, *do not judge in the slightest. Neither of us need feel shame. You are simply keeping a pale old man company. You are at perfect liberty to tell me what must be the case — that from time to time others wander into your thoughts. I will not chastise you for the truth.*

I sensed a dreadful submerged struggle. Dear Boy's being was a rag over which two contradictory impulses quarrelled — the urge to take offence, the urge to remain a consummate professional unto the last. I almost felt sorry for him, yet would not give up my front-row seat for this fascinating wrestling match. I was beginning to realize he was a stronger presence than previously supposed. His strength, I came to see, lay in a metal imperviousness that blow-torch and red-hot tools struggled to trouble. At long, long last, he turned eyes upon me that were beautifuller for being flecked with rare latent anger. I will remember his words until my grave. They may not have far to travel. *I can answer your question truthfully*, S replied. *It will mean that I never return to see you again. Would you like me to answer?*

My damned body failed me. I was shaking like an old fool. I was foaming like Pavlov's dog, from the moment S said *never return*. — *Dear Boy*, I replied, quivering, with pathetic speed, *do not tell me the answer. The question was poorly framed, and requires no response.* We looked at one another. The anger, receding from his pupils. It was the first time in all those years that we had looked at one another. He will not return for our regular Thursday session, I thought, with utter conviction. I was still trembling.

The truth was worse. He came back, fulfilled his duties with perfect diligence. I lay down after, complete and empty. Then as I was ready to hope again, to try to hope, that he would come back, come back and come back, until I would cease to torment myself, as I had those past seven days, only then did he miss the following Thursday session, without notification, ignoring all my messages, my increasingly frantic messages, my letters that I signed with a flourish and dispatched first class, as if that would help, all my unsent messages that I crumpled for shame and cast into the open fire, those endless pages where I scrawled his name, S, S, S, S, as if I could bring him to life, and even now, when you offer me the proof of why he vanished as he did, even now, I cannot prevent myself from thinking that in truth *I* brought it about, that I have disappeared S, with my stupid question, which I did not even want him to answer, for I realized, as soon as I had put it to him, that I did not know which of the answers terrified me more, whether he thought of others when he was with me, or whether he did not think of others when he was with me. My dear, it is as well I took the fourth blue pill. It is as well, for both of our sakes, that my voice is giving out, and that a shutdown approaches that I am unlikely to survive. Let us at least be honest at the last.

B I

I suppose I should get it out of my system, before it all starts. There's this horrible calm at the care home. Each of us going about our duties, trying not to let on. If the

94

patients catch on, we'll have to face facts. We're lucky we stopped ordering in the papers years ago. We've switched the TV to the channel that shows old repeats. Not so much as a headline makes it in. They talk about the old days, while the reruns play. Not so different from what I'm doing here, with you – now I think about it.

We didn't so much jump through hoops as fall through them. The lucky generation. Worked just enough to pass the exams, chose redbrick unis for the clubs and bars, took budget holidays, found jobs in the service economy, learned all the roundabout ways of answering, when people asked at parties what it was we actually did. Never occurred to us that not so long ago people had fought for what we took for granted. Or that soon after there'd be younger people for whom it would all be impossible as a fairy story. Blair's children. At uni we stayed up late at the end of our second term to watch the first bombs fall on Baghdad. Crisps and lukewarm Heineken in the communal kitchen. 'We' means the housemates I was trying to persuade myself were true friends.

When I first started at university I'd barely heard from S, since the night I told you about, and I was happy enough to keep it that way. He might have mentioned the kiss with the boy whose name I'd never even known and made it real. Then, in the computer room, horrible airtight bunker, as my first term came to an end as winter began, I saw it, on the screen – his name. Almost nobody sent emails yet. There he was, addressing me directly, without a 'dear' or a 'hi' or a 'hey', asking me without preamble, *Is it too early for us to start feeling nostalgic?* Then asking, same lack of logical connection as ever, *Shall we go to the seaside?*

So to the seaside we went. Checked into a beachfront hostel, paint peeling off the rotten beams. I fancied myself for a photographer back then – brought a chunky camera that took wide-lens panoramas. In one of them – I still have it – he's standing, bedraggled, on a pebbly beach, duck-egg sky, expanses of shingle and nothing else stretching out either side of him. Looking ironically, dead at the camera, as if to say, *So, you developed me after all.*

At first it was heavy going. We knew too much and too little about one another to speak. Boarded-up stores, Poundland, betting shops – I fancied it a throwback, when in fact the town was ahead of the times. We took refuge from the sea wind in a pub, which was about the only option. It can't have been past four. The scattered locals raised a collective eyebrow when we entered. Maybe that was why I ordered a pint, though I still didn't like the taste of beer. To fit in. I sat down at a bar stool, and a big moustachioed man with old tattoos turned purple said to me, *That's Dave's seat.* I leaped up, and the pair of us retreated to a little table set in an alcove by the fireplace.

We sat in silence. *This is a mistake*, I remember thinking. *Turns out it is too early for nostalgia.* Then S cupped his hand over my ear. *Do you think*, he whispered, *that Dave's gone for a piss? Or that Dave's been dead three decades – and you sat in his memorial seat?* We sat, watching the stool, which was never claimed by Dave. I didn't need to look out of the corner of my eye to know S was smiling with me.

We got another round. That was when I started to like the taste of beer. Taste adapts to circumstance. We were drinking on an empty stomach, talking about this and nothing. The fire slowly warming us. *S*, I said, because I couldn't keep it back. *Do you remember the photographs?* He smiled. *Don't worry*, he said, *I've been capturing it all. The foam. The table. Dave's seat. The purple tattoos.* I smiled. He blinked straight at me, ostentatiously, as if he were winking. *You should hold that pose more often*, he said. I can't shake it – the feeling that telling you this makes it untrue.

The pub started to fill up. A group of men suddenly entered, smelling of the sea. Every other time it was my turn, and I remember thinking, *All you need to do is walk in a straight line and say* same again *and go deeper into your overdraft and empty your bladder from time to time – and keep him talking.Whatever you do, just keep him talking.* After it rang for the fourth or fifth time, I didn't believe the bell for last orders. *What did you make of the sailors?* S asked with a grin, and I saw they had left. At some point in the evening we'd gone back to whispering, even though by now we were the only customers. The whispering meant we had to sit close, lean in, to hear what the other was saying. I remember thinking to myself, *He's doing it, he's putting his hand on my shoulder, in this pub, in full view of that bartender who mouthed* poofter *a while ago – at least that's what I'd imagined was the word.* I'd felt this touch somewhere before, maybe the night of the kiss, maybe in the fragments of images that came to me sometimes on waking. *B1,* he said, *you're gay.* It was so out of the blue – phrased so much like a simple observation – that I was lost for words. In the silence, the bell rang, but by now I knew it wouldn't save me. I remember looking at condensation, lit up on a window against the black night sky, feeling just like the window, see-through, heating with the pressure of trying not to cry or make eye contact with the bartender, or the sailors, who'd only pretended to leave. *B1,* he said – and I realized he hadn't removed his hand from the shoulder of the tweed jacket, which I'd bought from the charity shop, thinking proudly how much it suited me, then S spoke again. *B1, you're queer.* He said it like a parent reminding their child to brush their teeth, or a daughter explaining her senile mother's name to her senile mother. The word hung in the air like the ringing bell. *Queer.* Back then it was less common. At least in my circles. I realized with a sort of mental flinch that the tweed jacket didn't belong to who I was – didn't belong to who or what I was. I wanted to tear it off, hurl it away from me, only I didn't want S to relax the light pressure that came to me through it. He didn't add that it was OK – didn't reassure me in any way – and didn't need to, even when, finally, he lifted his hand from my shoulder.

What did I blather to him? It says it all, that I remember his words verbatim, down to the last syllable, even in that state – as to mine, I've no idea. I know I told him something about church, which I'd started attending in secret. I must have told him I couldn't be gay because I was a Christian. My cheeks are blushing even now. *Did you ever act on it?* S asked. I shook my head. *But you feel guilty?* I nodded. *It sounds to me*, he said, *like you want to not have your cake and to throw it up.* He couldn't be that drunk, I remember thinking, panicked. And then he went on to tell me, in a slow reasonable voice, how sorry he felt for Jesus, poor Jesus, stuck in a made-up world that people had invented for him, forced to go around performing miracles when all he ever wanted to do was love people non-magically – much more difficult, much more miraculous.

I didn't know if he was being ironic. By then, I didn't even know my own name.

Come on, S said, *we're going to the nightclub that the sailor recommended while you were on one of your bathroom breaks.* It was hard to get out the words I needed to say. *Thank you*, I said, *for before*. I felt like a stroke victim relearning language. *Silly*, he replied, and offered me his arm. We must have entered the club shortly before closing time. It looked like a warzone. Our Baghdad. Neon lights, prone bodies, smoke. I started dancing, which sobered me up, made me self-conscious – but by then my body could just keep going through the motions. I tried to take off my tweed jacket to reveal some colourful me underneath – realized it was in the cloakroom.

S was dancing, off in the corner. I'd never seen him dance before. It was like he was dancing himself backwards, away from the world. I couldn't stop myself approaching. Shoes sticking to spilled beer. He was grimacing, under the strobe lights, as if in pain, at this music we were forced to endure, whatever it was – happy hardcore, handbag house. He was patiently suffering it, transforming it, with his body. I didn't know a man could dance like that. I knew his body was trying to tell me something. Like *Maybe this trash could save us, if we hear it right*. Like *Come closer*. Like *Don't come too close*. I could see the little beads of sweat. Eyes glazed, like he saw me but didn't see me. Not a drug stare – university had taught me that already. I wanted to dance with him. I moved closer – the lights went up.

We were halfway to the beach before I realized I'd left my tweed jacket behind. I stopped fighting, let my body shiver. Breathed out a long breath, right as a distant foghorn sounded, had to put away the stupid thought I'd made the sound. Why always so ashamed, I was thinking, and after some delay I felt his mouth on my mouth. I thought about church – about that boy, wondering all over again whether S had seen me, wondering why I was wondering anything at all, when S's tongue was working in my mouth. And then I succeeded in thinking nothing at all, not hearing or feeling the water foaming on the pebbles, close to our heads, because by this point we'd toppled over. I thought of nothing, until from nothing formed the bare wooden planks of some attic in an empty adobe house in a desert. I'd never been there before, never even left the country – yet I had the strangest feeling that one day I'd live there.

We must have clambered to our feet – my memory has filtered out all the awkwardness, leaving this false impression of fluidity. The key to our beachfront hostel turned smoothly. I'm grateful this time you're not cutting me off. I saw you cut the timer – in case you didn't know. Mounting panic, on account of what might be required from me. Having my cake, eating it. I moved the single beds together. It calmed me to consider the angles, the geometry, but when that task was accomplished, the panic set back in. *Does he even like boys?* I kept asking myself, when the true question – I knew it – was *Does he like me?* I took off my shirt and he did the same and I kissed him and he kissed me back very gently. There was a cleft where the mattresses didn't quite meet – I felt it under me, I'd wanted to be the one that came to him. At one point I wondered if I stopped kissing him, what would happen, so I tested it. The answer was, he stroked my neck in a way that completed my happiness. I no longer cared whether he did or didn't like them, whether he did or didn't like me. He'd brought me as far as I could go – that night at least. I'd figure out the rest tomorrow, if tomorrow ever came, which seemed implausible. I remember watching the dark sky, happy we hadn't drawn the curtains. Before I could move into the adobe building, my body fell asleep.

Next morning we were silent again, but it didn't matter, because the silence was filled with our old conspiracy. I watched S brush his teeth. When I brushed mine, I shut the door. I needed to be by myself. When we got off our train to change to different platforms for our connections, I felt relieved. I'd managed not to spoil it. I didn't look across the tracks to where I sensed he'd be sitting. Even now I could spoil it – with a stupid wave. A couple of days later, finding it impossible to sleep, I got up to write a short story about it all. Stream of consciousness. For sentences at a time I tried to evoke the feeling of S's studded belt when it pressed against me. That paragraph never really ended.

A3

Sorry for the last time. I told you I hated the sound of my voice. Well, I've been imagining it – the sound of my voice – ever since. It wasn't a good day. I was run-down. Trivial little things, all of which pale in comparison to now. They're shutting the schools. The four of us, trapped in a small end-of-row semi. Wish me luck. They say it could last for a month.

I've got a confession. I looked you up online. I watched the talk you gave for that conference, the first time while I was doing the washing-up, then over again, this time paying attention. Even the jargon-heavy parts started to make sense the second time around. You said some things that really made me think. I even had the thought – *Maybe I could do a master's in something similar – once the boys grow up.* What a time to make grand plans.

He's here right now. S. It's why I changed my mind – about talking to you. Not that it makes any practical difference to you – whether he's a thousand miles away, or however many metres we're allowed to be from each other. It's not like he can talk to you, or anyone else. I wanted to get rid of the taste in my mouth. I knew that, as soon as he clambered down from the bus. He'd told me he couldn't drive. I didn't dare ask what 'couldn't' meant – whether he wasn't in the right frame of mind, or whether he's had his licence revoked. He climbed down and we stood at the proper distance from one another, smiling like idiots. In some way I was grateful for the restrictions. I'd have had to decide whether to give him a hug.

I had to insist he come to ours. *You can't stay in that apartment,* I told him, *with nothing on the walls, no one within a ten-mile radius.* I looked it up on Street View. Newbuild, cul-de-sac, in the back of beyond. I told him to come to the garden studio. *We've poured what money we have into it. It might as well be useful for something. We can socially distance, either side of the garden. We can cook and clean for you.* I had to stop myself. I could tell I was sounding like

Mum. That if I carried on any further, he'd say no – that he'd said yes, in the only way he could, by staying silent.

I told the boys their uncle was too tired to play the animal game. It's all they want to do whenever he calls round. S's own invention. You impersonate an animal impersonating another animal. Dolphins imitating ducks – worms imitating lions. The others have to guess. They play for hours at a time, roaring with laughter. I remember the last time S dropped round – it must have been more than a year ago. He folded his arms, pulled a silly face. They were stumped. *I'm a human being*, he explained, *doing an impersonation of a human being.*

He'd packed next to nothing in his rush to make the bus. They'd laid on a last extra service. Packed with people, scrambling to get to wherever they needed to. Or away from wherever they needed to escape. I told him we should go out and buy a few basic items. So we went to the shopping centre, where we used to smoke rollies, on the days he decided he didn't mind me hanging out with his friends. It was busy. Controlled panic. People shopping furiously for cargo shorts and T-shirts – before the world ended. I picked out a bunch of things from the basics range. Practically had to push him up the escalators and into the changing room. I saw through the gap in the curtain how thin he'd grown – or how thin he'd always been. *They're fine*, he said. *They're all fine*. I said yes on his behalf, when they asked if we wanted a loyalty card.

I knew the kids would be getting twitchy, stuck for this length of time with their dad. But I didn't want to leave the shopping centre – as if it would disappear tomorrow, taking all the memories with it. When I moved back here, it didn't feel like where S and I had grown up. All of a sudden I now wanted to see them again – the old places. We tried to find the bookshop where we used to read books we never bought, perched on those little grey stools. It took us an eternity to find it – I'd forgotten what a warren the old town is. I took the lead, pushing us forward, even though we were thoroughly lost. He put his arm on me, I didn't have the heart to tell him not to get so close. I thought – from the look in his eye – *This is when he'll tell me everything*. Instead he started reminiscing, from nowhere, about the time our hamster escaped from the plastic cage we kept forgetting to secure, leaving a trail of sawdust as it climbed down the stairs, into the living room, up the back of the fireplace – where we could hear it rattling around for hours, until we hit on the bright idea of coaxing it down with a chocolate finger. The hamster grabbed it before disappearing back up the fireplace – the hamster's lucky day – so we gave up and watched television, until hours later it sauntered across the carpet, without a care in the world, the chocolate finger filling one cheek pouch like a tumour.

At some point I'd stopped laughing and started holding back the tears. For everything he hadn't said. For the hamster with the chocolate finger being the only way he could say it. I recognized the building from the little gargoyle looking down at us, covered in soot. The bookshop had become a Starbucks, which is how come we'd missed it. We stood there a while, letting it sink in. *Give me a sec*, said S. *All these places will be shut in a couple of days – we might as well take advantage of the situation.* I was strong and didn't check my phone while I waited. He came back out with a tube of coffee capsules. *I stole them for you*, he announced proudly. *Don't tell the authorities.* He stopped smiling. I knew he needed to keep the joke up, to keep it just funny enough. But I didn't have the heart to join in. I just thanked him and put the tube in my inside pocket. Remembered the hamster. Remember thinking I'd tell you about it. Just to put it somewhere. I didn't tell S he'd stolen decaffeinated tablets.

He started coughing later in the afternoon and carried on for most of the evening. If he's got it, he might have gone and given it to me, when I didn't pull away, to stop him from touching my arm. I don't have the time to worry about that right now. When I stood out on the garden path, I could see the light was on, I could see his silhouette, stooping – we had to scale down the original plans for the studio. You can probably see it for yourself – for all it helps you – S's silhouette. We waved from time to time. I'd call, only his phone's gone. I imagine him throwing it from the top of a high building. Sometimes I just want to stop thinking what it is I'm supposed to feel. Looks like that wish will come true, at least. Soon we won't have the time to think about anything. Those of us who have a family to speak of. On the news they call it 'distancing'.

II

23 MARCH—28 MAY 2020

('Distancing')

DIRECTIONS TO INTERVIEWEES

From this point on, interviews will be conducted using
the voice memo function. As before, do not over-prepare
in the form of notes, script to self. Voice memos permit
you to record your reminiscences in several takes – but
please try to keep these to a minimum. Recordings should
be unbroken where possible – bearing in mind that, as
before, you do not need to avoid silences and digressions.
It may prove harder to stick to the twenty-minute
format – while you might record shorter voice memos,
please try to resist the temptation to record longer
sessions. Recording reminiscences while alone can present
logistical and psychological challenges – please do not try
to anticipate the potential response of myself, or any
other auditor. Continue, as before, to reflect for twenty
minutes in silence, before commencing your reminiscence
of S. Should you decide to take a walk during the week, so
as to build up the unstructured recollection described
above, please bear in mind the social-distancing
restrictions that have recently come into force.

B I

That birdsong you can probably hear comes from the terrace. I'm glad you found a workaround, so I can keep on telling you my little story. I can even control how I say it, now. Redo the bits I don't like, to make myself sound very clever indeed. I'll force myself do it in one go. Strange, to think of you somewhere, hearing this. Though as you probably noticed, I got into the habit of closing my eyes, even when you were in the room.

I floated through those days, after the seaside. Kept flirting with the idea of telling them, the two or three good friends I had – interrupting their chats about student politics, or who got wasted last night, to tell them something true about myself, to tell them what I'd learned. But I kept my mouth shut. Revelled in it, having all this power I never used.

I started to dress differently. To talk differently, now I knew who I was. If my friends had been in the least bit perceptive, they might have suspected. They weren't in the least bit perceptive. After a few weeks of holding out, I invited S to visit. Beginning of the spring term. I wanted to show him the person I'd become. How even if he'd given me a shove in the right direction – I could handle things from here. Crisp, sardonic, in my tightly fitting shirt that an old woman had taken one look at, sitting in her pew, and turned away in disgust. I hadn't gone back. I was making myself believe I didn't miss the church services.

I took S to the student bar, pretending not to notice the group of friends and nearly friends sitting at a large table. I was worried they'd call me over, make me have to introduce him. I was caught between who I'd been and who I was working hard to be. I tried to drink quickly, to get back the feeling from the seaside pub. S was telling me about a friend of his. She was going to be a big artist, she made site-specific art – choreographed ballets that took place in a carriage on the Underground, where the dancers had to work with the turns and the speed of the carriage. It seemed a world away. I'd been to London once, on a school trip, to look at old portraits. S helped his artist friend produce a series called *Morning After*. The pair of them would arrange blow-out parties and wake early the next day to photograph all the mess. The passed-out people, the fag ends, the dregs. She'd put on an exhibition at the student gallery on their campus. I didn't want to let on I was intimidated. I didn't want to wonder whether they were an item. I reached for the glass and spilled the drink – hating myself for my clumsiness, hating myself for showing it mattered enough to mop up with a napkin.

S hadn't seemed to notice. He was staring off to the right. I followed his gaze to where an older woman sat at the bar. She must have been a mature student. She sat with a large white wine and a look of total desolation. *Go and talk to her, if you want*, I said to S. He didn't give me the satisfaction of a contradiction. Instead he turned back to me and asked me what I thought was her question. I showed with my face that I didn't follow. *Everyone has a question*, he said, *a question that, when it's asked, in the right way, transforms them.*

That's very nice, I said to S, *but you could stop with all the pretty talk and just admit you want to fuck her.* It had sounded good in my head, but out loud it came out different, in my Midlands accent. S didn't even register I was trying to provoke a response. Trying to make him see me. He took the tiniest sips of beer, while my glass was empty, half of it spilled, half of it drunk so quickly it gave me the hiccups. I hated him for his restraint.

Everyone has one question they're desperate to be asked, he said slowly, as if warming to the idea. I looked at him, not cutting him off, not giving him any encouragement. And the best way, he said, the best way to figure out what that question was, was to put yourself in the most contrasting situations you could find, to track down the polar opposite of the person whose question you want to work out. Make yourself dance with your new friends at the nightclub – I saw him, back at the seaside – then tumble straight to the morning-tea session the old biddies put on at the local community centre.

So that was it. That was all I'd been to S. A person whose question he could work out. I could feel it welling up in me. I hated the stain under the napkin. Even now, if you looked at it closely enough, it was spreading. It couldn't have been worse than if I'd woken that morning, to the sound of the sea, and found him gone, without so much as a note. He'd asked me his question after first finding my opposite, whatever my opposite was. The alcohol hit me, not as drunkenness but as tiredness. I hated myself for having even formulated the questions in my mind. *But why do you need to work people out? Go on then – what question are you hoping to be asked?* I knew what he'd say to the second. *Well, B1, that's for you to work out.*

I was through with it. I was through with S. For the first time in the evening I relaxed, realizing it. But even then I couldn't keep it up, my indifference. I needed to hate him instead. Couldn't even hate him, fully. Because somewhere inside me, a little voice had started saying, *You might just be another person whose question he's learned. But you're the one he's choosing to tell about it.*

Shtum, I told the little voice. And I kept it shtum for the next six years I went without seeing him. Came out to my friends, some of whom stopped being my friends. My family. My stepdad was the big surprise – he was absolutely fine about it. Told me to enjoy myself. I wondered then – whether S and I had needed to turn him into a villain, to have something to fight against.

The birds are still at it. This moment, the fifteen minutes after the sun goes down, always makes me melancholic. But the paving slabs on my patio have banked the heat. Spring hasn't got the memo about lockdown. She's starting up as if life could just go on.

C7

My dear, can you credit it, here I am, C7, the silly old man with the face you may have been trying to forget, speaking to you through this contraption from far away, in my hard-backed chair! The wonders of technology. I am most grateful for your precise instructions on how to use the vocal memorandum. So I am to be encrypted just like a Rosetta Stone or wartime missive. The prospect of posterity brings a flush to my face. The thought of speaking to you was my main reason to relent and let my niece order the mobile telephone, which for several years now she has been insisting, in that patronizing tone of voice, will massively improve my quality of life. The word *massively* is hers alone. I tried to reason with her, but these young persons are painfully distracted. You can see that they have several – what does she call them? – browser tabs, open in their young heads at any given time. They complain that we old folk repeat ourselves – then pay us so little heed that we have no other option than to repeat ourselves.

I sat glaring at the mobile telephone for several days, as it lay on the porch tiles in its shiny packaging. Whereupon – as I must confess is sometimes the case with me – I pivoted from haughty disdain to utter dependence in a matter of hours. Yes, dear girl, read between the lines, deem this silly contraption my surrogate S. Certainly I do think of composing him text messages, if only I were to be in receipt of his mobile number. This confabulated pandemic has proved good for something after all. It has made me feel less alone. Perhaps you can hear a change in my voice. Perhaps had I relented sooner, my last years would have felt quite different. But the hour is too dusky for this much *perhaps*.

You will find me very silly, but I have begun to play a little game called *Bejeweled*, compulsively. My good arm now aches. One must arrange opalescent gems into a monochromatic pattern that causes them to explode from unbearable beauty. My doctor suggested that such games might arrest my cognitive decline. I now profoundly regret the way I glared back at him. I have even begun to employ emojis, when I text my niece, who it transpires is less incorrigible than I had previously believed. She does think deeply about certain things, in her own way. It is most peculiar how these little symbols change your voice. They are ideograms and hieroglyphs for our own age. In fact I feel quite bereft now speaking without them. Perhaps I will simply say them out loud. Winking face.

Damn it, I have been brooding on S, since you and I last spoke. Trying to connect what I knew of the lad to those absurd allegations in that article you shared. I should like to defend him, but how, to whom, in what tribunal? I was never much of a one for guilt, given that I believe only in the episodic self, but there has come over me, these past days, a crippling pain in my side, which at first I took for another stroke before realizing the new feeling of regret. I regret profoundly some of the ways I treated him. There, I said it, it is on the tape — now, please, encrypt me. I regret the little things I did. The littler they were, the more I regret them.

Darling Cherub was so uncomplaining. I would tease him mercilessly with other boys whom I fantasized about hiring in his stead. For a whole fortnight the running gag was Kyle Walker. He is the professional sportsman to whom I briefly alluded when we first met in the flesh. Kyle Walker is a throwback to a time before association footballers became effete and afraid to muddy up their tunics. He possesses a cartoonishly square jaw and a goatee beard so quadrilateral that he may have stencilled it on. He gallops up the right wing, overlapping the slenderer winger, indefatigable, making periodic and uncertain contact with the ball, thighs like the last German *Wurst* of the batch, stuffed with all the excess meat. Kyle Walker would not have been so clumsy with his hands, I complained to S. Kyle Walker would have made for better company. Kyle Walker would by now have read all of Andrei Platonov's works in the original Russian. Dear Boy smiled, unconcerned. Happy face.

I am working myself up to it. I am working myself up to what I truly regret. It has nothing in fact to do with Kyle Walker. It has everything to do with the very final time that S graced me with his presence. The final time that I did not know would be the final time, and so conducted myself with the same reckless abandon that has been my life. There, I am opening up – my niece would be proud. The next thing I know, she will have signed me up for social media. That autumn day brought such relief that Darling Cherub had emerged again, after my stupid questioning the week before – relieved and resentful that he had reduced me to that pitiful state of quivering longing in the intervening week. I hate need. Do not we all, deep down? I greeted him somewhat more brusquely than usual.

As our session continued, I took to punishing S, for making me need him, with the only weapons available to me. My words and my low cunning. He had just changed me into fresh clothes. I feel acutely vulnerable when I have just been changed. Having it lifted, my bad arm, above my head to fit into the gaping hole of the horrid sweater my regular carer has bought from the mail-order brochure, never so quickly that I cannot escape the sight of my blotched skin – puckered, jaundiced, inert. I speak beautifully only so as to compensate for my awful skin.

I mutinied against my helplessness, disgustingly snug in my beige sweater. I turned to S. Perhaps I would have hit him if motor function had permitted. Instead I began to speak. *Well, Dear Boy*, I started, realistically enough, *soon enough this will all be over – you will be finally disburdened from having to tend to this vile old man.* S told me softly that, from what he could see, I would be around for a good while yet. He was ruffling my hair, in the way that overpowered better judgement. But I pressed on. *No*, I replied, *you fail to catch my drift. I am taking matters into my own hands. Next week I go to Geneva for the appointment with EXIT.*

S looked at me then. Even his consummate professionalism could not extinguish the flicker of doubt. *Yes*, I said solemnly, warming to my theme, *I have no wish to see my body and mind decline further, and thus am resolved to take matters into my own hands.* Dear Boy now was ruffling more slowly, his hands as a dying breeze. He told me, softly, not to be silly. *Silly*, I announced nobly, *has nothing to do with it.* For I had looked into the schedule of the budget airline, seen that flights resumed with the coming ski season. It was my fixed intention to fly, for the first and last time, on this budget airline, so as to bequeath the largest possible estate to my niece. I would leave this world with the ghastly inflight music still jingling in my ears. It was a moving performance, I can assure you. I well-nigh welled up in sympathy with my own plight.

Inamorato's hands betrayed preoccupation. He was clearly at a loss. At long last he bent over my ear, told me in a new voice not to do anything hasty. Dear Boy was speaking in clichés. But damn it if I didn't like hearing those clichés. *No, no,* I said grandly, mindful of the dangers of overplaying my part, *I have engaged you these past months precisely to this end. To acquaint me with pleasures I never knew that I needed, until the gloaming. Having known these little pleasures at last, I may pass unregretfully into the night.* I sniffled. Dear Boy was still. His hands lay on my scalp, applying no pressure.

Of course not! I spluttered. *Dear Boy, forgive me — had I but known that you were so credulous, I would never have gone this far. It was all my little joke. I do not plan to take the budget airline to EXIT, nor anywhere else.* I could see he was not amused. I, on the other hand, was roaring with laughter. *Dear Boy,* I said, *Dear Boy. Forgive me.* I say it to him now, though I do not have his mobile number. *Dear Boy, forgive me. It was all but the folly of an old man alone.* S seemed genuinely put out. I inclined my head. *Hm?* I said. *Hm?* Finally the lovely ruffling resumed.

I was exultant, as he turned to leave. The old dog had had him good! But my exultation faded with each of his retreating footsteps. In place of it came something else. It is dangerous to sensitize your body to feelings when it is so used to being numb. Dear Boy had his revenge. Had his revenge by never coming back. Had his revenge by making me need him, all the more, making me need to call him up in the crypt of my mind, until there is no mind left, until there is nothing left to say. Very well, I will tell you it all, till nothing remains. Allow me my blushing face.

A4

It's only the different format that makes me able to do this. I just couldn't do face to face right now. However persistent you were. However convincingly you described what it is you're trying to achieve. I can't be seen. Not while I talk about this. I'd only worry whether I sound just like the others. All the others.

I couldn't even have done this a couple of months ago – speak into a receiver. But it's been growing, the part of me that wants to say it, as it was – at least as it was for me – without anger, or pity, or shame, or justification, or self-punishment, without covering anything up – without needing consolation, judgement, forgiveness. To get back the details, without their being destroyed by what comes next. They belonged to me, those details. Belong. To not hate or need to deny the beauty. Because no one – not S, not anyone – can take the beauty away from me. And then if I do it, if I can get it out – maybe, just maybe, I can begin to draw a line. I was trying to unscrew the lid of a jar of pâté the other day. Red in the face, twisting the lid –

when it suddenly came loose, I felt disappointed. I'd been enjoying my frustration. I don't want to enjoy my frustration any more.

*

I can only do this in short bursts. I need to clear my head from time to time. Start from the beginning. I can do that. I first met S at a party. He was known for them — 'concept parties', the more pretentious students called them. I never received an invite. Then one day a nervous fidgety boy came up and asked me if I'd heard of *Plus One*. It was the latest concept party — the concept being that you had to invite someone you'd met for the first time no more than an hour before attending. I told the nervous fidgety boy I could be his plus one. *Oh*, he said, *there's one more specification — you're not allowed to have already had sex with the person that you bring, by the time you arrive.* I told him I thought we could manage that.

*

I've just put her to bed. It's hard to try and get back the thread. *Be careful of him*, my friends said, when I told them about S the following day. *It sounds like he might be one of the new-fangled boys.* The *new-fangled boys* — that was what we called them. The ones who made a show of putting on their emotions, who might cook you lasagne if you were lucky, to get you into bed. The party had got better, once we paid the street busker to leave. He used to sit on the campus, playing his ridge-toothed saw with a violin bow. Somebody's bright idea of a plus one. He sent this horrible shrieking through the whole room until we clubbed together and paid him to leave. At last I could hear myself think. Got talking to a bunch of strangers, who were deep into a discussion about the US dating scene. They were very sociological about it. The prohibitions and tacit regulations of first base, second base. *I've never been on a date*, I announced simply. It sounded stupid until one of the students, S, rescued me by saying in that case we'd go on a date tomorrow – 6 p.m., in the café that did bottomless milkshakes. Just like Americans.

I'd presumed it was a joke – a kind joke, to stop me from sounding like an idiot. I turned up just to prove myself right. Hovered on the opposite side of the street, as if S would be looking down at me from some vantage point, laughing at how I'd fallen for it. Then I caught sight of him – even more on time than me. We didn't get close to finishing our bottomless milkshakes before moving to the bar on the same street. My wine had a bug in it. I was caught between fishing it out or downing the glass. We were stuck on fake date-talk, until we realized we were as wooden as whatever we were sending up. We invented narratives about the others in the bar with all the cockiness of those who are sure about life, not having lived it yet. That woman with the smudged mascara. *A lot rests on how quickly she drinks that cocktail*, I said. *Steady*, S said, *she's coming over.* She thought she knew us from somewhere – perhaps she'd caught us staring. *So how do you two know one another?* she asked, and I saw she hadn't been crying – the mascara was just badly applied. S launched into a story about how we'd met at a swingers party, leaving our respective partners, and were celebrating our wedding anniversary, happy to have left that whole world behind. He deadpanned it all on the spot. I went along – found to my surprise I could do it too. Lie. I spoke in great detail about our menagerie of animals, our hopes for the future, how it felt when we passed the door of the swingers club. Speaking with the total sincerity that comes with forcing yourself not to laugh.

That story made us into something. It was where we began. Even if from the start the thrill came laced with fear. That if lying came so easily, it could work against me as well as for me. I told him I should probably go. *Getting drunk's a moral imperative*, S said. *You have to have to strain to sympathize with someone with whom you have almost nothing in common — your hungover self, the next morning.* I felt sure, then, that he was one of the new-fangled boys, only cleverer than most at getting what they never stop wanting you to do. I need to pause here for a bit.

*

We lived in the same direction, so we could get the night bus back home and make it seem non-committal. The upper deck was deserted. S started stroking my arm very lightly — I let myself lean into him a little, zoned out. I came back to myself — barely awake — strangely sensitized to the rattling sounds, as the bus brushed or bent back unseen branches, to the swerve of the turns, stronger at the back. I felt his hands moulding the brushing and bending of the branches and the motion of the swerve, and I looked out of the corner of one eye, sure he was now touching me unambiguously, that I'd have to make a decision, either way, consent or not — but he was still barely brushing my skin with the faintest touch. Coming back to myself, I noticed we'd passed his stop. I don't know how I made it down the winding stairs, my legs trembling like that.

I was waiting for what felt like an eternity while he went to the bathroom — had started to drink the glass of wine I'd poured for form's sake. I was mortified by all the photos of me, surrounded by my friends. I wanted to hide them all away, but was afraid he'd come back and catch me in the act. I was worrying stupidly about what we'd do, if we stayed together, after I'd exhausted the only five outfits I looked good in. Would I just wear them out, or let him see who I really was? With each second, it seemed more implausible he'd ever existed, but then he was in the doorway, grinning sheepishly – the bathroom lock had got jammed. He's nervous, like me, I realized – I would never have shouted for help either. His nerves gave me the courage I didn't know I had to pull him on to me. I kept taking his hands and putting them on my skin – to remind them what they'd done, unthinkingly, on the bus. I needed him to pretend he knew what to do with me. I'd turned the lighting down, to make it flattering, forgiving. But even the dark let me see his eyes were shut – he was groping for me like a blind man. His jeans were bunched at the ankles, the unwrapped condom in his hands – I didn't want to look for fear of making it worse. I was mentally working myself up to the speech that somewhere I'd learned off by heart, without knowing it. The speech about how it doesn't matter, or if it does matter then I must be to blame. My skirt was winched up and I didn't care about smoothing it back down – my own shame was beside the point. I thought to myself, *Just make the noise, the noise they make in the movies*, and as I groaned, groaned into what I realized had been dead silence, a little lie of pleasure, his eyes flashed, as if remembering something, and even though I sensed now he wasn't one of the new-fangled boys, he slid down to part my thighs with his lips, and I knew that after all we'd both be able to pretend, until it came true.

The next morning, I woke, frozen – afraid to trust that the bed felt warm, then relaxed at the sight of him, still there, before freezing again at the thought that the slightest twitch might wake him – yesterday's make-up caked on my face. I tortured myself with images of me drooling, snoring – rolled over, to bury myself far from him. He stirred by folding me into his arms. He stroked me. *Only this time*, I thought, starting to doze off again, *there can't be any reason to stroke me – he's got what he wanted.* By then I already knew I was going to struggle to stick to the line I'd agreed with myself.

We had two months until we graduated. Everything made it impossible to stay together after that, which is how we could spend those two months joined at the hip, barely sleeping, not bothering about our exams – the course was mainly coursework anyhow. We could be carefree in the certainty it was coming to an end. We never fought, because we didn't want to stain the little time we had left. It was only when we started to fight, just before the end – dreadful rows, the likes of which I'd never had before, have never had since, storming out of pubs in full view of everyone – that I realized. We both did. That despite all the irony and the rational acceptance of reality and the little stories we told ourselves about how, settled into middle age, we'd look back at our little escapades, this actually meant something. Inconveniently, it meant something.

I never told S explicitly not to take the teaching job in Thailand he kept stalling on, until it was too late to do all the paperwork. He was irritated about it, and then came the really dreadful row we both knew would put a stop to us once and for all, put a stop to our little stop-gap experiment in a miniscule studio flat in Zone 4 sublet to us by a friend. When the anger faded, I regretted the relationship that, in another world, under different conditions, we might have had. I told him, with the sad honesty you only get at moments like that – where the truth makes no difference – how he'd nearly made me cum, almost a year ago, just from his hands on the double-decker bus. I could see – for once he couldn't hide it – what this meant to him. Six months later, keeping it secret from our friends and family, we were married, in the registry office, before two witnesses we'd met a couple of hours earlier. Just like in our lie.

C4

I know you scheduled me for later, in the last group of people — but I wanted to contact you ahead of time. I'll tell you the full details of my story, don't worry — but it's important for you to prepare properly. Because this isn't just about my story. It isn't just about individual stories. What you need to do is stop focusing on individuals — whoever they are — and focus on the *structures*. The structures of power.

This whole lockdown is a case in point. You want a good summary of the whole situation? Rich people cowering in their insulated homes — waiting for poor people to bring them stuff in cardboard boxes. So then they get to write about their lovely epiphanies, reading Proust in the garden. Feeling good about themselves for throwing the cardboard Amazon container in the recycling bin. Must be nice to be able to afford an insulated home. Must be nice to be able to afford an epiphany. Well, I'm one of the people who brings them stuff — one of the people who doesn't have a choice about signing up for the peak-time slots.

But, like I said, it's not really about me. You've got to not let yourself get distracted. You've got to think about the bigger picture. People say we live in an age of compulsive oversharing, and it's true – but only because private life has been abolished. Maybe my generation does share everything with total strangers. But only people with privilege get a private life nowadays. Take S. He didn't have a single social media account. Didn't have a single page under his real name – where he could be responsible for his own actions. But I'm not going to go into all of this now. I'm going to hold myself back.

I'm going to send you some useful links. I was researching S long before you started – I've built up a whole archive. A little tip – use a VPN. You don't want people monitoring. I'll send the password codes separately. Whatever you do, don't share them. You're going to need a strong stomach for some of it. What I recommend, if you start to feel queasy, is that you think of all those third-world people who have to do content moderation for the big social media companies. They have to look at filth 24/7 – and earn two dollars a day for the privilege. At least you're getting paid for this. Plus you can actually make a difference. You can move the dial on this. You can help make sure he gets his just desserts.

For all I know, S didn't even work alone – he probably operated in league. I'm limited with what I can look into. I wouldn't be surprised if it all goes much further than him. He's really just a placeholder. There are a few books you should read before you get started. I suppose you have got started – but better late than never. I don't want to tell you how to do your job – but you need critical distance from institutions of power. You're embedded within them – academic university, prestigious research institution, national funding. All that influences what you can and can't say. Maybe you think you'll subvert the system from within – but there's a reason these places haven't changed for centuries. My best friend at school – she had an internship at the World Bank – told me how, in the front lobby, there was this big sign, written in huge gold letters, saying OUR GOAL IS TO ERADICATE POVERTY. When she came in for work every morning, she heard the clickety-clack of those high-heeled shoes on the shiny floor – nobody once looking up at the sign. She couldn't stick it for more than a month. I'm not telling you to quit – though you might have something to gain, by doing without institutional support. It's all crumbling anyhow. They'll try to co-opt whatever you say. They'll bury your research – at the back of some dusty archive.

Anyway, those books. *Diverse Voices of Disabled Sexualities in the Global South*, edited by Paul Chappell and Marlene de Beer, Palgrave Macmillan, 2019. A proper intersectional analysis. You can find all these on the Russian mirror sites – the password's in the bundle. David Graeber, *Bullshit Jobs*, Penguin – I don't have the date written down here but, anyway, Graeber's timeless. Rest in power. *Revolting Prostitutes: The Fight for Sex Workers' Rights* by Molly Smith and Juno Mac, Verso, 2018. I'll explain how this is relevant later – when I come to talk about the petition. *Fascist Epistemes, Black Time, Cultural Anthropophagy* – a bit of a mouthful but it links a lot of stuff you otherwise wouldn't think to put together – by Margaret de Vrjin, De Gruyter, came out this year.

I'd give you some of the sources arguing the other way – only they don't bother with books. They already have the power – so they don't need to argue, they don't need to convince. Anyhow, we're way past being able to both-sides it. You want to have a defence of S? Just listen to any talking head on the MSM, not what they do say – but what they *don't*. I've got a pick-up. Poppadoms and chutney. I've got to cycle four miles to deliver poppadoms and chutney. Like I say, I'll tell you my story. But try to think about everything I've told you, before then.

A4

It's twenty to seven in the morning. I might get fifteen minutes to myself, if I'm lucky. I just want to set it down for you – before it vanishes. I dreamed about it so vividly. Our first place. We ended up staying for a year and a half, when we were only supposed to be there for two months. Our friend kept delaying his return from South Africa. You remember each corner – each speck of dust – when the space is small enough.

The kitchen was tiny, without an oven – we had to cook everything on a gas hob with burners that glowed in the candlelight. We both hated the bright ceiling lights. We were learning to cook together, with limited space and time – we only realized how elaborate the recipes were once we were halfway through them. I remember us frantically repairing curdled hollandaise sauce, with five minutes to wolf down the eggs Benedict before running to the Underground. All our furniture came from the street. Stuck a beautiful old mirror on to the wall, with the strongest adhesive we could find, because we couldn't drill holes. We willed it to stay up, then forgot. One evening we were eating, when there was a huge crash. Fragments of our faces in the shards, which we picked up, when the shock had worn off, and glued back on the walls – impromptu mosaic. The falling glass had made little divots in the laminate floor.

Sometimes I tried to fight it – the heaviness that came over me – but it felt so good when the candle sputtered and he stroked my back. *Let me hold you*, I sometimes said, but my voice was already half gone, and he answered with his hands. *I don't want to fall*, I'd protest. *I don't want to leave this – you.* And he'd whisper he wasn't leaving me – that he'd meet me there, in my dream, he knew how to scale the security fence. He'd find me at the crossroads – the words got blurry, each time the places changed. He'd meet me there at the foot of the cherry trees blossoming telephones – the alleyways of the candyfloss villages – mid-air in the plane we'd pilot together, which started to soar, above the clouds, now I was dreaming. Once I dreamed myself as a glass vase. If he touched me any harder, I'd smash – if he stopped touching, I'd fall.

We lived hand to mouth, at first, the obligatory internships, finding excuses to leave the office and sign on – back when the state didn't check as much – me at the publishing house, S at his consultancy firm. One morning I woke and knew I had to take the day off. *It hurts*, I said, in a quiet voice, when S woke, surprised to find me still in bed, when I had to start earlier than him. He asked where and I put his hand to my belly.

How long has it hurt for? he asked. *A little while*, I said –
though by now I knew I hadn't been letting myself feel
the pain.

He took the day off, though he was due to give some
big presentation, accompanied me to the GP, and then to
the gynaecologist on a same-day referral. Same-day
referrals. Another world. I needed him close to me, and he
was, holding my hand tight, as I told the gynaecologist, a
little man with thin-framed glasses, that I thought I'd been
experiencing moderate to severe distress for around a
week. No, around a fortnight. I used the vocabulary they
gave me. I could tell from the pressure of S's hand how
much it hurt him not to have known.

Hop on over here, said the gynaecologist in a cheery
voice, and I was lying on my back when I registered that
my legs were in stirrups, being hoisted up. My whole body
froze, except my legs kept lifting, against my will. *Steady*,
said the gynaecologist. *Lovely*. I tried to get my breathing
under control. Closed my eyes, instinctively, like I did as
soon as the dentist said, *Open wide*, like a kid playing hide-
and-seek who thinks that if she can't see, she can't be seen.
But I was exposed to all the world – had visions of myself
as some heifer, in lipstick, spread out on the operating
table, anaesthetized. I'd slowly relaxed and stopped trying
to control the angles from which S could see my body,

over those months. I was trying to recall exactly where he was sitting, in the consulting room, whether he could see me – whether he could see me through the thin-framed spectacles of the gynaecologist.

Neither of us spoke on the bus back. I knew he was thinking the same. We hadn't ever properly discussed it, except in passing, and I resented it being forced on us in this way, having to consider it, having to regret it – when we didn't even know whether we would have wanted a family. I'd told the gynaecologist the three different birth control pills all gave me different symptoms. *Well, then – that's one less thing to worry about*, he said. I wanted to break the silence. *S*, I said, *I'm sorry I've been shutting my body down lately.* He hadn't let go of my hand from when we'd filled out the registration form. He told me now he understood why I'd needed to.

I was the first to land a proper contract. The publishing house kept me on for a three-month maternity cover. The irony wasn't lost on me. I bought a bottle of Prosecco to celebrate. Got back late – put it in the freezer, to chill it more quickly. S came back even later, distracted, something had happened at work – but when I pressed him on it, he didn't answer. I kept thinking – now I'll tell him, but the moment never felt right. He went to the toilet and I suddenly recalled the Prosecco, rushed to the freezer, afraid it would explode. I ran my hand along the wire wrapped around the cork to check, pushed the bottle to the back of the cupboard.

A couple of weeks later, he got taken on, on a trial basis, by the consultancy firm. It was only then I could tell him about my own success. He wanted to know when I'd heard. *A week ago*, I said, splitting the difference. I thought about getting the Prosecco out – this time we had the time to cool it – but S didn't seem in a mood to celebrate. *I think I can learn*, he said, *what consumers want*. It sounded halfway between a justification and an indictment. *You'll be great*, I said. The words rang hollow. But what else did I think he should do? I'd told him, once, how he should collect the stories he told me as I fell asleep. I could even get them past the slush pile. *Artists need money or real talent*, he snapped – when he nearly never snapped. *I grew up poor, and B2 was always the brilliant one*. He sometimes used that friend as a shield. I'm not saying he should have been an artist. I had no idea what would suit him. When I forced myself to think about it, the Foreign Office was the best I could come up with. A diplomat – he would have made a good diplomat. But I never told him. The thought of him being far away terrified me.

*

I've got another five minutes to myself. I forgot to tell you about the flowers. We spent far more than we could afford on flowers – then couldn't bear to throw them out. The lilies turned paper-thin, translucent – most beautiful just past their prime. We only noticed how they stank of urine after a long weekend away – even then it pained us to tip out the stagnant water. I saw them both, last night, tipping out the stagnant water, repairing the curdled hollandaise. It's so easy, when you see someone from a great height – in your dreams – to think you know better. But the truth is they know something I can't.

B 2

I never really got to know A4. She seemed nice. Sometimes I wondered what made S move so quickly – marrying on the sly, moving in together. I can't remember us ever talking about it. Not that there was any taboo. We just had other things to talk about. Fuck – am I supposed to tell you who I am? I'm terrible at introductions. Even worse at being introduced. Well, I'm B2 – S's artist friend. You may have seen some of my work, dah-ling. Don't worry, I'm not up myself. S and I are friends from university. He helped me get a lot of my thinking straight, when I didn't have a clue what I was doing. Not that he ever wanted any of the credit. We made a stupid decision to hook up one night — I didn't really need whatever he was trying to give me — and from the morning after, we could stop pretending and be friends. Post-flirtation, we liked to call it, whenever anyone asked. Maybe that's the only reason I'm worth talking to about this — S was never trying to seduce me.

We got into the habit of sleeping from time to time with one another. Not fucking — sleeping. Or not even that — talking, as we lay in bed. It started from when he was helping me out with those parties. We went to bed late, had to photograph early in the morning, before whoever had crashed woke up, so it made no sense for him to go back home. Then, from that point on, one of us would stay at the other's, talking until the small hours. I used to stare up at these curves cut into the polystyrene ceiling in the awful bedsit I moved to after graduation — imagining continents, lit by the beams of the cars passing in the night. We stopped only when A4 came on the scene.

The one night you asked me to talk about was the last time we lay in a bed together. A4 was out of town for some literary festival. I'd been running through some ideas for a new ballet. Or trying to. It was one of the reasons I was drawn to S, I think, the way he moved. Completely untrained, weirdly clumsy — but for some reason you couldn't take your eyes off him. Anyhow, I shared my little idea. Normally he helped me make it better, but that night he didn't want to engage. *That's your world*, he said. I asked him what *his* world was, and he said he'd give me a window on to it – if that was what I really wanted.

Two nights ago he'd been at an office party – convened at short notice to celebrate landing some major contract. You'll see as I tell you – I remember all the details. No time to hire a venue, so they'd dimmed the lights, rigged up speakers – office space and cocktail bars being increasingly alike anyhow. Dissolving boundaries, work and leisure. Smart-casual, blazers and hoodies. I could picture the scene. Minimal techno. Brushed steel. Checking BlackBerries, queuing for the toilet, doing a line, sending an email. He'd tried to dance, S said, but felt on edge – forced to enjoy what would have come naturally, his body flinching a split second before the beat each time. So he left. Walked out early – which here meant three in the morning. The Underground still didn't run 24/7, but rather than phone a cab, he took a turn round the station, trying to sober up. Got on the first service. I love those morning carriages – early risers with briefcases, brought together with late revellers.

S's voice had drifted off. But he hadn't finished. The summer morning air hit, as the lift climbed. Residue of cocaine on his gums. He'd missed his stop, dozing off, so walked home along an unfamiliar route. None of us knew the city then – ten minutes beyond our comfort zone and we were lost. An urban fox padded across the street. Ripped-out cord of a public telephone, trailing like a metal snake. Maybe you see it like I do. The box, plastered with flyers and other advertising for escorts – palimpsest of faces, limbs, incomplete numbers, catering for every taste. S dialled one of the legible numbers at random – just to hear the ringtone. My body had stiffened at his words, and at the silences between them. S hung up. He was walking home. His phone was in his pocket, his hands knew where to press redial. He brought the BlackBerry to his ear – standard office issue, like everyone's – and he was actually speaking. Her voice was husky, of course it was. He saw the madam tapping ash from her cigarette, saw the lipstick stain on the dark glass – I saw it too. He heard his own voice respond – thin and reedy. S realized, in the way you realize you're very drunk and have broken your leg – an unreal realization – that he was committed to this course of action, committed to becoming the punter with the thin, reedy voice, saying he was only five minutes away.

Chip cartons from the night before, blowing in the wind. I see them, whether they were there or not.

There was a buzzer. She was exactly as imagined –
minus the ashtray. Gave him the key, told him he could
choose another if she didn't suit his taste. The morning
gloom of the room with the curtains drawn made it hard
at first to see the stockinged legs. She was lying on the
bed and turned as he entered. She didn't suit his taste –
he didn't think of changing her. His body was exhausted
from the climb up the red-carpeted steps – she removed
his clothes while he sat like a child, letting her take off his
layers. It was strange hearing S talk in this disembodied
way about his body. In any way. The small make-up mirror
revealed the crumpled expensive suit and the wearer's
body thrusting in miniature. She slapped his wrist from
where he'd moved it. He tried to put it back, she slapped
it harder – asked him what it was he wanted. *To love you*,
he said, pathetically. She was used to strange clients, she
said – but *he* was something else. He put his hand back on
her clitoris. S didn't use the word. Not from any excess of
delicacy – he just didn't talk in specifics – but I presumed
that's what he meant. *No*, she said, *it makes vibration.* He
was trying to place her accent. He was trying to locate the
miniature thrusting person in the mirror – but the angle
was wrong. She told him, *We need finish soon.* He made an
effort, for somebody's sake, for form's sake – giving up and
buttoning his shirt as he nearly fell down the stairs,

looking at the legs of the commuters who had started to gather on the street, to see how to do it, how to advance forward in a straight line, before he turned the key in the lock, like a real person, crawled into bed with A4, who was starting to struggle for sleep – they'd never spent a night apart.

I realized, when he stopped, the tension that had been holding his body together, his voice. I was thinking. I can't say about what, without sounding unfair. I was trying to work out what it was that made him something other than a freshly married young professional who felt regret at visiting a prostitute. That couldn't have been the meaning of his story, but I couldn't find the deeper thing I needed – beyond the simple fact of our friendship. We lay in silence. For the first time in a long time, I wondered whether one of us might reach over and touch the other.

Then I did something stupid. I tried to make S feel better about himself. Experience has since taught me – it's a bad idea to make people feel better about themselves. *S*, I said, *you need to please people. It isn't the worst thing in the world. We all do it. I do it.*

Not you, he said, *you're strong – you've become so strong – you're only beginning, you'll do great things.* He was starting to frustrate me. I'd often been angry with him, but he'd never frustrated me. *No*, I said, forcing it a little – I went out of my way to please people. The one person in the third row who leaves early and ruins the ovation. The licensed critic in my head. All that had stopped being true for some time. But I ploughed on. *Believe it or not*, I told him, *all women feel the need to please. Your first thought, when you enter a room, your principal concern — how to set all these people at ease.* Maybe there was some truth in that. Maybe I did still feel that. Maybe I still do.

It was the first thing I said that broke through. *That's it*, he said. *I need to set people at ease. Maybe*, he added, pensively, *maybe I'm a woman.* Now I really was irritated — so irritated I couldn't hold back. *You're forgetting something*, I replied. *Forgetting that for every woman there are two things — the need to please, and the constant unarticulated threat of violence. So perhaps you want to rethink whether you're a woman.* He was quiet again. I knew he was working himself up to it. I didn't want to hear the apology. *I love you*, I said to him. I must have spoken indistinctly. *I miss you too*, he replied.

B4

S, barely got to know him — strange how you can sit in a booth with someone for the best part of five years and still know next to nothing about him. Couldn't even tell you his football team. We ended up neighbours when they reordered the office, went open plan. Transparency, they called it. Top brass kept frosted glass, I can tell you that for nothing. Transparency, my arse. We used to joke it was cheaper to get us to monitor one another, rather than buy cameras. The joke was really on us – seeing as it was true. There were times when we used to have a right laugh together. You need some way to get through the daily grind. S got frosted glass soon enough. I knew from the start he'd go places. With some you can just tell. Not that he ever showed much ambition. Colleagues used to get uppity – not that he beat their numbers, but that he didn't care about beating their numbers. You ask me how I knew he was destined for the top. It's like asking how you know you're a legs man or a tits man. You just know.

He always waited to speak in the morning briefings. I could see when he opened his leather portfolio – nothing was written on the lined paper. He must have been carrying them all in his head – the ideas – or else just made them up on the spot. Some people can do that. My first reaction, without fail – S had finally gone stir-fry crazy. But the ideas somehow went *beyond* stir-fry crazy, so you didn't feel you could laugh openly. And then you go by the reactions of the top brass, who were starting to nod along – and then you didn't know any more what to think.

There's a knack to this business that isn't easy to put your finger on. All those lah-di-dah people who go on about advertising being this brainless profession – they can take a walk. It might not be rocket science or brain surgery, but if it was that easy – well, then, we'd all be hitting our monthly targets, we wouldn't have this personnel churn.

Maybe I'm no S, but I worked my way up from entry level, back when you still could. People should show some respect. It isn't easy, to think like the average punter. To put yourself in the mind of the guy who sits down and watches TV. You might think to yourself, *Yeah, that's me, guy in front of the TV* – three beers in, starting to digest your Indian curry, Friday night, beginning to relax in front of the box, probably you won't go out on the pull after all. But no. You're wrong. It's not you. You're just *a* guy that watches TV. Not *the* guy that watches TV. *The* guy that watches TV is more of an idea than an actual person. Inside him are all the actual persons – all the different actual persons, with their different ages, different backgrounds, different jobs, different haircuts. Different ethnicities – now we have to factor that in too. You have to reach them all.

'THE PULSE'. We still write it in capital letters, in the chat on Slack. Having 'THE PULSE' means understanding the guy who sits down to watch TV. More than that. It means being him. Beyoncé has it – not that I've ever been mad for her tunes – but I have to credit her with that. The *Star Wars* franchise has it. Boris has it, more than ever, now he's caught this virus – he's coming out smiling. Think of it in terms of Lego. Nobody says Lego is too stupid – nobody says Lego is too clever. Nobody says Lego belongs to kids – nobody says Lego belongs to middle-aged geezers. That's what we aim for, in a nutshell. Lego, only with slogans.

S was the only one who didn't seem afraid to lose 'THE PULSE'. Maybe because he knew he never would. If you ask me, more likely he didn't care. I remember his first presentation, I was shaking my head, thinking, *S, S, you could've put a little bit more effort in with the PowerPoint.* He'd put up some quote from a famous writer in a tiny font, about negative something or other, about how he, this writer fellow, liked to feel himself into other objects. Bit weird, if you ask me, imagining yourself as the black ball travelling along the snooker table. What's the word for it – the surface? Baize. Nice word. Could fit it into a jingle. S only had two slides. Pretty soon he was off and talking about what it would be like if we lived through this negative whatever it was as the objects we sold. Not just sold them, lived as them. Spoke *through* them, rather than *about* them. Learned to see as a purse does – he was getting into his stride – or a picnic hamper, or a chiffon scarf.

He was on the verge of getting a bit too eloquent for his own good, but he reeled it in. He was always good at that. He had another quote – and this one was only by Karl Marx! That was the second slide. It was about how in capitalism the objects started to talk. *People want their products to speak to them*, S said. This was apparently what Marx had understood. So if you could imagine the weight of the black snooker ball – next you could begin to imagine the customer who would take it in their cupped hands. This got some of the execs hot under the collar. You have to put yourself back in the mindset of a few years back – when you didn't have all these organic bags saying, *I'm bio-fucking-degradable, recycle me*, or your bloody smoothie saying, *I'm made from crushed berries, drink me*. Things were more traditional, if you see what I mean – companies spoke on behalf of their wares, as we called them. When S suggested it, it seemed crazy. It took the chief exec to say after a long pause there might be something in it. Pretty soon all the lads in their pinstripes were off in their breakout rooms, pissing themselves laughing – imagining themselves as Anglepoise lamps. The office had a different vibe back then.

We got our first big contract on the back of that idea, so then it was champagne breakfast, cocaine chaser – leave that out, obviously – but then it's strange, you feel a bit empty. So much time investing in a project, to suddenly be done with it — what you need is a proper blow-out party. One of those blow-out parties where the pot plants stink because everyone's too wasted to get to the loo. Good times. Not that S was much of a party animal. He came to one or two — maybe just one, now I think about it — then he stopped, can't have been his thing. You can put in your profile that he was more of a family man. For all I know it might even be true. I'd kill for one of those parties now.

Things changed after the takeover by the Yanks, when they hired all these chinless wonders who were required to have university degrees. They'd have liked to have got rid of me, only my numbers have always been steady. That didn't stop half the new recruits being above me in the pecking order within a couple of months, telling you how to do your job, but when you tried to put them in their place, you ended up with a formal complaint. Why they need to put in a formal complaint and not say it to your face is beyond me. No wonder S had mentally clocked out by the end. It wasn't a place for ideas any more.

There were times when I wondered what he was doing with his days, gazing off into space like that. I noticed his new business card one day, just before he got his own office. I've always had an eye for a well-made business card. This one had lovely kerning in Garamond. Nice texture and weight to it when I picked it up, 14 pt cardstock, the best. Then I looked at the card itself. Instead of having S's name, it just had this weird message written on it. *Over long obscure years, your nervous system slowly knits you like a sweater, so you can respond involuntarily to the person who will wear you.*

S, I said, *help me out here – what the fuck does this mean?* He came out of his little reverie. *Nothing much*, he said. *I've been playing around on a little side project with a friend.* I made the 'and' gesture with my hands. *Imagine being at some function*, S said, *where someone gives you a business card, only instead of selling you something, instead of selling themselves, it communicates something true. You can keep it if you want. – No thanks*, I told him, and put the card back on his side of the partition. *Then here's another*, S replied. This one said, *Stave off the terror of the negative by drawing a line of best fit through it.* I've still got it somewhere.

I wanted him to explain this one, but he wasn't looking at my 'and' gestures any more. To be honest, I couldn't wrap my head around it. *Terror of the negative.* Fuck knows. Maybe he was trying to get out of advertising and into the art world. That used to happen sometimes. People would start in our business – understand how to sell shit – then before you knew it, they were calling it art. The exact same thing, only now it was called art and the price tag had quadrupled! Shown in galleries and what have you. Then we'd get them back in, paying top whack – old colleagues, to offer us training sessions at away days, where they helped us get in touch with our *creative side*.

But I heard S didn't go down that route – people said he'd gone freelance, after he left all of a sudden. Makes sense, with the ideas he had – though it's strange I never came across him again. He must have been successful enough – otherwise, you wouldn't be doing this profile. This far in, I still don't know who you're writing for. It's not *Forbes*, is it? *Forbes* would be amazing. I wouldn't put it past him. What more can I say? S kept himself to himself. I feel like that old biddy on the news – the one who has a neighbour who did something, like made a scientific discovery or murdered somebody, the one who says, *He always kept himself to himself*. Seems they always do. Why is it that there's always an old biddy next door?

A 4

S's first proper commission let us put down a deposit. I could finally understand what all those people I got stuck with were talking about – overheating markets, sealed bids – but it never felt real. Not when the broker showed us lines, graphs, variable rates, tracker rates. I stopped feigning interest, let S handle things. *So this is his professional voice*, I remember thinking.

It still didn't feel real when we moved in – more like a child's idea of a house, scribbled in crayon. It came unfurnished, newly renovated. I liked those first nights. Sleeping on cushions, then on a mattress, which arrived before the bedframe – morning light streaming in through the curtainless window. We subtracted from nothing, ripping out the carpets, sweating as we pulled the fabric from the spikes pushed deep into the floor. We'd hoped to expose pristine boards, but the wood was rotten. Then – reluctantly at first – we started to add. You buy one piece of furniture and it makes you see the gap next to it. We drilled holes in the wall. It gives you a mad kind of energy, triumphing over yourself. Once we'd triumphed over the provincial people we'd used to be, learning how to hold chopsticks. Now we were triumphing over those impractical, self-satisfied, head-in-the-clouds people, who ate sushi and considered it a moral virtue not to know how to drive. Now we knew best! Now, at last, we knew best.

We got paint samples from the showroom, dabbed minute variations of sky blue on the chimney breast – a thousand pretentious names, none of which mentioned 'blue'. The morning sun lit them up in relief – little blue clouds in a magnolia sky. The wind howled down the chimney that we reopened – making the protective plastic sheet swell, like a mouth breathing. S exhausted himself with physical labour. His teeth clacked on the point of falling asleep – like a cat, when it sees a bird. By then the frame had been delivered.

*

I could have gone on remembering details for ever. I want to try to be more honest with myself. In the mornings, when I told myself I was getting ready for work, I used to look in the mirror – as if my body would reveal to me what it needed, to get back to what it had felt that night on the bus. By then I could just about phrase it to myself – the feeling had never come back. I knew it was bound up with the low-level pain I'd started to feel constantly – or just started to notice. I'd had to tell S about it, one night, when there was no other way to try to explain, why I couldn't go through with it. *You can tell me I'm a disappointment*, I said afterwards, into my pillow, so that I wasn't sure whether he heard. Then we did make love and it even felt good. I knew it was linked to the tears on the pillow – that somehow by breaking down, my body had relaxed to the point that it could. But knowing you need to relax isn't the same as actually relaxing.

It never worked up to the crisis I was half expecting. There were times when, out of the blue, he started kissing me frantically – saying, *Thank you, thank you, thank you*. What deserved thanks was beyond me. We were both able to glide at work, after the difficult period of adjustment. S seemed to be going from strength to strength – not that he ever wanted to talk about it. It used to upset me, only hearing about things in retrospect. Once he'd fully digested them. *Sorry for having been a pain*, he told me. *The new contract's been getting me down*. I didn't know there was a new contract. I didn't know he'd been a pain. *I sell things*, he'd say, when people asked at parties. In the end I gave up telling him not to be so self-deprecating.

Instead of talking about work, we made plans for escape. Plans you make for the sake of making them. Move somewhere sunny, set up a restaurant with the modified recipes in our turmeric-stained notebook. Find a rich donor to fund our loss-making but influential cultural magazine. Teach English as a foreign language, moving country every couple of years – working fifteen hours a week, living off the exchange rate and the rented-out house that it had dawned on us meant nothing. When the details got specific enough to seem feasible, we stopped talking.

We got talented at going on holiday. Could perfectly synchronize the Metro-Goldwyn-Mayer lions roaring before the in-flight film. I remember midsummer in Sweden, when the sun came back after half an hour away – miraculously. We gave up trying to sleep and instead walked through the forest in the middle of the city. Smell of resin. That sensation in my body – it was the absence of pain. We ordered the Swedish breakfast we'd underlined in our guidebook – croissant, prawns, mayonnaise, dill, parsley, sliced boiled egg. I've forgotten the name of the dish. Took the croissants outside and set them down on a round table whose glass top glittered in the sunlight. I looked at the mayonnaise oozing, glinting – noticed I hadn't begun to eat, because to begin would be to end our holiday. The airport shuttle left in an hour, our bags were at our feet. The croissants looked delicious. The last thing we'd savour, having remembered how to slow our pace – relearned how to chew, our food, our thoughts. S was silent, too, in the good way. Flakes of pastry ruffling in the light breeze, warmed by the sun's rays. The dill was in clumps – I told myself there was no reason to chop everything up so finely. I'd no longer eat just because the clock said so. I'd stop making resolutions, the sort of resolutions you make when your holiday is coming to an end. I felt happy S was there with me, declining to eat, like me – a beautiful vision came to me of our leaving our untouched croissants for the puzzled Swedes to clear up, not realizing it was a tribute.

But then it occurred to me – perhaps we're not sharing this silence. Perhaps we were stuck, without my having realized, in one of those stand-offs couples get into – where you both refuse to budge over the smallest, most pointless thing. Perhaps I've done something small to upset him, I thought, and now he's punishing me by not being the first to start eating his croissant. That was always S's form of punishment. Withholding. Withholding the sadness I knew he felt, when my body couldn't go through with it. No cloud crossed the sky but it might as well have. S picked up his knife and fork. I thought to myself, *Does he always hold his knife in his left hand and his fork in the right – what else have I failed to notice about him?* He put the cutlery carefully back on the table. I imagined him suddenly starting to wolf it down – to prove a point. Or sitting there, immobile, neither eating nor doing anything else, forcing me to miss the shuttle bus. He had a strong power of resistance – when he needed it. He nearly never needed it. *Or maybe*, I thought, *all this is in my head. He's still here with me, on holiday, enjoying the sun that never goes down.* The glare was making me dizzy. I closed my eyes – sensed on my skin that the shadow really had stolen over me. All this will go, I knew – as soon as I open my eyes. I saw it for one last time, the glimmering mayonnaise. It can only have been a moment later when I realized we'd both started eating.

*

Räkscroissant.

C 6

Agnes has given me a communication to transmit to you. Hello, by the way, this is C6, in case you did not recognize my voice. Agnes has written a poem that she would very much like you to experience. She insists that it must be read aloud, to be fully enjoyed – only she is too painfully timid to declaim it herself. For that reason I have agreed to recite it on her behalf, although I am sure that my shaking voice will make many mistakes. Speaking in public has always made me nervous and this is only more so when you cannot see your public, or even know whether they are there. Here I am jibber-jabbering, as if I could

put off for ever what I promised Agnes I would do – and
so I had better get on with it, her lovely poem.

When the bell in the tower of yon church strikes
    midnight
And the stars up above 'gin to glimmer most bright,
Lo! when most of what grows or what creeps is abed,
When the cat dreams of cream and the dog rests his head,

Like a coin in a purse made of dark velveteen,
The fair moon peeks up out with her luminous sheen;
Her gilt net she casts wide o'er nocturnal skies
Till the shining bright light a wan damsel espies.

Woebegone creature! Why bow'st thou thine head?
Why strain'st thou thy bright eyes for a light that is fled?
She has walked and still walks, over hot desert sand,
Till at last by a flowing dark brook she must stand.

What a garden she finds there, reflected at night!
In the ripples and wavelets, unearthly delight:
Drowsing lily dissolves as each petal unfurls,
Rose unfolds her white buds in loose quivering curls,

Then a drop plashes hard on the dancing parade,
Scatter rose and sweet lily in rippling charade,
No sole drop falls from heav'n, for no cloud mars the sky,

Then a voice comes from thence — *Sweet, wherefore must
   thou cry?*

As she turns, she espies, 'mid the shrubs, glimm'ring dark,
An outline detaching from foliage and bark.
No tree, he, as she'd thought, but a flesh-and-blood man
Who is stretching towards her his soft moonlit hand.

I am sad, quoth the damsel, *to be thus alone
In broad night, where save twig and bare branch and hard stone,
The sole creatures that keep a dear soul company
Are hunters most furtive, all alone just like me.*

*Mouse creeps and bat sweeps and owl swoops and rat gnaws,
Each lovely in ways that blithe mankind ignores;
Lovely but lonely, so that when they pass by,
I am moved by the sadness to break down and cry!*

Light and water make worlds, he then breathes in her ear,
*But come breeze and form clouds, soon those worlds disappear,
Yet one thing can make worlds that do suffer no flux;
Now that thing, you shall see, is reciprocal touch.*

And with that, he pressed firm, pressed her hand firm and
   warm—
Now saw she a world that from soft foam did form.
Close your eyes, hear no sound, he whispered in her ear,

Then she found with surprise – the new world became
   clear!

With light touch those hands pressed, so that shapes came
   alive,
Multiplied, sprouted legs, now did duck, now did dive,
And though bat and owl clawed, it was not as before,
For each creature was bound by a strict yet kind law

To their others, to each living thing: bats nocturnal
Now friended and frolicked with lapwings diurnal,
The bouncing red squirrel brought cheekfuls of nuts
For his friend, badger-rat, who then dropped them – the
   klutz!

What fountains rushed on, as he stroked and he
   stroked . . .
The kitten with string and cool shade under oaks
That the damsel recalled in desert of sand
While above stretched the sky in a lapis-blue band.

And the lily that gaped and the winking pale moon
And the patch of yellow grass slowly burning at noon,
The new world left a space for the great and the small,
Even for robins, who are horrible creatures and will fight
   to the death for their territory,

Then a cloud hid the moon, and his hand it withdrew;
The kittens and lilies and squirrels all flew
Away, but not like that other world, liquid twin—
For the world made by touch lived on through her skin.

A4

Part of me just wants to linger in the sunshine in
Sweden – I listened to that part again. I sound calm, like
another person. But between the holidays, I was less and
less calm. I was starting to torment myself with visions.
Of the other person there had to be. Or persons. Perhaps
there were several. I even gave myself a hard time for the
paucity of my imagination. The blonde and brunette
women I imagined were like stock photos from some
brochure.

S didn't make it hard for me to imagine. All I had to do
was extend the narrative a few frames on from what was
happening right in front of me. At parties – anywhere
really. He had a way of making whoever he was talking to
feel like they were at the centre of his world. That for as
long as it lasted, only they existed for him. There's nothing
more addictive than attention. I could recognize it from
personal experience. I watched him and saw, from the
outside, what he'd done with me. He always drank at the

same speed as whoever he was with. His posture, his movements, mirrored theirs. Women mainly – but sometimes men too. They followed him, with their eyes, when he left.

After the first couple of aborted attempts, I gave up trying to pick him up on it. *You certainly made an impression on her*, I'd tell him – or some formulation that tried to salvage a scrap of dignity. I never knew whether he was putting it on, that oblivious look. *Who?* he'd ask, confused and incurious. I gave him whichever name it happened to be. *Her? I'd forgotten we even talked*, S'd say. *Well, I don't think she has*, I'd respond. He was giving me nothing, so I tried another tack. Told S that if he treated people this way, made them feel special, lavished them with attention, only to forget them as soon as they left his field of vision – he'd end up hurting someone. Me and my feigned concern for the blonde woman from the brochure. *I don't think I'd cause anyone to be hurt*, S said distractedly.

But it wasn't so much the visions that tormented me as the rationality. I explained it all to myself in patient detail. He'd find somebody who could give him what I felt sure he must need. I might be able to live with it. I might even have deserved it. The problem would come if the second or the third one he found knew how to do it so well that the novelty and excitement of it would go to his head and he'd end up ruining everything we still shared and could still share. Don't think it hasn't occurred to me – how pathetically weak I was to think this way. But I'm trying to give you the truth. And the truth is I was pathetically weak. I was always on the lookout for signs – without ever being prepared to take the plunge and rummage in the drawer, or undelete his trash, when it would have been so easy, with all the passwords autosaved.

That's it, I'd think, when his body was unusually warm beside me. *It's running through his veins, his skin is starting to wake up again. That's it*, I'd think, when he sang along with a song, unlike him. *That's their song. That's it*, I'd think on another occasion. *He's been distant with me for two days.*

But then he'd come back, love me in the way that, until two days ago, I'd taken for granted. I'd relax into the thought there was nobody else. For all of a few hours. Then they returned, stronger than ever. Tormenting thoughts. He was loving me again like he used to, because the brochure woman existed after all. I'd been such a fool for thinking the love he was giving someone else would be subtracted from my account. As if love were zero-sum. When the truth was much more unsettling. The truth was that his love, his generosity, his giving were endless. The more he loved, the more he loved – it came out of him, oozing like some black syrup. I had to make myself stop. I have to make myself stop.

*

I can go on now. If I don't take breaks, I'll have to stop for good. I know now what I was scared of. That he loved me for my need for him. I needed him to make me better. And so I became his project, to cure me, with care. Perhaps I was scared of actually getting better. Because how then would he love me?

I'd long since given up trying to hide the pain. Now we talked about it a lot. S would get energized each time he hit on a new potential solution. He got a friend to bump me up the waiting list at the chronic pain clinic. I remember his deflation when I told him about the advice — *Try to transition from a pain elimination mindset to a pain management mindset*. So we needed other potential solutions — S as much as me. He tried to talk to me about my childhood until I had to tell him I didn't need a therapist. That there was no trauma to dredge up, just as there was no pivotal moment where I'd fallen off a horse. That perhaps there was no origin to explain what I couldn't put into words but had to keep giving a number on a scale of 1 to 10.

Then S gave me his next solution. The definitive one. *Maybe it's me*, he said. *Maybe I'm somehow making you ill – unintentionally. Maybe something in me produces this effect.* Looking back, I think he was right, only not in the way he thought. Because the way he told it, he was the cause but he was also the solution. He could make me better, in the gift of giving me up. When the full truth was it had to come from me – I was the one who had to free myself.

*

I need to say it, how it felt at that time. It felt like being buried under heavy layers and not being able to get warm. I made him keep the winter duvet on through summer. I wanted him to give me his heat. Sometimes I wrapped my legs around him. He'd trace a circle with his fingers on the small of my back, meaning, *Turn around now, so I can stroke you off to sleep.* We fell asleep locked together. I used to surface in the night – sweating but too heavy with sleep to kick off the duvet. Once I dreamed of us being buried under molten lava – ready to be dug up by archaeologists from future millennia, perfectly preserved, still entwined, like some exhibit from Pompeii.

People were well meaning. They were so fucking well meaning. At parties they offered me their seats, and I sat down with such bad grace, thinking, *But what more can you rightfully expect?* I tried not to worry my mother, though on one of the occasions when I couldn't hold myself back, she told me that she could understand if pregnancy seemed like the last thing I needed, given the state of my body, but that a lot of women with problems felt they'd never felt better, during and after – something to do with the hormones changing everything – until she started sobbing at the way I was looking at her, telling me how sorry she was that I had to have such a stupid old mother who didn't understand anything, and then I had to soothe her and forgive her everything. *I like S*, she said, once the tears had dried, *but you two are too dependent on one another. It isn't healthy.* I hated her then, forced to carry on hugging her while she carried on making assumptions, having no idea of how right she accidentally was – I'd never told her, nor anyone else, that I couldn't conceive.

She liked him. Of course she did. She and S would talk for hours. About Tupperware. I often worried he wouldn't leave me for another woman, but leave his mother-in-law for another mother-in-law.

Sometimes the experts were nice, sometimes not so nice. You were lucky to see the same practitioner twice. I remember the doctor who told me under his breath it sounded like wandering womb syndrome was making a comeback. One person really made a difference – a young neuroscientist who gave a talk at the chronic pain clinic. She specialized in placebo effects. People talked about placebo effects as delusions, she said. To explain why idiots made themselves believe that homeopathy was making them better. But we should start to think about the placebo effect differently. As a tribute to the amazing capacity of the brain to take something that strictly speaking didn't exist, and make it real – real as being punched in the face. And all these vicious cycles came about from this amazing power. If only we could learn to make *it* serve *us*.

I still had her words ringing in my ears when I reached into the back of the wardrobe for the pair of heels I hadn't worn since the wedding. It was full with the dresses I used to buy and never wear, because I could imagine them getting frayed and worn. Sometimes I kept them in the plastic packaging in which they were sold. My feet just about fitted. I went walking without a destination in mind – like the neuroscientist had suggested. It was autumn, sodden leaves on the ground, my heels sank into the turf. I walked through the park and into a clearing, sat with my back against the trunk of a large birch tree whose leaves had just fallen and were still dry. It didn't hurt too much. I was sitting in a ray of light that streamed through the leaves that hadn't fallen. I could feel myself drifting. I remember wondering whether I looked like a character from a fairy tale, asleep in my red dress at the foot of a tree. I came to, a few minutes later, in the shade. I'd been pressing myself into the tree trunk, to try to hold myself down, fighting the turning of the page in which I'd dreamed I'd lived – the picture of a woman in a red dress. A child out of view was trying to turn it, and I realized my stupid mother was right again in more ways than she could ever know.

B3

My English is very limited, just to let you know. I make even more mistakes when I am self-conscious, like now. It would give me pleasure if you could find the just words to express my experience. S would disagree with this point of view. He liked to say that the precise words do not matter. He had his chosen metaphor to express this. He said to me a long time ago that learning a new language is similar to packing a small suitcase. As you are packing you discover what is essential baggage and what you only thought was essential baggage. Well, my suitcase is very tiny! It only has space for essential baggage, and even then there are some required items that I must let go. S. How bizarre it feels to have his name on my lips. In our time together, I never needed to say it. In private moments I did not have to catch his attention. In public moments – then I never dared to speak to him at all.

English people have the habit to eat their words – but S is not like this. He speaks so clearly that I think I understand the language truly for the first time. One day I asked him if this was because he was a professor. He laughed at this idea. No, as a professor he would be fatal, because he lacked the necessary patience. I never discovered what was his true employment. I mean the employment before his other life started. He had learned some of my mother tongue when he was a young person, although he pretended modesty. But he was very good. It was easy for him, to make metaphors about tiny suitcases, when he travels with two big ones! Pretty soon we had become accustomed to speaking a bizarre mixture – half his tongue, half mine. I nearly forgot to tell you – I like your mission. We have a phrase for it. *L'histoire orale.* Perhaps the idea is less popular in this country. There are many things that translate with difficulty. The English enjoy saying how liberated they are – but if they were so liberated, they would not need to tire your ears about it. I also like S's mission. Perhaps the correct response is to be disgusted. But I am not disgusted. I am merely sad because he is gone.

We encountered one another at a party my friends obliged me to visit. It was when I was still depressed because my husband had left, after I was the one who followed him to this island where I never asked to live. It is crazy for me to think about that depressed person. She apparently was me, but I cannot believe it. S expressed to me how much he liked my disguise, so I had to explain I had simply come as myself, because I did not read the email about fancy dress for the stupid murder mystery party. I was the killer. The card said it in big letters when I turned it over. We had to pose questions to one another, and S kept choosing me. I felt sure he knew I was the killer but instead of making the direct accusation, he wanted to continue to pose questions, just to see my response.

We saw one another in total for four months. My body kept a diary. *Un journal intime.* My small ground-floor flat is on the route to his office. This was why, at first, I stopped myself from becoming too excited. This is all just easy convenience, I insisted, to the bathroom mirror the first few times when he had left. I had moved my bed to the front room because I like to be waked by bright morning light. S would press lightly on the door and practically fall straight on to my bed. He smelled of toothpaste and aftershave. A mystery, how your body can be so alert when your mind sleeps. I left the door on the latch. *Latch*, what a strange word. Drunk people and street sweepers sometimes waked me. Then I would fall back to dreams and see strange creatures pressing open the door, with the walls of my house as my skin. My body was so sensible I could nearly not breathe when S laid his hands upon it. It was like he painted my body – with my body. He would go below and come back and kiss my mouth and tell me he was carrying honey to and from the bee. Honey to and from the bee. Is this too explicit? It is not pornography. Pornography is not explicit, not really.

There is a small window – I thought I knew it. A small window when the sex seems like it cannot get any better, before the fear begins. The fear that it will become routine. That even if it is just as good, it will not be the same because it will become routine. At this time I remarked the tiny details of my body. Good and bad things. They must have always been there, only unseen. The little hairs that grow back always. The word is on the tip of my tongue. *Chaume*. It comes back whatever the salon talks about *l'épilation définitive*. S tells me he likes the little hair on my *nuque*. Here I think you English do not even have the word. He protests always that he does nothing – it is not he who moves – my little hairs rise to meet his hands. I feel them even now. My little neck hairs. His hands. I realized that this window was not small like it had been before.

We slept through the night only once. Sleep is a funny word for it because we obviously did not do that. S announced he could stay without warning, so I had no time to be nervous. When our feet touched it was like electricity passing through the ground. Sometimes I begged him not to make me *jouir* – here I must use my word – and I wondered to myself, *If you force pleasure, is this really forcing?* It is funny how you can think such distinct thoughts when you do not even know that you are a person. The next night, alone, I slept right through the drunks and the sweepers. In the day I remarked all these little aches and pains in my body. *So this is it*, I said to myself. *Now I am an old broken woman.* Then suddenly I connected the location of the aching to the movement we had been making. Then I could enjoy the pain. Even now when I try hard I can still feel the rhythm of his moving in me, when I breathe slowly in and out.

S only became shy when he made a little speech about his wife. I do not comprehend why he had to tell me about her ailments. I can see he felt bad, but it was a lack of respect for her and for me. I tried to explain this to him. I tried to explain that there is no free love – this was just a word the English imported from the Americans, who never believe in what they advertise. Then the English buy it and take it seriously. For love you must pay, always. *Fine*, I said to him, *I am prepared to pay. So now shut up about your wife, for her sake*. And we went back to reading a book that our bodies kept interrupting. When we read more than three pages, out loud, I could forget my terrible pronunciation. The story described a man who returns to his desert homeland, to make his old community happy with communism. He finds his mother who is old and nearly dying. But the desert land is so hot and primitive. One day he falls ill with fever and lies on the sand, until large black birds – I ignore the exact name – circle in the sky and swoop down. They take small bites and then get braver, take bigger bites. The story is horrible but we cannot prevent ourselves reading it.

Now even our naked bodies do not interrupt. Even though we can see only a few pages remain, it feels like these birds will never stop swooping down – like this man will never stop dying. The story was always realist, but now time slows, like in real reality. The man has a gun but is too tired to fire it in the right direction. He can only scare the birds – but soon they come back. I hate these birds as they swoop down and cannot read because my eyes are wet. *S*, I say, *I wish they were dead*. The same stupid voice how I used to tell my baby brother, *I wish you were dead*, when he was behaving obnoxiously. S dries my eyes with his wrist, which no longer wears the watch – it makes me so happy how it is gone – and says to me to think from the birds' perspective. *They also are hungry*, he says. *They also wish to save their community, even if not with communism.* He asks me to imagine, if the story was from the birds' view, if the man had no name, but simply was described as red meat – then, he says, we would feel another way. Maybe we would hate the red meat, how it shoots metal bullets at the hungry baby birds. I remark how S's eyes are also wet. It is true, everything is perspective. Probably you have already spoken to his wife. So I am the black bird with no exact name, swooping down, having no story.

A5

Hello there! It's me. A5. Hope you don't mind me getting in touch like this. My sister gave me your number – just thought I'd contact you on the off chance. In case you needed any more information. I enjoyed our little chats. My body seems to have adjusted to the medicine. No more cognitive fog. We were talking about the Spanish flu – do you remember? I don't think I had the exact number to hand. Well, it turns out five hundred million people were infected. Anything between seventeen to fifty million died. Not that we need to talk about Spanish influenza. It'll be interesting to see how all this kerfuffle compares. I imagine you're looking at the tables and the statistics, like everyone.

Sorry for this constant dinging, by the way. I signed up by mistake to this women's fitness newsletter – texted STOP to the number, but they just keep on dinging! Suppose I'm really just killing time. Like I said – let me know if you want anything more. About the whole family situation. We're a strange old bunch – but which family isn't? We could go for a walk – if you wanted to. The only time I can't make is one to two. That's the deliveries slot. Amazing these nice people who come out of the woodwork to help the golden oldies. Amazing to realize you're a golden oldie, come to think about it. Mine's a nice lady – one of those complicated names, from here or there or wherever. Food's not to my taste. All these vegetables I had to look up – celeriac and whatnot, which you can't do much with. I appreciate more bog-standard food. Hospital grub suited me just fine. You get in a routine – peeling off the metal foil, knowing exactly what you're going to get. The smell hits you and you tuck in.

Picky children make for picky adults – that's where a lot of today's issues begin. Listen to me, off solving the world's problems! Oops-a-daisy, I pressed a button there.

Well, I'd better be going. I wonder whether all these birds and foxes and whatnot have been here all along – or whether they've moved in, now humans have given them the run of the place. Funny the thoughts that get into your head – when your routine's out of whack. I keep thinking how much this will cost, my gabbing on. I know it's all free – because it goes through the cloud – but you can't shake the feeling you're going to have to pay, one day, one way or another. I can work around your schedule. I'm sure you must be busy – I read lots of professions just keep going remotely. It's another world nowadays. Suppose this must count as work for you – hearing me go on. Another world! Like I said – any time outside one to two. We could go for a walk in the park right by me. Distancing – the full monty. My assigned lady even brought me a nice mask – very fetching, you should see it. Union Jack, only all sort of glittery. You notice a person's eyes, with the masks on. But I've always been one to take in the whole face. I should stop rabbiting on. It just seems an awful shame for the daffodils to go unseen – before they're lost for another year.

B3

From the start I kept telling myself any moment now S would leave. I was continually wrong, until I was right. Then I got angry for letting my guard down. Angry with S for being stronger than me, strong enough to leave. When I have never been able to leave. I have never allowed myself to comprehend that I want to leave. My husband was gone before I realized I no longer wanted him. I cannot even leave this rainy island, even when all my friends tell me how Brexit makes it the moment for departure. I am humiliated by the paperwork of Settled Status. Yet for some reason I want to leave less than ever.

Near the end I had given up stopping my son from coming into my bedroom when S lay with me. Most days we had to be quiet because soon he would rise up to go to school. Quickly he began to enjoy running into the room with his uniform and stupid compulsory tie all in a mess and jumping on the bed. We secretly put our clothes back on under the duvet. S made up stories and I made up silent stories in my own head about how we were a family. Sometimes his out-loud story and my silent story were near enough alike. One of S's compositions was called 'The Congress of Clouds'. All the cloudlike things, the mists and vapours and fogs, gathered in a circus tent in a hidden location in the sky. They were angry and had convened a summit. The vapours believed people did not give them the same respect they gave to solids or liquids. My boy never liked stories but he liked this. The clouds and fogs made a tight heavy ball that came out of the circus tent. It came toward the humans who were on the beach happy there were no clouds in the sky. I do not want to tell you the ending.

Perhaps this is why S left. Because I told him how one day he would become a great father. I regretted saying it from as soon as I saw the look in his face. For a week, after he was gone, I trailed around the back alley, where sometimes we walked in secret late at night. I looked through the frosted window of the gastropub to try to see our ghosts holding hands under the table.

Sometimes I feel I cannot prove he existed. That we existed. It is somehow mixed up with the fact that he never wanted to *jouir* inside or outside me. It is stupid to consider it this way, I know that, but it is like there is no trace. Sometimes I nearly begged him to accept pleasure from me in exchange for what he gave. I could tell he was irritated when later I asked him about it. Once when I insisted a little too much, he made another speech about how for centuries men had forced women to give pleasure. Forced them to their knees to give and take.

How in our small way we were restoring this imbalance. We still had some way to go. But we could. Because I was talented for pleasure. This is what S insisted. Our world presents the compulsion to enjoy, but almost nobody really has a talent for pleasure. My body is unique in this regard. I blushed. Perhaps it is – but I do not think it is the only one to be unique. This sounds like a contradiction. It is not.

My friends all tell me the same thing. *B3*, they say, laughing, *you are crazy. When all of the men we have known only wanted one thing, whether or not they admit it directly, you have found this person who does not want you to do this act – and still you complain!* They asked me for his name until they were blue in the face. This expression I like. I would not tell them. They believed I had made S up. I gave up. I could not explain why they are wrong in their attitude.

I remembered S when defrosting the compote, because we had raked together the leaves that had been piling up for months in the garden, brown, red, black, to reveal apples from the tree. Worms crawled in some but many were still good. We rinsed the apples under the taps and I cut out the bad bits while S told how everyone says the English are stiff upper lips but see, they do go to extremes, just look at the taps – you can choose between burning hot or freezing cold. A bit later that day we argued, and I could recognize neither of our voices. Then we stopped suddenly and in the silence heard the jazz music sound even more strange than we had been sounding. We realized at the same time – the record was spinning at the wrong speed. We changed it from 45 to 33 and the jazz was beautiful again and we never went back to our argument.

One day I told S how delicate he is. But he surprised me by looking sad rather than happy. After a long pause he replied that he thinks something is missing in him. He lacks the capacity for violence. He has never felt it. He has never even had to fight to suppress it. *But this is good!* I say. *You are the exception! Most men are the opposite.* But I cannot make his face happy. He repeats that something is missing. He tells me that delicacy is not the opposite of force. That delicacy is not even the opposite of violence. Now too late I understand.

When S was on top, I could always feel how he protected me from his full weight. Only once near the end did he let go of his body so it crushed me – a little – and I fought to breathe. Now I sleep with the door locked. On our street there have been several burglaries. The wall of my house has stopped being the skin of my body. But I still remember the feeling of S falling with all his weight and crushing me only slightly.

I've only got a very small memory to give you. I'm not
sure I'm going to be able to get used to this format – it
feels different speaking into a phone, without you sitting
here by my side. I try to make myself close my eyes and sit
for twenty minutes, just like we used to. My mind's filled
with all this useless rubbish. Let me tell you the little
memory. S was seven or so. He was round at the
neighbours'. Their eldest was a couple of years older – she
was celebrating her birthday. I was enjoying some rare
peace and quiet – when the front door opened abruptly,
and S ran through the porch and inner doorway. His face
was painted on one side. He was crying – the tears
smeared the make-up. You could just make out whiskers,
drawn in black crayon, dissolving.

I took him in my arms. Tried to console him – but
between the sobs, he wouldn't tell me what had happened.
He only calmed down when I washed the make-up from
his cheek – but still wouldn't tell me a word. I had to go
to the neighbours. The party was in full swing. They were
all made up as tigers, panthers, other animals. I took the
mother to one side. Asked her what had happened. S was
fine, she said. Sat down in the chair, where the children
took it in turns to have their faces painted. He started to

look uncomfortable. They were halfway through. Without warning, he ran from the room – muttering something to himself. The mother followed him. *They're going to fix my face* – that's what she told me my son had said.

*

It's not quite true – that I think of the things that cross my mind as useless rubbish. Sometimes I think it's worth putting down on tape. So I do just that. Press record. It sits there on this device. I flirt with sending it to you. These little things have nothing to do with S. So it won't be of much use. Not to you and not to me. Because this is supposed to be about him. So disregard it, if one day I do it – if one day I send you a little message that has nothing to do with anything.

B1

I lost S in our twenties. Happened with loads of my straight married friends – loads of my gay married friends too, come to think about it. The new platforms – they gave us an excuse to touch base. *Hey! I'm on Facebook! Hey! I'm on WhatsApp. And look, we still have nothing to say to one another.* Call me old-fashioned – I missed the telephone. The way we used to talk – lying back, eyes shut – a bit like this. I'm speaking for myself. As if by now that wasn't abundantly clear.

He was busy. I learned to claim I was, too. When we could find a moment, when we could find a mobile signal, he parried all my efforts to find out just what was going on in his life. *I'm pathetically heteronormative*, he'd say, *pay me no heed* – self-deprecating, disingenuous, to the last. Your life must be far more interesting. Tell me about the interesting life I helped facilitate. He didn't say that part. By now I knew – knew at how cheap a price his curiosity came. But I still couldn't always resist it – the urge – to talk about myself, to be listened to. I tried to limit my self-revelations. Caught myself halfway through the latest litany, the latest sob story. *He sounds like David*, S would say, *only without the muscles and hang-ups* – I'd forgotten having ever dated David.

I tried to imagine his evenings, his days at work. Not because they were interesting. Because S was doing them. He told me he'd been subcontracted to a company that was trying to automate flirting. The app would compute the optimum response time – lock the keyboard to prevent you from responding, until you seemed sufficiently hard to get. I didn't tell S I could have done with the app. The full service cost extra – it dictated optimal responses, based on feedback from previous successes. Users signed away their data, so future flirting could self-correct. S told me this in his faraway voice – baffled and amused. *This world*, he said with a sigh, *is a negative feedback loop of desire*. I asked S, with false innocence, whether he'd come up with the whole idea. It was something in the distance he seemed to need to put between himself and the product. He laughed, caught out. *That's advertising*, he said. *You don't sell a product – you sell the buyer the illusion they came up with it.*

One of these stilted conversations must have touched a raw nerve. As soon as I put the phone down, I picked up pen and paper, wrote how I was sick and tired of social media, truncated phone calls – that if he wanted to speak, in future, he could write me a proper letter. Here was the new address in Cali – unfortunately I couldn't vouch for the Colombian postal service. I'd been proud of how I'd concealed my impending move. A little secret all of my own – punishing S by its sudden revelation. My little ramble was barely legible by the end – it was a while since I'd picked up the fountain pen my mother bought me for Christmas. Maybe I scribbled a little more than I needed to, for effect – the scrawl on the back of the photograph taken all those years ago, on the beach, saying 'to the afterlife'. A dramatic flourish – but I didn't expect a response. Two days later, a letter came through the door and landed right on top of the cardboard boxes packed in haste, just like everything in those manic three weeks – resigning in haste, finding an emergency subtenant, to see out my lease, deciding in haste to go all in with Andrés.

Deciding in haste my relationship with S was at an end. I had to do it then and there. If not, I'd lose the force that had been building up in me, the force Andrés had given me – through the love, the terror I'd lose him, that we'd never stop fighting, that we'd stop fighting and lapse into the blandness we observed out loud in others, to draw stronger lines around what we were. I knew S from the spindly writing – besides, who else would write? I was aggrieved to have ceded the final word, the final flourish. Just like him, bursting all over again into my life – his personality perfectly expressed by the envelope falling casually and weightlessly on to all my packed resolutions. I fantasized about leaving it there – unread, in the dust, for the cleaners to discard – the way you fantasize about impossible things. The month it would take for my possessions to arrive by sea, via South Korea, made the move a positive commitment. I'd be cutting out the extraneous.

But I read it – of course I read it – quickly and dismissively at first, my mind made up, then more slowly, unmaking it. My handwriting had fallen apart the longer I wrote – S's composed itself, till it was calligraphy. He told me he'd been waiting all this time, without knowing it, to be addressed – just like that, with ink and paper. That now I'd chosen this medium, we should stick to it. That he'd write to me as often as he could, once I arrived. That if I wanted, I could write back to him. That it'd be interesting to imagine what correspondence might emerge – between two men with our history, singular, representative – in such different times and places. Me, living my grand new adventure. S, heteronormative, married – even then he couldn't shake the self-deprecating nonsense – at a completely different stage in his life, masturbating unenthusiastically to pornography to produce the semen sample for the expensive IVF procedure. Our words might reflect upon masculinity – upon whatever the hell masculinity might mean today – on becoming a father, not becoming a father. On the weird contours of male friendship. On the ways that it could make and unmake and make and unmake and make itself. By this point his handwriting was becoming very clear indeed. He was dotting every *i*, crossing every *t*. He was returning the photograph to sender, he said – to its rightful owner – and I could feel inside the envelope that it was true. He told me he could never compete with Andrés, pasty-skinned as he was – but that affixing this old memento to the walls of my future Spanish Mission mansion would make him very happy. Rhythms of his words still carry me.

I was astonished. I hadn't ever pried into his relationship with A4 – he never volunteered details. I'd presumed they'd decided against children. Sometimes S alluded obliquely to her being ill. I couldn't work out whether he was apologizing to or for her. I tried to recover my irritation, at his revelation trumping my own – but the sense that, after all these years, I was finally holding him in my hands, won out. It was so good to feel his presence. *Is it near Bogotá?* That was all the others said. *Do be careful not to get mixed up with Pablo Escobar.*

All I remember from those early weeks in Cali is being dazed, disconcerted. Trudging through the sun like quicksand – through narrow streets that went nowhere but offered shade – feeling pathetically unable to cope with myself so soon as Andrés left for work each morning. Not because I was a foreigner, but because he made me feel foreign to myself. I only recognized myself at his touch, so it was hard, to walk down the streets unable to hold hands – because in this neighbourhood, he told me, they hated queers. In the long hours when he was at work or with his family, waiting as he waited for the right girl, just shy of forty – *yes*, he said with a smile, *people start late here* – I'd stumble round the Barrio San Antonio, feeling no longer a tourist, not yet a resident, conjugating irregular verbs, wondering over the difference between *ser* and *estar*, essential being and temporary being, wondering how to say *I am a bald man*, because soon this would be my essential being. But grammar and shame melted in the heat, and so I returned in my mind and often my body to the little kiosk that Andrés had arranged to act as a forwarding point for my mail. For some reason he didn't want me to be traceable to the apartment he'd rented, five minutes away from his bachelor pad. Bachelor. In the end I stopped trying to fight the happy feeling that stole over me when the kiosk man said, *Gringo!*, putting the latest letter in my hand.

I don't know how many letters there were in total. Now they're tied in string, securely kept under lock and key. The delivery was unreliable, so sometimes the sequence broke down. I imagined blanks in the story where letters might have got lost. I wanted to live up to whatever he imagined about me. The beautiful things validated my upheaval – the terrible things would make for good stories to tell S. I sought both out in equal measure. The way the bottle of beer smashed into a thousand tiny pieces when it hit the ground – when Andrés made it hit the ground, as he walked from me that night, straight into his mother's house – yes, a real mama's boy, the prodigal son – while I waited for his bathroom breaks, for the double ticks to turn blue. He had a bladder like an ox. No wonder I wrote letters to S while I waited for Andrés to piss.

S, on the other hand, tried to live down to his false modesty – to what he insisted was his mundane life. He told me all the terminology. Downregulation. Blastocysts. Ovarian hyperstimulation syndrome. *Teach me some Spanish instead*, he begged. *Let me live in the subjunctive – I'm buried in medical textbooks, drowning on Mumsnet.* He spoke about A4. For the first time – to me at least. How the clinic treated the women like battery-farmed chickens. Rows of beds, cordoned off by pale blue surgical curtains. Shuffling footsteps as the nurse passed from bed to bed, sound of the curtain yanked along its rail. The nurse bent down – you can see I really read these letters – took the vital measurements, injected another dose into another arm, drew the curtain. Muesli in the mornings, as S stuck a hypodermic needle in his wife's belly, to induce an artificial menopause – shutting the body down to wake it back up. What little I know about the female body comes from that time. The embryos all had ratings. A, B – like being at school. The British class system starts early. They took the best of the batch and froze the rest. I remember thinking – not just thinking, dreaming, dreaming vividly, while I was awake – about these frozen embryos, souls in a state of permanent suspension. I don't go to church any more but I want to call them souls. I imagine them thousands of years in the future, unfrozen into a ruined world, their brothers and sisters dead thousands of years before. I need to press the fucking red button. This is all bringing back too much.

A3

He's not better and he's not worse. Right now, that's about all I've got time for.

A1

I was lying on my back on the sand. I was a young woman again. My husband on his front beside me. From the sounds I could tell he was sleeping. On holiday he liked to drink a beer at noon. I let a thin stream of the sand in my cupped hand trickle down on to his back – like an hourglass. He doesn't wake. His skin is peeling – the layers look like gradients on an Ordnance Survey map. I trickle a little more sand. It reminds me of the way I season steaks – just as he likes them – sprinkling on the flaky salt before rubbing it into the meat, letting it sit. His body feels strange, because it is strange – to me. He grunts and I remember where I am – see my paleness and freckles and stubble, the scar, through my faded magenta bathing suit. Even when it's dead, they call it an abortion – if the foetus is big enough for them to need to deliver it. He's up now, staggering sleepily towards the sea. Each wave makes me tremble even when it only comes up to his thigh. He holds his nose and dives down. I fight the worry until he appears once again. The sun comes out at moments and then contradicts him entirely. Then I see him swimming, less strongly than before, towards a long, frayed black line, stretching over the surface of the sea. I can barely make it out. Too small to be buoys. He pauses – dives deep – surfacing on the other side of the black line. I think he'll never come back to me, until I hear his footsteps on the sand. The angle makes his body huge. *Bees!* he says. There were bees, hundreds of them, floating on the surface – they must have been drawn to the sea on account of the drought but then drowned. *You should go in. The water's lovely.* What he always used to say. *Go on in. You know you really should.*

The thought of the bees makes me tremble. But I'm compelled towards the water, which laps against my feet, washing away sand with each wave – out from under me,

forcing me forward, until the water's around my hips. I
think of the salt kissing my scar – seawater, the best
natural remedy, the doctors had said. To my surprise it
feels good to be covered – to be in the process of being
covered – and I'm nearly up to my neck when a wave
comes suddenly and picks me up, the bubbling in my
ears and the stinging in my eyes, and when the wave
lets me go I see a blinding light – a blinding light that
eclipses then reveals the mountains that were there all
along – and I realize the expensive sunglasses I'd forgotten
to remove got carried away, by the tide, and I decide not
to shut my eyes to go down looking for them. And I
remember this actually happened – is actually happening,
in the Turkish valley, in 1978 – happening later enough for
me to understand, the meaning being simply that it
happened to me.

BI

The letters kept coming. I was fast running out of
experiences and observations. That's not quite true – I
was running out of the exciting experiences and clever
observations I wanted to be able to give S. I had to
combat little surges of excitement, that one day soon we
might publish our correspondence, fight the publishing

house's requests to tone it down, tell our story, say something about friendship and masculinity – oh yes, big abstract ideas like friendship and masculinity – until I forced myself to snap out of it, stop forgetting my decisive break with the past. Half the time I felt I wasn't in Cali, but in a hospital waiting room – watching his wife be cut up on an operating table, or maybe being his wife, cut up on an operating table. Seeing through his eyes – now he had finally let me, for the first time. In the grey room where men produced semen samples, the big screen offered several varieties of pornography – softcore, except for the channels with Asian women, who were made to say things like *You can do what you like with me – you can't break me, but you can have fun trying. – Write to complain*, I told S.

But there was no time for morality. Things had already moved on – to the antenatal classes, where a mother-to-be had asked how she could tell whether she was pissing herself or having her waters break, if they felt so similar. *Best question all week*, wrote S. I had to hold back from reading the letters too quickly.

For a month I heard nothing. I don't know whether the silence made things worse with Andrés – or just made them feel worse. Emailing would have broken the spell. Finally the misplaced letter told me how they'd been convinced the foetus had died, for one whole awful bank holiday. A4's blood pressure was higher than the doctors would have liked – they were worried about pre-eclampsia. If it rose beyond a certain level, the baby would have to be delivered early. It felt the heatwave would never pass, as I worried about A4's blood pressure – he'd got me weeping at the words 'bank holiday', remembering barbecues and lawnmowers and all the other things I thought I hated. I'd never really dwelt on A4 – now all of a sudden, I couldn't stop thinking about her. I realized how much S loved her – or maybe, I told myself, feeling at once magnanimous and special, S was realizing his love for her, in the act of writing to me. Love needs a third party.

And the foetus hadn't died. Indeed, the kicking resumed with greater force. S juiced smoothies – beetroot, ginger, kale – placed the tray on her belly, when she was too heavy and it was difficult to get out of bed. Once the unborn kicked so hard, the tray overturned and stained the sheets with beetroot. Under the right light, you could just make out the silhouette of a hand – tiny, but with five distinct fingers. It didn't show up on photos, else S would have sent them. I saw the hand anyhow.

My drama was beginning to feel painfully teenage by comparison. I was already regretting all those emails I'd dashed off to old friends and even family – forgetting that the time difference meant they'd receive them mid-morning, stone-cold sober, at the office, far from me in every way. I was addicted to sudden honesty, apologizing to lapsed friends for trivial things they must've forgotten. It was easier to be honest about all that than it was about the present. I had to force myself to write to S about what was neither happy nor exciting. About how, now that I knew Andrés had no plans to come out any time soon, I had a decision to make. About how, after a sleepless night in the rented flat, I raced over to his, even though it wasn't one of our approved nights, marching in grim determination and then breaking into a run in the sure knowledge I'd find him barebacking another guy, but when I opened the door, breathless, I found him passed out in his bed, so I undressed him while he grunted in confusion, falling back asleep almost immediately. About how I cradled his beautiful head in my arms, smelling the anise stench of guaco on his breath, being unable not to like it – finding even his fucking snoring beautiful – thinking to myself, *I can sleep through his sleep, I can do without the little rest I am still able to get*. I told S all this. I wonder whether he tied my letters with string.

A gaggle of nurses had gathered from nowhere, surrounding the obstetrician. They were whispering, very slowly, so as not to let on, S realized too late. Her blood pressure was rising – A4 would need a Caesarean. Prostrate on a trolley, she was wheeled away. By the time S was let in to see her, it was all over but she was still woozy after the general anaesthetic. She squeezed his hand – he wasn't sure whether it was involuntary spasm or conscious communication. Only when the nearest nurse told S to stop frowning did he realize his daughter wasn't dead. A4 remained in the hospital for the next few days. The drugs in her system ruled out breastfeeding. He told me – beautifully, his letter still long and spindly – how her nipples leaked useless milk. There I was, at the intersection of Carrera 3 and Calle 4 Oeste, wailing like my own unborn newborn. I never got to grips with the grid system.

S handled the feeding while A4 convalesced. Sometimes he had to fight the nurses for the bottle. The doctors had told him how sometimes the fingernails of a premature baby might never grow to full size. The heartbeat could go fast or slow, but so long as it stayed regular, there was no cause for concern. Sometimes he put his head to his daughter's chest, he told me – this letter was barely three lines long – heard her heart beating, and realized why it reminded him of putting a shell to your ear and hearing the sea. Because you suddenly go from feeling very big to feeling very small.

It was harder for A4. She didn't feel she'd given birth – birth had been taken from her. S sat by her bed reading a book – I think it was *The Moonstone*, something that let him put on different voices. He was under strict instructions not to make her laugh too much and so split her stitches. Hospital policy dictated that the lights were always switched off at the same hour, so they read with the torches of their phones until the nurses complained. Three times a day, he placed thirty milligrams of codeine under A4's tongue. The nurses let him do that – they were starting to like him. He'd begun to write me letters on his phone, while she slept, when he couldn't see for tiredness – though even the false autocorrects improved them. Sometimes he talked about publishing the correspondence without my prompting. My pulse raced until I realized this meant something was coming to an end. Now we could live on and be dead for ever in a finished product, I thought, sitting in the departure lounge in Amsterdam, on Andrés's priority pass – the last anonymous gift he ever gave me – on a layover that seemed to last for ever. By then I'd had to tell S everything. It felt pathetic, to be intruding upon what was now his family life. I'd have liked him to keep telling me stories about codeine and *The Moonstone* – to help me forget I existed. But by then the letters had dried up.

B 2

The evening you wanted me to tell you about took place in S's house. I hadn't been there for years. The child was nine or ten months. Curious, beautiful eyes. S's eyes. Not in their colour – his were hazel, hers were changing from blue to green – but in the way they looked at things. With steady attention. Fatherhood didn't appear to have aged him.

It was an odd assortment of people. There were some work colleagues, a childhood friend of S's, who followed him for the whole evening with sad eyes, a fidgety couple who kept worrying about the babysitter. Two old university acquaintances, talking about superfood smoothies. *They've changed*, I thought – until I realized they used to talk about recreational drugs in exactly the same tone. I got the sense S and A4 were trying to relearn how to be in society. The sound I'd taken for ambient music turned out to be background noise from the baby monitor. They twitched at the slightest sound, whenever she so much as moved in the cot. Just before dessert, she got a bit whiney. A4 rushed to bring her down. We cooed over the child. She fell back asleep – from that point on, we started talking in hushed voices. Children improve adults – particularly the adults that don't have children. They stop taking themselves so seriously.

S talked about his latest project. By now he'd relaxed –
had stopped checking the griddle pan every thirty
seconds. His office was in the early planning stages for a
new app that would bring people together in a new way.
It was going to be called the Courtyard. S described it as
if he actually cared. Perhaps he was simply good at his job.
The market was flooded with dating apps – but people
were dying to make friends outside their echo chambers.
Look at us, said S. *We all agree.We all agree about absolutely*
everything. Our idea of disagreement is whether or not we liked
the big abstraction show at the Whitechapel. So this
application was created to put people in touch with
others unlike them. *Consensual difference* – that was one of
the tag lines they were toying with. S showed us a beta
version.You could specify how many people you wanted
to meet – how unlike yourself you wanted them to be, in
terms of politics, class, social background.We all had a
good laugh at that – how can you measure unlikeness? But
S was unfazed.With enough data, he said, you could
measure anything.

A4 was watching him persuade us. I couldn't read the
expression on her face.There'd be no ads, said S, unlike
the other platforms. Bars and restaurants would pay a
subscription charge to affiliates – in turn, they'd host the
meetings. Meeting in large groups would mitigate safety

concerns. We had to agree it seemed well thought out. The only concern, said S, was scalability. It couldn't build gradually. There had to be enough different people signed up for the system to make diverse connections. So they were planning a marketing blitz. The venture capitalists were prepared to lose huge sums for a year and a half. It was a point of honour for them – the size of the sums they were anticipating losing. S had a meeting, Monday, with angel investors. He was dandling his child.

That was when one of S's work colleagues started speaking. He was French, or Belgian – I confuse the two. He spoke even more quietly than the rest of us – but somehow he made the room fall silent. *You think you can fix social isolation*, he said, or sighed. He was shaking his head. It wasn't clear whether he was asking a question or making a statement. I don't remember him having said a word all evening. He would tell us, he said – he would tell us about social isolation. He'd just listened to a radio show, on French public radio. He stressed *public* – as if to make a point. The show profiled unusual professions. A recent episode featured a man who worked as an *accompagnant sexuel*. He didn't translate. Told us with a wink perhaps we Anglo-Saxons wouldn't understand the term. An *accompagnant sexuel*, he explained, offered services to individuals who felt prevented from experiencing physical intimacy. Perhaps they were handicapped. Or had body-image problems. They might have had traumatic experiences. Or never have had any at all. They might have specific tastes – fetishes, which required unusual patience or discretion.

After each sentence he paused a little – as if waiting to see whether any of us would jump in, be outraged, protest. He seemed sardonic but also, somehow, in pain. *These workers*, he said, *they possess amazing sensitivity. Only very few people do. Love, passion – these are poor words to describe what they feel. – Feel for their job as escorts?* someone cut in. The Frenchman smiled. *Perhaps*, he said, *we should consider that word's etymology. Escort: it means 'to carry'. To carry through a life. We couldn't call what they do a job. The only adequate word is métier. – Vocation?* somebody suggested. He shook his head. *No*, he said, *not vocation – métier. The variety, the difficulty of these needs*, he added. *The humanity.*

I wondered whether all this was malicious sport – to unsettle all these uptight Brits. But it seemed just as likely he'd burst into tears. These *assistants sexuels*, S asked—*Accompagnants sexuels*, the Frenchman immediately corrected. OK, OK, said S – he didn't usually betray irritation – *accompagnants*. Were they – legal? The Frenchman told him, told us, it depended on the country. I remember the glint in his eye. Germany, Netherlands –

they turned a blind eye. It was technically illegal. But their police had more important matters. Elsewhere, he said, it depended. There was another silence – the silence that feels like several people struggling to formulate a joke. We were stuck, between the wistfulness that had come over us – and the joke someone would end up cracking. This being England.

But no joke came. The Frenchman went on calmly. We British should welcome the *accompagnant sexuel*, he told us. Because it exposed the burned-out shell of our Thatcherite economy, where care was outsourced, privatized at the going rate of the national minimum wage – a world of spiritual isolation and tactile prohibition.

At those words, S's old friend suddenly came to life. I learned later he was training to be a care worker himself. Bi. His name was Bi. He was trying to control his anger and nearly succeeding. He told the Frenchman his *accompagnant sexuel* sounded in actual fact like the perfect embodiment of Thatcherism. A good entrepreneur. Getting rich off the backs of vulnerable individuals – building up dependencies – then getting people like *him* to praise his *exquisite sensitivity*.

The Frenchman met his gaze directly. He had the eyes of a cat playing with its prey. He told his *dear friend* he was forgetting many things. That vulnerable people had bodies too. That capitalism only ever changed when something came along to raise its contradictions to a higher level. This contradiction was simple – the universal need for touch, pitted against the privatization of experience. The *accompagnant sexuel* showed capitalism sowing its self-destruction. We should all read Marx on prostitutes – if we were in any doubt. We were nice, we British – with our lovely institutions and associations. But that was the problem. We did not burn things down – we formed associations. Our supermarkets stocked the worst-quality meat – raised under the most appalling conditions. Our response was to form associations – until we had the biggest animal-rights movement in the world. But if we had not forgotten to kill and to taste – how to kill an animal with dignity, looking it in the eye – we would never have needed these associations.

With sex work it was just the same. We had forgotten how to touch – if we ever knew – and so now we had to form an association to fight for sex work for all. *Really?* said S. It was the first time I ever heard him blurt out a question. Yes, said the Frenchman – this association had a memorable acronym, which naturally he'd forgotten. SHADE, or SHALE – we should look it up. They were fighting for the universal right to fellatio.

Not one person was sure whether to smile or frown. But I saw what was going on in S's eyes.

Looking back, it's so easy – to claim you always knew.

Once I wrote a part – for an early urban ballet – loosely modelled on S. I never talk about the intention behind my works. This'll be the first time and the last. I prefer to call them 'site-open' rather than 'site-specific'. The choreographer can work with the environment however she chooses – but she has to work with it. I tried to write a part open enough for S to fit. That could fit around S. The dance notation itself is as minimal as it gets. Have you ever seen dance notation? It's beautiful – in its own right. The single curving strokes against the stave – they capture the sweep and fall of the human body, even if you can't read them. They recall Japanese calligraphy. They remind you that all language is a body. It's almost a shame it has to signify at all. But all language does – signify, represent, cue. So I kept this notation to the absolute minimum. All the cues can be disregarded – so long as the performer has a clear rationale for what to replace them with. In this role – the role I wrote for S, the role that never quite fitted him – the performer dances not against but with whatever forces resist them. I suggest several sites. In one possible realization, the performer simply lets themselves be carried downstream.

III

28 MAY–30 JULY 2020

('Easing')

DIRECTIONS TO INTERVIEWEES

Although some lockdown measures have now been lifted, the same stipulations given in the previous section ('Distancing') continue to operate. Please note also the consent form that has been sent to you separately. This form permits the disclosure of any material contained herein to the relevant legal or law-enforcement agencies. It applies to all past and future recordings. There is no obligation to consent to the sharing of any material. Should you not wish for your reminiscences to be used in this manner, all extant audio recordings in which you have participated will be destroyed.

A4

S was a good father. Such a good father. They all told me that – so it had to be true. It had to be true, because I wasn't able to contradict them. The only things I could've said would all have sounded so petty, ungrateful. That he never knew when to stop. Making me the one that had to put a stop to it. The practical nagging one, with a stopwatch, saying, *Very good, the pair of you, but we need to get a move on.* Sometimes I felt that was my only role. I dreamed, once, that he was pumping milk from his tiny nipples, straight into the empty bottles – to replace the formula I'd been forced to give her. I hardly needed a therapist to unravel it. My unconscious wasn't making much of an effort to dress itself up.

But I want to talk about it – the times when I couldn't stay exasperated for long. When she was three and a bit – watching her toddle down the front garden of every house on the street, because S had told her some houses liked to be stroked. He purred when she tickled the tumbledown cottage under its letterbox, while I watched from the kerb, unsure whether to laugh or to worry that the old woman who lived there was about to twitch her curtains. Total strangers made compassionate eye contact with me, when they played their little games, on buses and trains. S had told her that somewhere on his body were three magic buttons. One would make him speak a magical new language, one would turn him purple and sparkly, one would convert him into a shooting star that orbited the earth. She'd poke at him with her pink little finger, for what felt like hours on end. *No. No. No*, S would say. She looked frustrated – frustrated and relieved – that her father hadn't been turned into a shooting star.

What was strange was how little he touched her – the magic buttons aside. It took me a while to notice. Then all at once it struck me – the contrast with what he'd told me about his mother. He used to defend her fiercely, even though there was never really an attack – as if he needed to find a reason to defend her. He'd tell whoever'd listen that she had the only kind of intelligence that mattered – knowing how to hold another person. So I couldn't understand why he held himself back with our daughter. I can only get through this if I don't use her name – I don't know why. It was all the stranger when I remembered how he stroked me. Even now he stroked me, though by now we were both fast asleep less than a minute after crawling into bed – I was long past being capable of insomnia. Couldn't even tell any more whether my pain had gone away, or just been crowded out by the crushing exhaustion. Maybe my own mother had been right all along.

Hold himself back – that's exactly what he did. Like he wanted to divert her attention – the attention he always knew how to awaken – away from him and to the world. He'd hunt for new objects, textures, for her to fondle. Wallets that opened out to release credit cards, which I always had to tidy away afterwards. Leaves she'd hold when he carried her around and leaned over the plants. Keys, which he had to stop her from cramming into her mouth. He was avid. He fed her need, servile, never tiring, running left and right for new things to experience. Until the inevitable – the one thing he could never see coming, and I could always see coming, being the nagging one – the moment when she wore herself out, grew more and more fractious, because she needed to rest.

I grew slowly attuned to little changes, over those first months. S liked fatherhood most at the start. He never told me that – I saw it. Saw that he liked how every day our daughter had to make herself into a new person all over again. Had to make a new world for herself. S would help her, starting from scratch – his favourite place to begin.

They'd touch the world together, trace its outlines. When it started to come together, from one day to the next, he liked it less. She was coming to be a person. Oh, he liked it, of course he did – the way she smiled, recognizing him. But something in him was quietly panicking. Panicking so quietly that it took me months to hear it. Panicking that she was learning to be a person, by herself. That she was learning how to fix him. Anyone else would have been glad. To be known. To get to be plain old Dad.

The truth crept up on me so slowly that I forgot to hold it back. I was tired, one day, snapped at him. *You know she doesn't need you to orchestrate life for her. She can pick the book from the shelf by herself.* Immediately, I saw it – the thing he was almost always able to cover up, even on the few occasions he let himself feel it – the hurt. I had to stop myself apologizing, instinctively – because I wanted him for once to be hurt. And I remembered, for the first time in a very, very long time, the look on his face that night – years back, when we'd decided to get married – after I told him he'd nearly made me climax with his touch alone.

*

I can't go on any more. Only one last thing I want to say – for now. We had a little ritual. Our carrying ritual.

Before and after my discharge from hospital, S would carry my bags. He carried on even when I got better. She noticed. She noticed everything worth noticing. *Mummy*, she said, as soon as she could turn the noticing into words, *let me take the bag*. S told her she was too small — but she could soon. She insisted. She wanted to carry something. S gave her a biro, the only thing in his pocket. She wasn't satisfied. *Carry our love*, he suggested. *Carry the love I have for Mummy and Mummy has for me and Mummy has for you and I have for you*. She looked at him with that scrutinizing face — the face I've never been able to resist. Then nodded decisively. OK! She'd carry our love!

S made a pantomime face of sudden concern. He wanted to know if she could be sure — that she could carry our love — when it was so very large. Sorry. Just give me a second. I need to say this. When it was so very large. Scrutinizing face. *I think I can do it*, she said, doubtfully. S looked to me for validation. I told her I *knew* she could do it. That's right, S said — because there was one thing she should know about love. It was infinitely large — but weighed next to nothing. In fact, it weighed less than nothing — because instead of weighing you down, it carried you up, like a hot-air balloon. She was smiling. She announced proudly she would take it. And she strode ahead — carrying our love. She marched along — turning back now and then, to check we were watching her carry her invisible suitcases, from time to time putting on a pretend straining face, then lifting her feet to show she was floating up. I want to cry but I can't.

C I

Do you like my voice? People tell me they like my voice. One of the few nice children at school told me I had a voice for radio. Then one of the others said I had a face for radio too – everyone laughed, including the nice ones. Nowadays all that's water off a duck's back. You stop worrying as you get older – by which point the damage is done. I've come to terms with it. I've come to terms with Hildegard. For a long time I didn't know her name. For a long time I didn't know she had one. I drew her every day for a week – my therapist's suggestion, to put on paper what was inside me. One day she came out as a black star – one day an old leather boot. Gradually, she started to resemble herself. When you looked closely enough, the leather boot was an old crone's withered face.

They say it does you good to give names to impulses. Lots of the others in the clinic did it, without needing to be asked. For the anorexics it might be Ana, for the bulimics Mia. *Ana doesn't like me to do this, Mia doesn't like me to do that.* That was how they talked. My old leather boot of a woman was mine – mine alone. I didn't know what to call her, so it was good she announced herself. When she said the syllables slowly, as if speaking to a simpleton – *Hil-de-gard* – I realized she'd been the voice in my head all that time, repeating what people said about me being too ugly to be a girl. She used to do that a lot – take things people had said, twist them – then all of a sudden she pretended to be kind, suggesting things to cover up the pain. Just as quickly as my family took my objects away, Hildegard would suggest new objects. She was always creative.

Strangely enough, Hildegard and I now get on reasonably well. We've learned a kind of grudging mutual respect. You could say we need one another. She needs me, because she lives inside me. I need her because – well, I don't know why, but I do. I can't say I like her, exactly, but part of me thinks she has my interests at heart. Like when she says to me, *You stupid idiot, go to that party, you're becoming a social pariah, wash your hair so you can wear it down and cover your face.* She's coarse, no two ways about it – but underneath it she means well. It's in both our interests to come to an arrangement. Like this virus. People talk about it as if it's hell-bent on our destruction. But if it gets too virulent, it'll lose its only way of getting around. Like it or not, we're going to have to learn to live with one another. Like I have with Hildegard. She taught me how to be strong. Stronger. I learned how if you speak with enough authority, she'll even take orders. I've learned a lot.

But it took me a long time to get there. She scrutinized every little action – every back-and-forth when I was agonizing about whether to make the appointment with S. She laughed when I switched the laptop on – laughed when I shut it down. She laughed when I clicked back a link – laughed when I went forward. She was wheezing. Sometimes I worried she was getting very old. *Look what you're about to do*, she rasped – when my finger hovered over the dialogue box. *Look at that coward* – when I deleted my browser history. *Look at those grubby fingerprints – you can see them when you finally shut the computer down and the screen goes black.* She was very proud of her ignorance concerning the internet. I tried to quieten her down by watching a documentary – we could normally find a compromise – but the first letter auto-suggested S's page. When I entered my personal details for the seventh or eighth time, this time I actually clicked send.

I found S on the Silk Road. This was back before they shut it down. I liked the way he described himself. I liked the way he described me – though I knew he wasn't talking to me alone. The text box allowed you up to two hundred characters, but he kept it simple. I didn't care about the lack of testimonials. I didn't want to be reminded of the fact I was shopping for a product. Bitcoin only, like most of what you could buy. Later – when they took the server down – he went on to the internet proper, was paid with real money. The people I mentioned – who came around asking questions – told me that. I listened to them, because I was curious. But I didn't feel comfortable – so I told them nothing, not even to contradict what they said about S.

I was nearly hyperventilating when I heard the ring at my door. I'd switched off all the lights to make it look like I wasn't at home. I had it all figured out. I'll ignore it, he'll ring three or four or maybe five times – conclude that some sock puppet, some adolescent, was playing a practical joke. I hadn't even needed to make a down payment – given the lack of testimonials. Then suddenly I had a vision of him knocking and knocking – until my neighbours, who hated to be disturbed late, late being eight, asked what he wanted, confirmed I did live here. I'd been stupid enough to put down my real name. Hildegard was breathing loudly, through her nose. I went down the stairs, opened the door. I'd covered my face with a shawl. Not that I needed the precaution – it was so dark we could barely see one another. I can't stand bright lights. I've felt much better since I replaced the on/off light switches with dimmers. I put a low light in the front room – to show him where to go. I was in no state to speak. He padded through silently – I saw he'd taken his shoes off at the front door. Just like a normal person. Polite. Just like the other one I'd tried it with – years before – after which I'd told myself, never, never, never again.

I sat there like an idiot for a long time. I was hyperventilating quietly – calmed myself down with the thought we could use up the whole time like this, in the almost darkness. I was more than happy to pay to be left alone. My shawl was making me hot – so I took it off, safe in the knowledge he couldn't make me out. Your body goes numb when you sit without moving too long. You travel somewhere else. I don't know how long we sat like that, until he broke the silence – asking me softly when was the last time I'd been touched. His voice reminded me of something. A shuttlecock falling. Feathers, weightless. I used to love watching them float across the net, when the girls did PE.

I sat there in the silence and cried invisibly while I thought about the question. I tried to remember the last time. It must have been months. I thought about how even the men who bump into people develop spatial awareness around me. Thought about the documentary I watched with Hildegard – about the Romanian orphans, thousands of them, abandoned on the street as the USSR fell apart, who didn't have enough carers, who were fed and kept warm but never cradled, so their brains never fully developed. Thought about the nice boy telling me I must be hot when I sat on the boulder overlooking them all, splashing in the pool – first holiday away from my parents. I already wore several black layers, to cover every inch of my skin. He was so kind – but he couldn't stop himself shuddering when he took off the last layer later that week. It took so long to undress me that we were ten times more awkward than when we started. He said the usual nice things – it was him, he was a bit shy. But that's the thing with bodies – they can't but be honest. We sat there for a bit, betrayed by our bodies. I told him to lie with me. When he did, I turned my back – the one part of my body I was never able to reach. To damage.

A long time, I told S. By now I had no idea how many minutes or seconds remained. I turned the dimmer until I heard the click and, in the dark, took off my outer layer. My eyes began to adjust to the dark. I thought I might be embarrassed to tell you this – but now I've started, I don't feel it. I could only see the outline of S – which meant S could only see my outline. I could live with outlines. His was softer than before, more curving, which meant he'd taken his own clothes off, without a sound. I turned the dimmer just a touch. The room looked like the world in the seconds before dawn. At low settings the dimmer buzzes. It bothered me, so I turned it up, just a little – the buzzing faded, light slowly washed the room. I went ahead, because there were only seconds left – so what did it matter? I have to be careful when I take off my leggings, so I hadn't noticed S move towards me – hadn't noticed him kneel by my side, leaning his head on my lap. He somehow knew the only way I could show my need to be touched was by touching someone else – someone whose skin was smooth.

He asked if I could turn the dial, just a little. The buzzing vanished. I saw his hands, moving along some of the healed parts of me – my thighs. It didn't matter because I didn't feel there. Sometimes I'd run my hands along myself, years after what I'd done – it felt like touching another person. I used to run my hands on those lines, reading them like Braille. Feeling nothing. I thought I knew every millimetre of my body. But S found a little parcel of skin that felt. It felt like pain – but every unfamiliar sensation feels like pain at first. *Stay there*, I said. *Please stay there.* He left his hand on my skin. It must already be over, I thought – my allotted time – maybe he charged a higher rate for extra. Only now he was inside me. First with his hand and then with him. It felt nothing like I thought it would – because my body was tensing itself for when he'd start moving, and he didn't start moving. We lay there. At times I thought I should move, for the pair of us. I've seen the videos, like everyone. But instead we lay there, on the couch, in the gentle light. I didn't want it to go anywhere. I didn't want to go anywhere. I was still crying silently, though he must have been able to feel it. *You're doing this*, he whispered. *I'm not doing anything*, was all I could say. *Exactly*, he said, and somehow I understood. Hildegard had fallen asleep.

I don't know how long we lay there, going nowhere, until I felt something deep in me contract – wanted to go on feeling it, only it started to pinch, to feel sore. It was so deep within me that I don't know how S could feel it. But he did, because he slowly pulled out of me. He felt my pain like – I was about to say, like it was his. There I go, inventing stories. *Stay with me for two moments more*, I said. I must have sounded pitiful. *Two minutes more* would have been too specific. *I can do that*, S said. That part of me had stopped contracting. *It's my first time*, I told him. He was holding my hand. *Mine too*, he said, *in a way*. I didn't dare ask what he meant. With a client, I presumed. I had to fight the stupid thought I was special – not just the first person who'd come along. Perhaps that explained why there were no testimonials. Or perhaps no one wanted to endorse him, because they didn't want to share him. I told him he seemed to know what he was doing. *I'm good with first times*, S said. *It's all the rest I find difficult.* He said it in a throwaway way, as we got dressed. But when I thought back over it later, I decided it was his way to tell me not to contact him again. I swore I'd try to find that part of myself on my own. I didn't believe a word of what I was saying. But it turned out to be true. I found it. S wrapped the cardigan around my shoulders – turned the dimmer until it buzzed.

B I

The government assures us we're slowly going back to *normality*. Ha! As if that were an option. For any of us. For me. Sometimes I think about all the things I've told you, speaking into this thing, in a darkening room. Whether I'd have told you half the details face to face. It's too late now to do anything more than wonder.

I didn't see S for a good two years after I came back home. This time I couldn't blame him – I was the one with the tail between my legs. We went back to scattered phone calls. Went back to patchy reception – this time worse, because we walked as we talked, going in and out of Wi-Fi coverage. He always seemed to be on the move. *Bear with me*, he'd say – and then I'd hear a metallic clang just before we lost reception. I tried to imagine what tunnel or remote place he might be travelling through. I'd always imagined he had a desk job. I never followed the thought through.

He talked in a flurry – sometimes bordering on some kind of manic elation. I couldn't work out how he did it. Fatherhood only seemed to have tired him out for a year. While I had no excuse to be as exhausted as I was, slogging through the theoretical part of my preparation – NVQs in Health and Safety – knowing full well how useless the theory would prove for whatever I found on the ground. My qualifications could have given me a shortcut to a more managerial position, but I wanted to see how things really were – to actually be a care worker – before deciding whether the small ideas I had to reform the sector might actually work. And here I still am, all these years on – taking down a letter dictated by one of our patients, which will probably never get sent, to Matt Hancock – she wanted me to address him directly – asking could she please have a ventilator, if it comes to that, because she has four little dogs that need feeding.

And I don't have the heart to mention her four little dogs lived at different times — that now all of them are dead. Reform of the sector seems a long way off.

I told S some of this. Not the letter about the ventilator and the four dogs — my training, my hopes for the future. He was interested. That part goes without saying. He'd show more interest during a four-minute conversation, with bad reception, offering you more of his undivided attention than most people could get over a twelve-course dinner. He wanted to know all the details. Was it true, what they said, what he'd read, that the state was cutting delivery to the bone? What about private providers? How did they outsource care? Tender contracts?

I answered as best I could. Half the details I didn't yet know. I tried to change the subject. Once day I plucked up the courage to ask whether we should edit our earlier correspondence. He told me, noncommittally, he could ask A4 for publishing leads. I didn't ask again. Then it was his turn to change the subject. He asked me, out of the blue, if I remembered that night in Paris. Of course I did, I replied. I didn't really. But as we started reminiscing, on cue, together, the way friends do, when they don't have the time or the will to forge new experiences, I found I did remember it, after all. It had been stored somewhere in me, all this time, with vivid colours.

The dirt-cheap overnight bus in the early days of the Channel Tunnel. The two of us, midway through our degrees, bleary-eyed, drinking real espresso – still hard to find in England. Vaulting the turnstiles at the Métro, because someone had told us it was easy – getting caught by a policeman with an automatic rifle, paying a fine that was half our budget for the whole long weekend. Making each drink last, in the Marais, depending on the generosity of locals – depending on the charm we could put on, with our shaky accents, depending on our young bodies and tight shirts. Noting down the address the man in the leather jacket gave us when we asked the question in bad French. The door without an obvious handle – standing there uncertainly, until we spotted the little button, which we pressed, because it was there to press. The silence, in which time we must have been looked up and down. The click of the door and the feel of it giving to our touch. By then I really wanted to stop being a virgin. I really wanted to stop being a virgin and for S to know it.

The fog of cigarette smoke and the smell of perfume covering up some other smell. Jostling past shoulders, all in the same leather jackets as the man from the bar who jotted down the address. Turning to the large television screen – because that's what you do when you're nervous and overwhelmed by a group of people, turn to the television screen – where I saw hardcore gay porn for the first time in my life. Feeling like a fraud for blushing – knowing if I looked over, I'd only see S looking unfazed, at the bar, buying us a drink, with the little money we had left. The pair of us, squeezed up anxiously in the overcrowded booth, out of place in age and dress and experience. Wanting to cry at how badly I wanted to belong – to belong, nonchalantly, in that place.

S needing to take a piss. Coming back after what felt like an eternity away, when the only guys sizing me up were the wrong side of sixty, a smile on his face. Him telling me, *I got more than I bargained for. Take a look for yourself.* Twisting down the narrow winding iron stairwell, though I didn't need to piss – it was hard to imagine I'd ever need my bladder again. Downstairs, unlit. Techno so minimal it sounded like a slowed-down jackhammer. Tripping over a limb – somebody's limb. Seeing the limb coil, like a snake in a nest of vipers, connected to other bodies and other limbs, clinging together on the dancefloor where nobody thought to dance – pale disco light picking out a pile of discarded clothes. Shirtsleeves tangled, another little orgy, this one made of ghosts. Deciding in terror to force myself to piss. Pushing the door of the first cubicle, feeling it swing back at the

contact of something moving and human. The same with
the second. The third. Finding an empty cubicle at last,
squatting on my haunches to block the door because the
lock was broken – wanting to let no part of me other
than the soles of my shoes touch the soiled floor. Hearing
the grunts from the neighbouring cubicles, feeling the
vibrating partitions – smelling the smell that was only
partly covered by the perfume upstairs. Thinking, *I want this,
I know I want this, I have to find a way to let myself want this.*

I remember it, I told S. Restrained myself from adding,
Too well. Asked him why. He told me he wanted to
apologize. For what he'd done when we left the club.
When we were walking along the bridge by the Gare du
Nord. I already saw it all in a flash. Then S started to say it,
exactly as I saw it, so it had to be true – had to be true
for us, at least. The four of us walking back, S, me, the
two Dutchmen in their thirties or forties who we'd
picked up along the way – or who had picked us up along
the way – who drew the line between what happened
upstairs and downstairs. The feeling of dread, mingled
with excitement. Wanting and not wanting to be invited
up to their hotel room – wanting and not wanting to have
to turn them away because we only had a bunk in our
backpacker hostel. Climbing above the railway track,
silver in the streetlights. Feeling a pain in my stomach that

stopped me speaking even small talk as S talked more and more, holding himself back from falling into the French he wasn't supposed to speak, that belonged to none of the four of us, that he seemed to have picked up from somewhere – maybe from the tangle of limbs on the dancefloor. Feeling tired, so tired, 4 a.m. tired, too tired to hate yourself or your friend, for having two smartly dressed Dutchmen eat out of his hand, when you would have taken either one of them, to get it over with, back when you still had enough energy to try.

I don't get it, I told S. *You're apologizing for what?* He told me how he'd been feeling it for a while – had been feeling sorry for what he'd said to those two men. For the way he'd said it. Because whatever he told me when we crawled into the bunk, his voice drifting up while the others in the dormitory snored – about how he hadn't realized, he'd just been chatting away, it hadn't occurred to him – was bullshit. *I know it was bullshit*, I told S. *I tried to tell you at the time.* He told me he couldn't hear what I was trying to say to him – wouldn't hear me. That he was a slow learner. Now there was no background noise. Now he didn't seem to be in a hurry. He was finally ready to hear the words I'd spat back down at him from the upper bunk. He'd twirled the Dutchmen around his finger – because he knew he could. Because it felt good. Because it had been a little game. But he didn't need to play the little game any more. He didn't need to satisfy people just to show he could. He'd come to see there was a better way.

That's good, I said. I was trying for his non-committal tone. It didn't quite come off. I've never been able to do impersonations. *That's good – that being a father and having a family have taught you the meaning of care.* There was a very long silence. I figured he'd been cut off – that he was travelling through another tunnel after all. *Yes*, he said, at last. *Yes, it is.*

C 2

I don't really need to say a word. You've probably already made up your mind about me, like all the other bluetick libtards – you probably read about someone like me in the Sunday supplement of some newspaper you subscribed to because they gave you a tote bag. See how it feels – to have someone presume? Bet I'm right about the tote bag. Don't worry, I'm more than happy to play down to your expectations. It's all true – *tfw no gf*, depressed Wojak memes. Too much porn – *that* goes without saying.

You want to know the worst thing about porn? It doesn't turn you into some violent monster like the media wants you to believe. It just makes you numb. It turns you into a fucking libtard. Because you know the definition of a liberal? Being happy to accept anything – because you just don't give a fuck. You know, this funny thing happened to me the other day. I was walking on the high street – the sun was bright, reflecting off all the buildings, so I couldn't see clearly. For this crazy moment I thought I saw this weird kind of monster walking towards me – all its skin peeling off. Then the shape got closer and I saw it was just some obese woman in a leotard. You want to know the strangest thing about the whole thing? How I felt – when I thought it was a monster. I felt nothing. *Oh, look at that monster, skin peeling off, coming straight for me.*

Just look at the sites, if you want to see what I mean. Oh, you must be too delicate a flower for all that – or let on you are. So you'll have to take my word for it, or pretend you do – don't worry, your secret's safe with me. Porn's gone strange. Everybody's bored. Nobody can be bothered any more just to watch a girl getting nailed. We've got too much knowledge. They still look at you that way, the camgirls – but even they know the game's up. It's like the mystique's gone – we all know every hole before they've even taken their bra off.

There was a time when it still worked for me. Even had one camgirl I used to visit exclusively. As if I were in a monogamous relationship. Used to get competitive when the other guys tipped more than I could afford. But now it's gone weird. This one camgirl, she doesn't even bother to strip – just talks to the guys. Sometimes she plays a guitar. Reads us all stories, if you tip ten tokens – for real. Tells jokes – she's actually pretty funny. From time to time one of the guys says, *What the fuck are we doing here?* in the chat. They still have the same stupid usernames – hardcock71 or whatever – but nobody seems to do any jerking-off. We're living in a post-jerking-off society. *I don't know*, she said to the camera. *I don't know what we're doing here.* My name is greyed out. I can't talk, because I don't have tokens.

It had been a while since I'd even got it up. There's one more item for you – *tick!* You probably know lots about erectile dysfunction. I started going to the gym, just like the guys in the videos tell you to. I bulked up pretty quick. You realize there's nothing to it. Was ready for the locker-room banter. But it turns out that's just a phrase. The only thing all those jacked guys went on about was protein shakes and how they had to spend the weekend in bed after overdoing the bench press.

I felt better enough about my body to put it to the test. A lot of us like to talk about how we can never get laid but really it's just that – talk. The truth is we don't really want to leave the community. Virgins only. Part of the code. It feels good to have a code. It's not that hard to get laid. I was getting undressed, psyching myself up for what I was going to do to her, when she said something about my hairy legs. Made me lose all my confidence.

So it was back to the gym – more desperate than before. By now I felt almost certain it wasn't something physical. I was catching my breath one day, dumb-bell in my hand, when I noticed – all those hipster retards had shaved legs. *Fuck it*, I thought, *now I have to do this too.* All this was getting to be serious work, for someone that couldn't be bothered. But I made the appointment with the laser removal in some town in the middle of nowhere. Was in agony, biting into the towel, while this guy ripped out the hair – it turned out the advertised price was for wax, not laser. The guy doing it was one of those Corbynistas – he kept going on about the coming revolution and how the Russian channel was the only reliable news source, while I had to just say *right* and *uh-huh*, trying my best not to scream. No, I said, when finally it was over – I didn't want my balls and ass crack doing. The Corbynista showed me what I looked like in a mirror. I looked like a fucking plucked chicken.

By now I was committed to leaving the community – that was how I thought about it, as if losing my virginity was just a means to an end. I got pretty tanked up one night and went through the street I'd heard about. The first woman that came up to me was African, or Caribbean, or whatever. I remember how the receptionist looked at me when he booked me into the room with the hourly rate – like I was dirt. I kept seeing his face when our clothes were off and I was trying to focus on the task at hand. She could tell it wasn't working – put herself on all fours so I could take her from behind. Now I'm going to give it to her, I told myself, but I couldn't get the angle right – it was asking too much for me to do all the work, with her just sat there on all fours. *I can't*, I said, but I sounded like such a loser, which is why I started to make the story up – about me being an undercover journalist, exposing illegal migrants. She could get in serious trouble with the Home Office – but if she gave me my money back, I'd make sure she wasn't named in the article. I got more confident with my trousers back on. I almost started to believe myself. I could look in her eyes – now I was in control of the situation. I could see she was weighing it up. She gave me half back. I didn't know if I was still technically a virgin. I didn't know if I was allowed to stay in the community.

Phew, I thought, at least I got out of that situation, but then I was walking back home through the rough area, when some guy came up to me. He's going to throw a punch, I thought – but then at the last minute he reached over, picked the fucking glasses off my face! I'm blind as a bat without them. I was trying to run after him only I was running through a fucking impressionistic painting – I could hear his footsteps fading. *Give me my glasses!* I shouted. *It's not like you can sell them.* The footsteps stopped. I didn't know if he was gone. *It'll cost you a tenner*, said the voice. *This is ridiculous*, I thought. I was puffing. I followed the voice. Waited with the note in my hand until he handed me the glasses. Like some gangster rendezvous. It was just as well the black woman had given me half back. I put my glasses on – saw this sad knackered geezer. We sat there wheezing. Two sad knackered geezers. I asked him, *Why the fuck did you do that?* when I'd caught my breath. Then he went and burst into tears. Told me how his dad has just died. How he'd been going through a difficult time. I got kind of emotional. *Promise me* – I told him – *promise me you'll never do that again. – I promise*, he said. For some reason I didn't want to leave him. *What the fuck was that about?* I wondered on my way home. I'd completely forgotten I had the body to punch him.

Then there was one more attempt before S. I got wasted one night. I'd started to drink once I got into crypto – needed to go somewhere after a day of staring at the screen. All those charts – candlesticks, bearish engulfing, evening star, time to sell. They used to flash in front of my eyes even when I switched the screen off. Which I almost never did. I found some site – pop-up brothel made it sound like a boutique hotel. She texted back, *Hi baby*. I was on my way when my phone vibrated. *Baby, can u get me cigarettes?* I asked what kind – she said Benson & Hedges. For the next two hours I set off on this wild goose chase, when I could've got Marlboro Lights from the service station, which meanwhile had closed for the night. Then when I finally reached the pop-up brothel, I found myself apologizing for the lack of cigarettes. *Don't apologize*, I told myself, *just take out all this frustration on this woman.* – *Hi baby*, she said in a sleepy voice, *I thought you'd never come.* Fifteen minutes later, I had to admit it was something deeper than the physical. She'd found a couple of spare fags down the back of the sofa. Offered me one, showed me the blinking setting on her fairy lights.

By then I was getting hammered on a more or less nightly basis. One morning the feeling didn't go away even when I'd vomited. I scrolled back through last night – couldn't remember a thing. I'd apparently searched for the camgirl who played the guitar and read stories, but she'd deleted her profile. Then a whole string of videos about men getting hair transplants in Turkey, which I watched again, remembering nothing – they looked like big babies, red bald heads bandaged on the plane back. That was when I saw S's page. Fuck knows how I found him. I'd even set up a profile. I fought the nausea, but I couldn't stop scrolling. *C2*, I said out loud to no one, *you've already shaved your fucking legs, now you're a full-on batty boy?* Couldn't bear to read what I'd apparently written to S – but couldn't bear to take my eyes away. *Who even is that person?* I thought to myself. *Not S. Me.*

It all got worse when I saw the amount of crypto I'd sent, the time we'd fixed, my address. *I'll let him in*, I said, *because none of this matters.* All this only mattered to prove to myself I wasn't – I wasn't going to get it up with *him*, in that state. He looked a bit uncomfortable when I let him in. He was probably expecting something a bit more lived in. All those crisp packets. I've always had a thing about eating in public, so I take the crisps from where I've put the pack in my inside coat pocket. Then I just dump them when I get home. I wasn't lying, when we spoke on the phone – I'm a long way past shame.

The bottle of gin had taken the edge off the hangover. *I've paid for this S for two hours*, was what I was thinking. *I might as well do whatever I want with him.* I tried a bunch of things. I tried to go back over past experiences – to correct them. Got him to get on all fours so I could pretend to be that journalist again. Or to role-play some of the scenarios the algorithm gave me – like the video where the guy puts his hand down her trousers and acts all surprised to find a cock. None of it worked. It worked as much as I was scared of the monster with the skin peeling off. So I just sat there, leaving S with nothing for entertainment but the crisp packets and the rectangles on the walls where I'd taken down the posters of the page-three girls – I'd started to think they were looking at me. Not like that – in another way.

I remember not speaking to another human being for two weeks when I was a child. Just to test whether I could. I imagined myself as this stone whenever anyone came near. Not moving a muscle. I was chatty enough before then. I don't know what happened. It's what I did with S. I made myself into a stone. He didn't seem bothered. He was getting paid, after all. Then I heard his voice, asking if he could trim my nails. I was so surprised I forgot I was being a stone – turned to him. He was just sitting there. *You've got quite delicate nails*, he said, *but they're a bit long.* That was true enough. I used to bite them, but then I stopped, because I don't like the feeling of needing something.

I never said yes – just let him do it. He found a grubby old pair of nail scissors somewhere in my bathroom. Went slowly – I guess he needed to fill the time with something.

He was holding my hand with one hand – he cut with the other. I could feel myself getting agitated, thinking how he'd move on to my feet and find my ingrowing toenail – before I reminded myself none of it mattered. He stopped – three fingernails still to go. *Slow*, he said. *Let yourself be touched.* I let my hand go limp, because there was nothing to fight for or against. *There*, he said. *All done.* I didn't want to admire my fucking nails. I nodded. My hand was still in his hand. I wasn't going to move it. I wasn't going to do anything. *Very nice*, I thought. *All that crypto for a fucking manicure.* The weird thing was I was getting hard. I might have said something – only I didn't want to jinx it. I was racking my brain for another situation we could try out while the iron was hot.

I suppose S felt it. He took my hand – put it on my fucking crotch. Let it lie there – under his hand, which had never stopped holding mine. I tried to move a little, to start rubbing – but he held my hand tight, to keep it still. It was weird how I kept getting harder. He took off my trousers, put my hand back there. First time a man had seen me in that state – first time anyone had seen me in that state. I didn't particularly care either way, I just noticed it. When he took me in his mouth, I wanted to say to him, *Save yourself the trouble, I can't feel anything* – except I was done apologizing. Done apologizing for myself. Done apologizing for forgetting the cigarettes. *Fuck it*, I thought, which is what I normally think – only it was starting to feel good. *Fuck it, this is starting to feel good*. I started thinking – now I'm definitely out of the community. The rule is you have to talk about the sexual experience that got you kicked out – the more humiliating or disgusting the better – but I could feel myself on the edge, and I told myself none of it mattered, but it sounded different, and then instead of saying that out loud, I was just moaning *sorry, sorry, sorry, sorry*, like a fucking liberal, saying sorry because I hadn't warned him I was coming and that he'd have to swallow some of me down.

He came over some more times and then he stopped. I gave up worrying what it meant. What it meant was I liked to have my cock sucked by S. There, I said it. To get my cock sucked and then talk. *Don't pretend to like me*, I told him once. *Don't pretend to care. Don't pretend we have a single thing in common*. He used to run his hands along my fucking stubbly legs. *We have more in common than you might think*, S said. I asked him, *Tell me one thing*. He was stroking my hair. *I have psoriasis too*, he said. Maybe it was the first fact I learned about him. Maybe it was the last fact I learned about him. I know. Tiny violin. Depressed Wojak. What the fuck do you want me to say – now he's gone? You want me to say how deep down I think it's my fault – for making him say one thing about him, so he had to leave? You want me to go to Hampstead Heath, set up a Grindr profile, asking someone to suck my cock?

I never told the community. I just left, without a word. Which is why I'm telling you, instead.

A1

My mother – more and more often – used to remind me of the children. People forget in the reverse order in which they learn. First children learn to focus their eyes. I'll never forget the first time S and A3 looked at me – really looked at me. Then they learn to coordinate their limbs – then control their bowels. Then speak. Mum was the mirror image. Her language went – she lost control of her bowels, her arms and legs went. Right at the end, she could only grip me with her eyes. When she lay on the bed, fed by tubes, immobile, her face frozen in that bewildered expression, even then her eyeballs still swivelled – still followed me around the room, still gripped me. I don't think it was a coincidence, how quickly she went downhill, as soon as both children were gone. As if she was telling me, *Now's my time, my time to be taken care of. I've been waiting so long for you to take care of me.* There was I – dreaming up all manner of things, now at long last I had time for myself. Time, for the very first time. Maybe the freedom scared me. Maybe that was why I slotted back so naturally into the role of caregiver.

It started with the automated calls – whenever she tugged the emergency cord – informing me that the ambulance was on its way. I tried reasoning with the on-site manager of the sheltered accommodation we'd put her in, explaining she only did it when she got nervous alone and started to panic – that sometimes I missed her calls, even when I took the handset into the bathroom with me, to hear it over the shower. The system was automatic, he explained every time – a private company was responsible for installation and maintenance. So I had to drive over, wait for the paramedics – they could've been helping someone who needed it – while she fussed over her overnight bag – *Oh dear, what a palaver I've gone and caused* – but delighted all the same with the attention, fixing her bob like a princess. She climbed into the ambulance like a princess – guided by solicitous attendants into her welcoming golden carriage.

Digestive biscuits – all she ever said she wanted, when I offered to do the shopping. *None of that chocolate tomfoolery.* She drew the curtains from 3 p.m. – which gave her an excuse to turn on all the lights, even in July. I knew she was going downhill when she saw the cat in the carpet pattern. *Look at that cat, dear — such a friendly smile!* I told her it was the carpet, that she couldn't have a cat with her allergy. *Is that so?* She said it with that tone of voice — as if I'd told her an interesting piece of historical trivia. *Is that so, Mother? — No*, I said, *you're* my *mum*. She fixed me with those eyes. They were beautiful — the way some eyes get more beautiful while the face around them changes. I tried to hold her gaze. It exasperated me — how much I still loved her, how I knew I'd never be able to make a clear distinction, to say this reduced thing before me no longer was my mother. Sometimes I had the crazy feeling she was testing me. To see how I'd react to the hallucinated cat. To see if I'd humour her — *That's your old moggy Tabitha*. To unsettle me.

But she was always on best behaviour when S called round. She didn't see anything in the carpet, then — except a carpet. She was so proud of her grandson. He'd announce she seemed fine — taking everything into account — at the end of their long chats. I used to hear them muttering while I scoured the sink. She'd look coquettish, a little flushed, like a schoolgirl, when I entered the room with a cup of tea she'd wave away on principle. *Would you just look at the clock — we've been rabbiting on like there's no tomorrow — nearly time for*

Antiques Roadshow — *it's getting dark outside* — *somebody should draw the curtains.* S would tell me, later, during our debrief, some of what she'd said. Stories about secret balls in air-raid shelters. Other men, before my father — I don't know what. He asked me whether I'd had any idea. I hadn't. She could have been making it all up, grown suddenly fantastical. Or have lost her filter. Either way, S'd say, she needed an amanuensis. She didn't remember two minutes ago, but she had 20/20 vision of a Saturday afternoon in May 1952.

I think I can tell you now. Sometimes I got aggrieved with how S would helicopter in — tell me how to care for my mother — when I was the one who had to fill the shopping list with more than digestive biscuits, to scour the sink. It's slowly sinking in — why this feels such a release. To admit I was angry with him about this. I never knew I was allowed to be angry. At anyone — particularly not S. To admit that I'm allowed to be angry at him, even if I want to protect him — even though I can't protect him — from whatever's coming. The process has started.

The times I liked best were when my mother and I both forgot she was going to die soon — when we could bicker just like the old days. *Mum*, I'd say, when I saw the Post-it note reminder stuck to the wall, *you don't need to polish the banister, you live in a flat now.* — *It's not my fault,*

she said, *if I'm overwhelmed with all these odd jobs.* Odd jobs
meant sorting free circulars and bank statements – I'd
transferred everything to direct debits. *Far too much on,*
she'd say – when I suggested bingo in the communal
room, after she moved into the sheltered flats, which
already felt like years ago, even when it wasn't. In the end
we played patience – it's really a game for one. *Are we
nearly there yet?* she'd ask, in a high-pitched voice – like a
child in the back seat. I never answered – for fear of
asking where *there* was. After she died, I took down all the
Post-it notes – hundreds of them, scattered across the
rooms. Mostly shopping lists. A few were messages for my
brother – I couldn't make head or tail of them. I noticed
the last note when the flat was practically bare – stuck
right where she'd fallen, for the final time. It read, *S says
don't ever forget again to look at the flowers.*

C3

S walked through the overgrown side path to the priest's
cottage. I'd had to give fairly detailed directions. It was the
only thing I liked about the place – that if you weren't
looking for it, you'd never see it. Even the postmen
mistook it for a side extension at first. The priest was
kind to let me stay. Didn't even try too hard to convert

me. Perhaps he thought all that would develop naturally. I went along to a couple of the services – more to show my gratitude than anything. It was nice enough – I liked the stories and the singing. He made a special point of introducing me by name – my new name – to each member of the congregation. I could tell he'd primed them. They were all friendly. I went a couple more times – stopped when it became clear they didn't understand the slightest thing about what they said they were forgiving.

I flinched when I heard his feet on the paving stones – force of habit. Weeds grew between the slabs – I saw how they'd grown, whenever I was on the lookout. Even though he knocked just as I'd told him to – two soft raps, two hard – I couldn't shake the thought he was one of them. Come back to finish the job. Still, I slid the bolts, moved the wooden plank. Hadn't bothered to tidy much. Before me, the cottage hadn't been lived in for years. You could try to beat the dust out of the tired furniture – it just floated for a while, then settled back down. I'd stopped noticing I was constantly allergic – or perhaps my body had adjusted. Antihistamines would've meant a ten-minute walk to the nearest pharmacy.

I need to make myself more comfortable. Any position starts to hurt after more than a few minutes.

S sat on the sofa bed – the only space he could find. Each morning I told myself to fold it up – turn it back from a bed into a sofa – so I could read sitting down, like a normal person. But as the days wore on, I never summoned the energy to click the metal frame back into place. What was the point, folding it up just to pull it out again, when I was spending the whole day alone in the same room? Anyhow, I prefer reading lying down. S didn't know where to put himself – between the bedding and the books. I was suddenly ashamed of the lack of a duvet cover. I hadn't come so far loose to forget that people were supposed to put duvets in duvet covers. *I must be relaxing*, I remember thinking, *to feel ashamed*. There are some situations where shame's a luxury your body can't afford.

I always have too many books on the go. I keep them open at the page – face down, though I know it ruins the spine. Back then I used to pick up one book, put it down, drowse for a bit, pick up another, till the different narratives started to merge. Not that I read much fiction. I couldn't make the mental effort to put myself into another world. Though I wanted more than anything to be in another world. I mainly read history, philosophy. Sometimes I left a book open so long that its page turned yellow. I only noticed when I turned over to the white page underneath.

S shifted a few of the books to one side. It felt like an invitation – to my house, to my own sofa bed. I couldn't go close to him. I saw stains on the sheet I hadn't removed – perhaps they weren't really there. I washed everything frequently, but there was so much damp that things smelled just the same when I left them to dry inside. There were holes in the wall outside – I saw them from the kitchen window. I suppose the priest had taken the washing line down for my own good. He was thoughtful that way. Not that there was any chance of me making it out into the garden. I stayed inside and watched the grass grow.

My mother always told me milk won't get unspilled, just by crying about it. It was just like her, to give a little twist to a proverb. I remembered her unspilled milk when I started to cry, with my back to S, so he couldn't see. I was facing the wall and I let myself go. I didn't put my hands out to break my fall, so my head hit the plaster. I wanted to feel it again – my head hitting the plaster – but without making the effort, to keep falling and keep hitting myself. I couldn't cry any more. I felt it then – S's hand – on the ridge of my back, where it hurts. He didn't take his hand away. It still hurt. I wanted it to hurt. Then I lost the feeling of pain. The body can't keep hold of anything for long. After a while it turns every sensation – pleasure, pain – into something else.

My voice came out muffled, speaking low into the wall. *Do I disgust you?* I asked. Eyes shut, forehead pressed tight. He took a long time to say no. But it wasn't the delay of hesitation – it was more like he wanted to be careful to say the word in the right way. The single simple word. I asked him, again – this time more clearly, moving my mouth away from the wall. *Do I disgust you?* – *No*, he said, after a smaller pause. It was like a caress, that *no* – not quite that much, like the lightest brushing – so I let my body fall, but in the opposite direction, so this time he might break my fall. And he did – break my fall – and carried me down to the sofa bed with the sheet that smelled of detergent. He took off the T-shirt with the stains that no one could see – so quickly I didn't have time to warn him. His hands traced the boundary of what he couldn't touch – I closed my eyes and tried to see the shapes he was making, like a young boy making faces from clouds. I'm not supposed to talk like that – not supposed to think like that. I'll try to do better – I promise in future I will try to do better. The line from one of the books I never finished. It came to me at his touch. *Abide in hell, and despair not.*

Then it all started pouring out of me — with the relief, the relief to say it to another person, after all that time mouldering. I can't tell you half of it, even if I'd like to feel that way again, because you're not S and you're not taking me in your arms. You're not here to tell me I don't disgust you — and I probably do. I'll tell you the little I can, all the same. Because what else is left? I told S how at eleven I didn't know what attraction was — and at fifteen I realized I was attracted to eleven-year-olds. That was the time Mother and Father had started to play their disgusting games. They must have known I could hear it all — the walls of that house were paper-thin. But I won't try to blame them — when I grew to like it, grew to like the noises they made. The hiss before the lash. I can't go there. Years on, when they were both long since in the ground, I stopped by to watch the demolition of the whole row of terraced houses. Compulsory purchase, to make way for the new railway line. The block disappeared in a second in a puff of smoke. But none of it ever really disappears.

I tried to make the thoughts stop — almost from the moment I felt them. Kept away from places, situations. Bunked off school. Wandered around the car park. When it turned icy, I warmed my hands in the public library — sticking to the adult section, hoping the adults wouldn't ask questions. Started to enjoy reading, because there was nothing else to do. Nobody seemed to notice me. At that time of the day there were only pensioners, jobseekers, the homeless. You could sign up for half-hour slots on the computers. I used to tilt the screen so others couldn't see, reading on chat rooms about the side effects of antidepressants – numbness, lack of libido. I wanted the side effects more than I wanted the primary effects. I persuaded my mother to book me an appointment with a psychiatrist – persuaded my psychiatrist I was depressed enough to need a strong dose. So terrified he'd see through my story that I made myself a nervous wreck – got exactly the diagnosis I needed. When the library was nearly empty, I researched chemical castration. At night I tried to sleep by imagining the magic horse that carried me to imaginary countries. But it hadn't come back since I was young, and the thoughts always led one to another.

I didn't go to university. I just went to the internet, where you learn more – which is the whole problem. Couldn't stop thinking about what I never – never once – acted on. Listen to me, pleading my case. Part of me wanted to act on it – not to do it – just to stop thinking about it. By then I was reading a lot. *Abide in hell, and despair not.* One day I got chatting with someone on 4chan. It was like talking to myself. I said more about myself in forty minutes than I had in ten years. He claimed to be twice my age – though who knows, everyone's an avatar. I never found his handle again, on the forums I plucked up the courage to visit. I got terrified he'd been an undercover cop. Though part of me wanted to be discovered. I used to stand at the bus stop thinking, *It's obvious, everyone knows – they're all just waiting to see how long you'll take to turn yourself in. Do the decent thing, turn yourself in, you might get a shorter sentence.* In some ways I came to want him – the undercover cop who'd out me. It was the one fantasy I'd allow myself. Hiding tires the body. That was one reason to set up the chat group. To find him. Or somebody. To expose myself to somebody.

People go on about the 'dark web', as if there was a simple opposition – dark and light – when there are just lots of shades. I knew right away the authorities could have found me – if I was a priority. What I'm trying to say is that I could have hidden better, if hiding was what I'd wanted. I could see the burns by the parts S was avoiding. Could picture the splotches, the mushrooming out. If you remove yourself far enough, look down on it, you can find it beautiful. The marbling. The livid tones. *Florid.* That was the only word I remember the doctor saying, when I sat there, high as a kite, in the hospital bed. Floating for days, before the pain kicked in. I made myself remember what Kierkegaard says – suicide is the supreme act of selfishness.

S took off the rest of my clothes and saw the worst of it. He started to massage me with an oil he'd brought. It smelled of lavender. My muscles stopped fighting and I told him what the *pro bono* lawyer had advised me not to say. The three non-negotiable conditions. A strong sexual urge for legal minors. A promise never to have acted on them. A commitment never to act on them. *Keep it to a minimum*, the *pro bono* lawyer said. *Don't go into details – and don't justify.* But I told S, as he worked the oil in, how that chat group gave all of us the only chance we'd ever have to express ourselves – to discover we weren't alone – without consequences, retributions. I got messages every couple of weeks – from people I'd never meet, telling me that group was the one thing that held them back from acting on it. Let me just get a bit of air. Time was I didn't dare open a window. Small mercies.

The server stopped hosting – we migrated somewhere less accessible. Darker shade of the internet. By this stage I was receiving disturbing messages – anonymous threats. Could just as easily have been from police, vigilantes, convicted paedophiles. None of it fazed me. I'd have gladly died for that community. After two more migrations we were running out of options. I say 'we'. Most of the others had got cold feet by then. Traffic was down ninety per cent. It was just the core group – and if we couldn't reach others, there was no point. I got a phone call. They told me to come into the headquarters – made it sound like they were asking, when really they were telling – under caution, not arrest. No need to record. Just a chat. A woman spoke while a man took notes. I remember the force with which he pressed his biro on the notepad. She was nice enough. I suppose they'd worked it out between them that way. She could see I had good intentions, but I'd have to shut down the site all the same – we were vulnerable to bad actors sharing illegal content. Insufficient age verification. Minors might come into contact with abusers. Downloading actually counts as distribution – in the eyes of the law.

I told them there were already a thousand ways to share illegal content – nobody would come to us to find minors. Knowing it was futile only made me speak with more passion. I told them it seemed fine for social media not to bother with age verification. That I was honest, owned it – didn't call myself a MAP, or an ephebist, or any other euphemism – that I was a paedophile, trying hard not to act. Told them however they reproached us was nothing in comparison to how we reproached ourselves – but it wasn't a question of choice, of will. It was in us. I offered to show them research, the neuroscience. They told me not to make backups. Back home, my mother asked me how the interview had gone – it took me a few seconds to remember my cover story. I said I wasn't confident of getting the job. The market was shitty.

Then I was in a bad place. I did think about killing myself – but was terrified to switch on the computer, when I knew they were watching. Pathetic as it sounds, I felt I couldn't kill myself without proper research. I knew there were threads listing painless ways. I have a low threshold, for suffering – I didn't want my parents to find me that way. I festered in the attic for weeks – trying to return my mother's smile when she was pleased to find me not on the computer, for the first time since I was ten. She was the one who suggested I upload my CV on LinkedIn. I looked at the images for less than eight minutes. I know because we checked, later, my *pro bono* lawyer and I, though the timestamps were ruled inadmissible. Deleted them immediately. I'm not stupid. I know nothing's ever really deleted. We press Control-X, think it's gone – but it's there floating in the clipboards of our desires. I was relieved by the knock at the door. I could picture the truncheons, though there were none. I shut the Velux windows, because I didn't want the attic to flood if it rained. Kissed my mother on the cheek. Her cheek was wet.

In the second meeting they recorded everything. It's bringing it all back – speaking into this thing. I suppose you'll distort my voice. They played it back to me – my distorted voice. To preserve my anonymity. *Listen*, they said, *you sound like what you are. A monster.* The woman was gone. They were police from higher up the chain. Inhumane. They didn't need to kick me around. I wanted them to. I told them none of this would have happened – if they'd only let me keep my community together. But I'd lost the will. They told me my little community *was* the problem. They quoted the chat boards, out of context, to make it look like we were doing exactly what we weren't. *What disturbs me most*, said one, *is that these little fantasies are so well written you might want to read them.* They casually mentioned castration, suicide. *Sounds like you got yourself some options.* I know these people. These are the people that rail about *those nonces* – by day. Then put their mistress in a chokehold – by night. Or who click a button, see a pixel explode, in the Middle East. That's fine. Society's fine with that.

It doesn't feel the same, saying this, without S to hold me. The sentence was short. Just like my *pro bono* lawyer had said. A first offence. The system's clogged up, they wanted easy convictions, to massage the statistics – for

the right-wing media, freedom of information requests –
while trying not to let too many get murdered inside. I
didn't get murdered inside. Kept my head down for the
six months. Practically the only person I spoke to was a
teacher, who put on basic literacy and numeracy classes.
She told me how, in nearly all her classes, the sex
offenders were the only inmates who wanted to learn. She
couldn't bring Blu-tack into the lessons – convicts could
use it to make a mould and use that to make a key from
wood or wire. More skilled than me – whether or not
they wanted to read and count. They never told us their
names, but I can see her face. It helps – to remember the
people who chose to show kindness.

The *pro bono* lawyer was right about everything else.
How the real hardship would start outside. The register.
Housing restrictions. No proximity to schools, school bus
stops, parks. As soon as there's so much as planning
permission for any of those things, you have to move.
People say councils draw up blueprints for things that'll
never get built, just to force offenders away. The grinding
fear, that some vigilante has joined up the dots – traced
who you are to the new name they give you.

I moved four times in two years – three times on
police advice, once because of a new free school. I liked
my last place up until they came through the front door

wearing balaclavas. They hit me around a bit and then tied me to a chair and set fire to a rag greasy with kerosene. The council house was full of old carpet and wooden furniture – it caught easily. There was one who wanted to stick around to watch me burn but the others said not to take the risk. I sat there, tied to the chair, thinking how I'd been willing to martyr myself for my community – but now I'd just passively welcome death. The flames were at my feet. I passed out from the smoke but came to again with the air full of burning. I knew the rubbery smell was the satchel my mother had bought me – before I knew. My old books would all quickly catch fire. I thought about how they'd smell. I don't know what force made me tip the chair over, prise open the door, roll down the stairs – breaking my shoulder and ribs, which took the full weight of my fall. I didn't salvage a single book.

I sometimes wonder where it came from – the urge to roll, to fall, to break, to go on screaming, for help. It wants to go on living dumbly, despite everything. Now it only sounds rehearsed. The first time I said it, it sounded differently – because S was there to take me in his arms. He hadn't stopped working the oil into my skin – he was delicate where it got sensitive, further down. My voice was getting drowned out by the sound of his running the bath – and I realized I had nothing left to say.

I started to shiver and so he wrapped me in my soft dressing gown – the only clean item of clothing in the house, which is why I never wore it. When the level was high, he peeled off the gauze bandages to reveal the worst spots. He lowered me into the bath, gingerly – until I leaned back and felt him supporting me. He asked me if it was too hot and I said a little. He turned the cold tap with his right big toe – the one unsubmerged part of his body I saw – because I was terrified to turn around and find someone else's face. The heat spread through me and I slowly stopped thinking all this was to lull me into a false sense of security, before finishing it off, slowly.

I hadn't bathed in weeks. It hurt too much. I could feel S scrubbing my skin. I was becoming numb. I thought of my body, carved up into sections, like the diagrams in the butcher's. Remembered the Bach fugue – I haven't felt strong enough to listen to it, since I stopped being able to play it. It was the way he moved over me – endless variations for two hands. When he hit upon the precise combination, I knew the world would end. When his hand went to my undamaged thigh, I saw my erection bob just above the surface of the soapy water. It sank down again. It surprised me – the little signal of my desire. So the medication didn't work after all, not fully. I didn't know what the desire was for any more, where it was going. I was going to say something, I wouldn't know what until I'd said it out loud, but S brought his finger to my lips. It was shrunken and wrinkled. Like my own skin. He started to wash my hair, slowly working up the gel into a lather. Then brought his face to my ear, whispered, *When liquid foams, it's a little miracle, all over again.* It was all he said while we bathed. The bathroom acoustics made his voice sound far away. Even when he was still with me. Though I wanted him to come back to me badly, I never phoned the number – when I'd risked everything to get it. *Abide in hell, and despair not.*

C 4

I knew something was up from the moment he started picking at his food. *Dad*, I said, *why are you picking at your food? – I'm not picking*, he said, *I'm savouring.* Well, from where I was sitting, some things seemed to be savoured more than others – the tofu wasn't among them. *Where did that extra-virgin olive oil come from, Nigel* – that's how I phrased it – *the one you're drizzling like there's no tomorrow?* He hates it when I call him Nigel. *Waitrose*, he said. *Don't be a smart alec*, I said. *What I mean is*, why *did you get it? – Because I like the taste*, he said. The taste. As if he could feign ignorance of saturated fats, mono being a no-no. As if we had room for luxuries. We're lucky to break even, when you take everything into account. His pension keeps going up – just not as quickly as my entitlements go down. I had to make a point of getting out of my seat and bringing the margarine. The information's written on the side of the tub – so he can't play innocent about fatty acids. I tried to drop off the extra-virgin olive oil at the soup kitchen later in the week, only they don't accept what's already been opened. It's the gesture that counts, though. I took the bottle home and hid it at the back of a cupboard.

I should have suspected even then. But I was busy, with volunteering and with my research that was already hard enough with the lousy connection. I never imagined he might actually get up to something while my back was turned. I kept a close eye on him at the bridge club, particularly when one of those widows asked, all innocent, if they could play a hand together – a whiff of her perfume and that would be that. Men carry on acting as men, long after they should have retired. We play every hand together. I got quite good at it. You have to remember every card played. You have to watch the body language of your opponent. I watched those widows like a hawk.

After the extra-virgin olive oil there were other telltale signs. He wanted one size down when we went to buy him his new shirt for spring. I don't care how much flab he'd lost, men in his age bracket shouldn't go near slim fit. Looking very pleased with himself, he was, checking himself out in the changing room. *Dad*, I said, *your eczema having quietened down doesn't mean you have to flaunt yourself before the whole world.* He looked one last time in the mirror – finally buttoned the button up. But he got back into that bad habit of contradicting me. It started with him being reluctant to go out canvassing. I honestly feel like his mother – tying his shoelaces, because when he does it they just come undone, pinning the badge to the lapel of his jacket while he sits on the bed. He kept asking why we had to go when it was raining and there wouldn't be an election for years. I explained how we didn't just want fair-weather friends. Pointed to the sky – once I spotted the link I'd made without knowing it – to prove my point. That unlike them we were committed. By then I was back to calling him 'Dad' – though I always reserved 'Nigel' as a threat. *As for the election*, I said, *you know they can call it any time. You really think they won't override the Fixed-term Parliaments Act?* Which is exactly what they did. Not that I ever get credit for being proven right.

Well, in the end he came along – although he mumbled the lines even more than usual and the wind blew away his badge, which can't have been properly secured, so I had to get my hands dirty fishing it out of a puddle. No thanks forthcoming. *Dad*, I said, though he was beginning to test my patience – he hadn't wanted to knock on the door as soon as he saw the big driveway with four cars – *it's good for you to get a mouthful from toffs like that. It shows we're getting through, provoking a reaction. Before they just smiled and voted Tory – now you can feel something's at stake, everyone's worked up for one reason or another.* I had to keep reminding him what they told us at the training sessions. Don't just preach to the converted – knock on the doors of the probablys, the maybes, the almost-certainly-nots. Otherwise, we're in the echo chamber. In his defence, Dad did do his best to learn the new terms.

Things seemed to pick up again after that, but then we were watching the news on TV – by TV I mean my laptop, connected to the screen by an HDMI lead, which I had to pay for out of my own pocket, to avoid the mainstream rubbish. We were watching the one show we pay to subscribe to – the analysis is that good – but then he got back on that old high horse about how some of these arguments reminded him of I-don't-know-what back in the 1970s. Look how that all turned out, and was I really sure, he just didn't want to see all our hard work go to waste — and so on and so forth. *Dad*, I said, through pursed lips as he was testing my patience once again. *We've been over this more than once. It's not like I haven't seen the documentaries. It's not like I don't know who Michael Foot is. I have a lot of respect for the politicians on our side back then. But just look at them, those grey men in their frayed jackets with the elbow pads — listen to the way they spoke, impossibly long-winded.* I explained to him how in the end it isn't really about the elbow pads — the elbow pads are just *representative* of something bigger. What matters is the energy and the ideas and the fact we're waking up and we have all these new ways of organizing. Because really, what's the point, if you think history will go on repeating itself? What's the point, if you don't believe in the possibility of fundamental change? And it frankly wasn't a great look — a boomer lecturing a millennial on the ins and outs of it all, given the mess they'd made, which we'd have to clean up. Then he went quiet, only not the usual kind of quiet, when we were paying attention to our show.

He kept spending more and more time in the bathroom, but when I pressed him he just said he was combing his hair. It did seem a bit less thin on top all of a sudden. His other excuse was those pamphlets I'd put on the shelf by the loo, to give him some ideas to mull over —

his constipation gave him the time – though he'd ignored them up until then. I wanted to disbelieve, even when I could see the light of the smartphone glowing through his trouser pocket. We opened up a whole can of worms with those devices. People go on about the dangers of exposing the young to social media. Take my word for it, it's the geriatrics you need to worry about. They never got to grips with desktop computers. You know Tony Blair didn't send a single email in his whole time as prime minister? Tells you everything you need to know about the man. But when the new tablets and smartphones came on the market, things got out of hand. They were so intuitive any idiot could use them. The thing was they hadn't been prepared. They hadn't been trained, like our generation, to understand the internet – how to discriminate – so they had the worst of both worlds, old habits and new access. Before you knew it, they were refreshing the *BBC News* homepage every three minutes. The more advanced even learned how to set it as their homepage. Everybody goes on about firewalls for minors – nobody brings up safety settings for pensioners. They got everything, then they used it up – fucking Triple Lock – and now you've got grandmothers dancing on TikTok.

He had a good grumble, about being monitored, using some of my own arguments against me – until he understood it was for his own good. So it beats me how he thought he was going to get away with what he was doing when he went off to the study and claimed to be playing solitaire while he listened to that classical music that just went round and round in circles. From time to time I quickly opened the door – just to test him – but I knew his reflexes were good for a senior citizen. Once we took him to the doctor who banged one of those little hammers against his knees. When Dad got compliments about his response time, I surprised myself by thinking, *That's how quickly he minimizes the screen.* By then my suspicions were pretty far advanced, only I was keeping quiet about them – because two of us could play that game.

One evening I let slip I was coming down with a cold and couldn't go to the bridge club. Made my throat sound hoarse for effect. Just smiled when he suggested in that case he might play a hand with one of the widows – which at any other time would've driven me potty. *No problem*, I said, *have fun.* I locked the front door after him, like I always do – I like to have some notice when he comes back, in case I'm watching something myself to relax. I deserve some downtime, with everything I have to shoulder for the pair of us. I left it ten minutes before I started to retrace the search history. It wasn't hard to find.

Seniors might be able to use tablets – but they don't have the faintest idea how to cover their tracks. The less said about the user name the better. As if there's any reason why a grown man of his age needs a second email account. I forced myself to read through the whole exchange. It was hard, but I managed. I only sped up at the end when I remembered he was due to come back. Went so far as to hope one of the widows was detaining him with her flirtatious smile. You don't want to imagine the quantity of messages. They seemed innocuous, at first – Dad was going on about his childhood in all this unnecessary detail. It was when he started talking about Mum that things went downhill. Speaking in his real name. Saying how he loved me but I could be touchy so he needed to be careful. In the end I found it – of course I did – the email where Dad gave his address. Our address.

You've been very clever, Dad, I'll take a leaf from your book. That's what I thought to myself. So I put back all the browser tabs just as I'd found them – deleted the search history from the last half hour. The mouse I'd smashed in that brief fit of anger posed more of a problem, but I replaced it with one that looked nearly the same from the box with all the cables. I hate using Amazon but sometimes it comes in handy. It was getting dark by the time he got back. I heard his key turn the lock, so I was prepared. I was very calm. *Sit down*, I said, *please*. Do you have something you'd like to tell me? He started blabbering on about how he only helped the widow put away the chairs. *Nigel*, I said, *I don't care about the widow*. That shut him up. *Have you got anything you'd like to tell me?* He looked genuinely confused. For a brief moment it crossed my mind he was more manipulative than I'd thought. Or maybe he was disassociating. Maybe there were two different personalities inside him. So I started to test the water. Talked to him, as if nothing was amiss, only dropping in some of his phrases, the ones he'd used in all those disgusting messages. It took him a while to cotton on. But when I asked him, using his exact words – whether anyone had recently made him feel things he hadn't felt for years – he knew the gig was up.

I've seen them, I told him, *I've seen them all*. I'd say my voice had less anger than regret. I was curious whether he'd break down – like people often do when they've been living a lie and are found out, but he actually tried to brazen it out! Spouted irrelevant rubbish about how it wasn't what I thought, how I hadn't met this S – makes me sick just to say his name – how with his help he'd been feeling so much better lately, that part of him even *wanted* me to know, when keeping secrets had been the only thing weighing him down. It took for ever to explain how he was the victim. I stuck at it. I was patient. *That's how gaslighting works*, I said – could see I'd need to explain the concept. That generation doesn't have the words, so they don't have the concepts.

But I could see I still wasn't getting through, so I had to take preventative measures. The tablet vanished, for a start, and the smartphone – I changed the password to the second email account, in case he tried to log on from the laptop. It was just as well I gave myself time to cool down, having been all poised to send an email telling that creature exactly what I thought of him. An email would only have put him on his guard. By now Dad was moping. Wouldn't come canvassing. Went so far as to protest that it wasn't so bad. That all this S had done was let him get in touch with himself. That there wasn't anything wrong with it – whatever society thought. My mouth feels dirty saying all this.

He came clean about how, during my volunteering training that weekend, the creature had come round and held him all night, in Mum's bed, while he cried and remembered their life together and slept more soundly than he had in years. I'm putting it the way he put it. That was when I knew this called for more drastic measures. Taking Mum's name in vain like that. Taking Mum's bed in vain. I took down all the photographs. The honeymoon one on the bedside table and the one on the mantelpiece and the one in the silver frame high up on the office bookcase – the one where she's smiling, not knowing she's smiling at him carrying on like that, hunched over the terminal – men are disgusting – and I packed them up very carefully and put them in the cubby-hole he doesn't know exists, let alone the combination for the lock. By this stage he could tell my mind was made up, didn't even put up a fight, though he must have noticed the gaps on the mantelpiece and the bedside table – this S hadn't made him completely blind. He didn't dare beg for them back. I think it must have been starting to sink in, what he'd done to her memory. She looks so lovely in those photographs.

I went straight into my story because I wanted to test whether you'd remembered what I said in the last recording – about not getting sucked into the individual accounts but remembering the *structures* of power. That's what matters in this case. Look, I signed the petition that sex work is work, but that doesn't make me a hypocrite – it all depends on the power relation. Most sex workers are marginalized and vulnerable. A high proportion come from immigrant backgrounds – their clients are mainly men with money and power. Whereas in this case the tables were turned. Do you want to know what this S was? I did *my* research. He was an adman. Says everything you need to know. Dressed up in a fancy suit and tie, leaving the office early, because his top salary still wasn't enough – it's never enough for people in that position. And his clients? *They* were the vulnerable ones, like my dad, who was a senior citizen, who hadn't even paid off the final instalments, who might be tempted by a passing fancy to remortgage what he had. So no, I wasn't wrong to sign the petition.

Once I'd recovered myself, I needed to prepare the ground carefully. The anonymous letters were a mistake. I see that now. Institutions of power always close ranks. I waited for him to come through the revolving doors of his shiny office and then walked at a safe distance to what I discovered was his house. With that stupid bounce of his – like he was enjoying the thought of what he'd got up to and what he'd get up to. Like he was dancing at the very idea of it. I could watch him from the bus stop opposite – the bus never came, given the funding cuts, which gave me the time I needed. S didn't leave the house while I waited. I suppose he needed time to shower, formulate his excuses – read a fairy story to the little girl who came to greet him at the front step. I got into the habit of watching S in this way. Sometimes the wife came out – I got into the habit of following her too, at a safe distance. Working three days a week, leaving around ten, back around three. Nice relaxed schedule for a busy Karen. She was the one I felt sorry for. Even if she was a Karen. Once the daughter walked along by her on all fours, like a cat. Poor child. The wife dropped her off at the crèche, and I followed the wife to the office. Another big company sign at the front. Another happy productive worker.

Then I could make progress. The wife looked even more innocent in the profile photograph on the company website – it must have been a few years old. You can't let sympathy distract you from the job at hand. They said they welcomed interns on a rolling basis, but it took countless emails to HR before they called me in for an interview. I picked out a new suit when Dad's monthly cheque cleared – he owed me that at the very least. Had some fun trying it on for size. I looked the part. She might have looked just like that when she was my age. Felt like a total fraud – dolled up in make-up, answering these idiotic questions about where I saw myself in ten years – and still it wasn't enough. Turned down for a job where they don't pay you to work, because you don't have the experience, because you can't afford to buy it. Sort of sums things up. It took me a while to remember that I was only there because of a different mission. To see the wife. Not that I had a very clear sense of what I'd do. Our eyes only met for a second, as the receptionist was showing me out of the building. But I recognized that look – the same look that was in Dad's eyes. That was when I saw what I needed to do and how to do it. I was already composing the letter to myself on the way down – trying not to slip over in those stupid high heels. They make you hand back the badge with your name on it, at the front desk – as if you were going to frame it, hang it on the wall. I started walking around in no particular direction. I knew I had another three days wearing these clothes. The big department stores let you take anything back – so long as you keep the receipts.

c6

My head is fairly splitting, but I must attempt to focus upon the things I wish to say to you in the small amount of time they have allowed me. This latest carer would only lend me her phone for a small period if I agreed to sign the document from the National Health Service with all its small print. I misplaced my reading glasses some time ago. Like all the other carers, this one has on one of those stupid beekeeper outfits – it is not as if I would sting her if she didn't have that plastic visor on.

Now that I am speaking all these words, I have begun to wonder if you even remember who I am. It is such a dreadfully long time ago that I told you about my little group of friends. You could well have moved on to other more pressing matters in the interim.

I must try not to become distracted, even though my head is splitting. The caretakers have assured me they have not turned up the central heating – although there is no other plausible explanation. I would naturally take my clothes off, were I wearing clothes that were easy to take off. There are many days when they do not even come to undress me, as was customary before. I have very little idea of what is going on, although I sometimes put my ear to the padlocked door to hear footsteps – running, running, running – down the corridors. They no longer come to clean my windows, and when they bring my packed lunch, they simply put it on a tray and proceed to stand at a distance in their beekeeper costume. It appears we are down to the bare essentials in that regard. A sandwich and an apple and a can of pop, without so much as the crisps that fizz on your tongue. The carers no longer draw close enough to soap me down. When I was a little girl I used to let myself get very dirty indeed so I could enjoy the thought of how good it would feel to scrub me clean. Now it is a little like those old times.

Even the medication deliveries have become irregular. When you tot everything up, it is a mercy that my friends have returned to pay me a visit. They have returned, only they are awfully faint. Teresa in particular – her skin is so pale as to be nearly transparent. You can nearly see through her to the chalky wall.

They sit or lie or adopt other poses in the four corners of the room. Christine suffers these restrictions more than most. She insists on moving closer to one of the other ladies in the room. All she wants is a little cuddle, she says – her skin pines for human touch. I must prove very firm. *Christine!* I say in my loud voice. *Christine – get back in that corner!* I explain to her once again about the necessity for social distancing. We must all stay far removed from one another till the day when we can take a walk together in the sunshine.

It is quite a nice thing to care for people, because it distracts you from your own symptoms.

My window is beginning to get grimed with bird droppings, but I was nonetheless able to see through it the other day an old lady with her shopping. Nobody comes that way normally, most of all these days, but there the old lady was. The heavy bag split and an orange rolled to the feet of a young man coming the other way. Two people in one day! That was a turn-up for the books.

He bent down and was all poised to return the orange to the old woman's waiting hands when he remembered the necessity of social distancing. I suppose we will need to find new ways to get dropped fruit back in a stranger's bag.

It is Agnes who gives me the most cause for concern. Her delicate mouth, her lovely little throat. You would not believe that dreadful hacking cough would come from it – but it does, at all hours. It is hard to get a wink of sleep with her coughing. I know how guilty it makes her feel, to keep us all up. I know because even when the room is black, I can feel her body trying to keep the cough inside her, so as not to disturb the other ladies – until her pale face turns blue and her whole frame is a-tremble. I am trying to describe Agnes as I know she would like to be described. Then at last she can fight it no longer – the hacking cough resumes. I feel it like it's mine. It just must be contagious, however far away you sit from each other.

One day lately I heard a small sound like the rustling of autumn leaves – I required time to twig that Agnes was trying to tell me something. I asked her to speak up, but she would or could not. Then I was in a pickle – for her voice to be audible, I would have to move towards her. In the end I thought better of my precautions and moved a step closer to her corner. Her voice was still very faint and muffled. I abandoned my health policy and got dangerously close to Agnes.

She gave me the message I now wish to relay to you. Agnes desired very much to know whether you liked her little poem. She was ever so modest about it – you know how these imaginative types are. She was wondering if – when you publish it in the book you are assembling – you could make the initial letter look like it does in traditional poems. You know the sort I mean – in big Gothic font, so it resembles a metal trellis, wreathed in lovely creamy flowers and creepy-crawly vines. Agnes was a little shy about her poetic production because parts had been emended by the other ladies. I believe this is one of the reasons she would prefer a pseudonym. You can take mine if you absolutely must. Perhaps you could call it *Lament of C6* – if you require a title.

Lovely Mister Squirrel still comes to visit. No need for a beekeeper costume for him!

Susan has been lying on the floor without moving for some time. The strangest thing of all is there are two of her here – in the north-east and the south-west corners. Oh my days, this shivery feeling is back and the phone will fall from my sweating hands if I do not have a little lie-down right away.

A4

We'd just got back from our first long trip away. S was carrying our daughter in his arms. She'd fallen asleep in the taxi. Babbling nonsense. Little West Coast expressions – she'd only needed three weeks to pick them up. I went first with the small suitcase. Pocketed the two letters on the doormat.

I went straight to run myself a bath, while S put her to bed. It seemed something was wrong about the house, but I couldn't put my finger on it. Jet lag does funny things to you. The heating was off, so I had to wait for the water to heat up. I remembered the letters I'd put down on the basin a moment earlier. The first was from the Liberal Democrats. Printed in a way to make it look handwritten. Addressing me by name. They photocopy the same things for everyone. There should be a place reserved for those pointless trivial things you fix for ever in your mind – because of what came just after them.

The second letter was handwritten too. But for real. It said, *Your pig of a husband has been sleeping with hundreds of people. When I say hundreds, I mean hundreds.* There was more but I couldn't read it. So I jumped to the bottom of the page. *Yours, a concerned party.*

I left my body. I left my body and went somewhere else, telling myself, *Just keep going, away from the body you've left and into the room. Don't let on, don't give in — it's exactly what the malicious person who wrote that nonsense wants. Go into that room and just ask him so you can return to your body.* I'd instinctively flushed both letters down the toilet — the Liberal Democrats and the other. The bath was still running. S was folding underwear in our bedroom. We'd put on a full load before heading to the airport — marvelling at our organization. We just seemed to have so much time. *S,* I asked him — shutting the door behind me, though I knew our daughter was asleep — *have you been sleeping with hundreds of people?* By sticking to the exact phrasing of this ludicrous accusation, I could be sure to refute it. He didn't turn around — didn't straighten his back — but he did stop folding the underwear. I knew it from his posture. In the past — years ago now, when I'd worried about the brochure woman, before she came into our life — I'd always known it would be this way. Nothing would make him volunteer any information — but if I asked him directly, he wouldn't be able to lie.

So the weak person I was, the weak person I'd moved beyond, the weak person I couldn't think of without a shudder — it turned out she'd been right all along. I was falling, backwards, but something stopped my fall – I slid along its surface, thinking, *That's the grain – of the wood – of the door*. It supported me as I slid down it and on to the floor. I was OK, so long as I lay there, with my back against the door, my legs straight as the laminate flooring we'd laid a long time back. I needed not to become formless. I knew chaos lay very close – but I'd persist in my being, so long as I kept this L-shape, floating through space. My eyes were shut. It wouldn't hurt so long as I stayed perfectly still. I couldn't breathe slowly – but I could breathe shallowly. This is the one and only time I'll ever talk about this – for some reason, it's you I'm telling it to. I don't know how long I sat there. I wondered whether S was still somewhere in the room, gone back to folding the clean underwear. I wondered whether S even existed. He couldn't have left. It felt good, to have finally blocked the one exit. I felt fleetingly powerful – more powerful than before or since. I couldn't open my eyes – even if it left me unprepared for when he put his arm around me. I hated my skin because I knew it would immediately relax. He hadn't come to console me. It was the barest show of respect.

I don't know how long I sat there – in that L-shape – travelling through space. I saw him, through my shut eyes – it suddenly made sense, that he was *this* sort of man, folding the clean underwear. A thousand images and words came back to me, filling in what until then I hadn't realized were gaps – in what until then I hadn't realized was a story, a story about me. An awful clarity came over me – I knew there was only a brief period when the violence done to you makes your brain plastic again. I wanted to figure out as much as I could before the pain set in. I was thinking hard, in my L-shape. *Understanding is just a way to cope*, I told myself. *What you're doing is coping.* I thought my voice might laugh. I was worried S would do something to himself. I was worried I wouldn't be strong enough to resist taking care of him. I was worried about one of us starting to talk, and then it would all begin – the satisfactions of shared understanding, working through it together, complicity. We'd always been simultaneously saved and doomed by the way we could talk through crises. I felt a twinge in my back for the first time in years – reminded myself not to fight it.

I opened my eyes. He'd collapsed in the other corner of what was still our bedroom. It was all still there. The wallpaper, the plug sockets. For some stupid reason, it had all persisted. *And so there really were hundreds?* I said. The dryness of my voice gave me the courage that I could actually do this. I looked at his face and his eyes that were looking at nothing. *I can actually see this man now*, I realized. *After all these years I can actually see what he looks like — now that there's nothing I'd rather look at less.* I repeated the statement to the ceiling. The ceiling didn't respond either. *I suppose I'm not enough for you*, I said. *You're too much*, he said. We were both talking to the ceiling. I told him not to talk rubbish — to stay silent, if he had to — only spare me the rubbish. I felt my back twinge as the wooden door pressed. *Mummy will be there soon*, I said. *Go back to bed. — She's still in her clothes*, said S. For a moment we both returned to the people we'd been a short time ago. She occurred to me with a stab of pain. *But our girl*, I said, *our baby girl. Why isn't she enough for you?*

I trapped him in the ensuing silence. I hadn't cared about what he'd said about me — but I wasn't going to let him out of this question. He waited a little and then started speaking quietly, quickly, because we both knew she was there on the other side of the door — because even after everything, after everything that was happening, she was going to need to be spared this and then put to bed. She was enough for him, he said, she was more than enough. That was the problem — she was too much. He was scared of the day that would come when he wasn't enough, when she'd outgrow him. I knew this was only part of the truth. But I also knew he didn't deserve my reasoned arguments. So I turned to him – with venom in my eyes. Such venom in my eyes as I looked straight at him. *S*, I said, *how much damage do you have to do before you stop speaking with perfect fucking syntax?*

It was only a retort – called for no response, from either one of us. But in the silence I knew what I had to say in the little time left. I needed to keep my eyes tightly shut, keep the tears trapped in, while I said it. I spoke softly and quickly. *That explains why you need all those mistresses*, I said. *Because you're scared of the moment that happens to every parent – every caregiver – of no longer being needed. Because I've become so strong you don't need to care for me any more. Because that, deep down, was all we ever had.* I paused, leaving a space he didn't fill. *But all your mistresses*, I went on, *they can't really give you novelty. I don't care how many there are. The thrill they give you will always turn out to be just the same thing.* I paused again, and he still didn't fill the space – I decided to make him. I opened my eyes wide. I knew I was frightening, because I was starting to frighten me.

I've got better, he said after a very long pause, in a tiny voice. Something was curled up outside the door – it might have been the cat or our daughter. *What does 'better' mean, I asked. You didn't fuck somebody in the fortnight before we flew to California?* I remembered, when I said it, what I'd thought, on the plane – we might move there permanently. S's company had a new branch – I could work remotely. It turned out I liked the sunshine, the gardens, even the driving. The words I'd said stopped being ironic as they died in the silence. I knew I had very little time left before the pain kicked in. I was trying not to think about the pet names we used to call one another. I felt – stupid thought – I can give everything up, but I'm not ready to give up being called by my pet name on Saturday morning. S, I said, summoning the strength I still had. *Tell me you didn't – fuck somebody – in the fortnight before we flew to California?* He said nothing. I told him, in that case, to break down 'better' for me. Told him to give me the digits. Told him I still couldn't hear him. Strained my ears. *Better*, he was saying in a tiny voice. *Better.*

I told him what I needed to say, because there'd be no other time. How hard I'd worked – to make myself strong – and now would have nobody to share my strength with. That she and I could pack our bags in minutes – after all, we had clean laundry, still piled neatly on the bed. I was realizing slowly how terrible it must have been – to be him, to be so utterly unable to take himself seriously. I sensed I could finally have got the answers I wanted – about his father, about why for all those nights he would never let me hold him. It was probably the one time in our expiring life together I could have got an answer to all those questions that only then occurred to me were the right questions. But I didn't have the room inside me any more – to be the person that understood him. I could feel the formlessness coming – I had to be able to carry her, sleeping if she were sleeping, awake if she were awake. I couldn't block any longer the thought I'd never cared about being married and so it meant nothing to be divorced – the most terrible thing would be to see something on the street, or in a field, or to hear something someone said, and not to have someone to share it with – and I cried, I couldn't help it, but I'd done what I needed to. I let the door open on to me while the tears stopped me from making out whatever had become of him.

I took our daughter and went straight to a hotel – I couldn't bear the thought of my kind mother taking us in and of her having to bite her tongue all the time. We spent a week there, as the dirty laundry I couldn't afford to wash piled up. Then one morning we got up early and went home, knowing there wasn't a chance in the world he'd still be there. He wasn't. The pile of folded clothes remained. One night I finally fell asleep – woke with a fright, sweating. Something was digging into me with its claws. I fought under the duvet to prise the wedding ring off my finger – threw it, burning hot, into the corner of the spare bedroom I'd moved into. I slept a little. By the morning I'd forgotten – until the vacuum cleaner made a crunching sound. I carried on, though the room was spotless, dustless. Then I fed the cord back and sat there, putting it all off. I've put it off ever since. The dust is piling up and I haven't changed the bag. Sometimes I think about that ring – buried deep in a cake of dust.

C4

I'm tired – achy – hope I'm not coming down with something. It was pelting down right until I clocked off. Then – naturally – the sun came out. I'll keep this brief – I want to mark myself available for the peak time tomorrow morning. Even pre-pandemic, people looked at you like you were vermin – opening the door, just a crack, to snatch their pack of processed meat, chopped into little pieces, so they don't have to think about the battery farm it came from. Lockdown just gives them an excuse not to open the door. You stand there, soaked, while they lecture you from behind the letterbox. *Your mask should really be covering your nose.* I've learned to keep my mouth shut, since the robot supervisor gave me my second warning. You have to smile — even if they can't see it, they can tell from the eyes. At least you can yawn in secret. The one good thing to come out of this pandemic.

I still prefer it to the office job I used to do. A miracle I survived two and a half weeks. It takes a special kind of temperament to bear it. Someone like S, I suppose. Forcing myself to get up every day at the same time — walking by the side of the motorway, at rush hour, to the industrial estate. I had to, because I couldn't afford to learn to drive — not that I would have, anyhow. Most days it was tipping it down. The cars didn't bother to swerve to avoid splashing me. No natural light in that underground bunker — when I finally reached it, soaking wet. The neon lighting exposed everyone's dandruff and skin conditions. We all came through the temp agency. Wearing that stupid headset all day long. It rots your brain — you turn into the sort of person who *should* work in a call centre. They don't need to replace us with robots. They turned us into them a long time ago. The way my line manager spoke to me — wanting to know why I'd booked the insurance claims inspector into two slots, Greater Manchester and Solihull, with ten minutes to spare between them. Why should I know where these places are – I'm not from there, am I? It's not my fault if the system lets me book things that are humanly impossible.

Don't get me started on my office colleagues. I used to try to talk to them – I mean a real conversation, a meaningful conversation, not blather about *Love Island* or who eyed who up by the coffee dispenser. I had to beg them to leave the basement for the lunchbreak – it was so depressing with the sandwiches they'd all wrapped in tin foil – to go to the café on the industrial estate, our one other option. They were blinking like moles that had never seen sunlight – complaining the whole way. *This walk alone takes up half of our lunchbreak.* Then we sat there in silence – I tried to get them to talk about something meaningful, but couldn't get even a flicker of interest about basic income or even unionizing. They couldn't see the point! The only good thing to come out of those two and a half weeks was the poem I wrote – that evening when I was really burned out, so exhausted I couldn't sit still. Dad was driving me nutty, so I walked by the embankment where it all sort of tumbled out of me – about an office worker like me who over time has a black dahlia that starts to sprout on her instep. It's a symbol. Think about it – I'm not going to do all your work for you.

After the two and a half weeks I couldn't take it any more – I'd given up engaging them in conversation on any meaningful subject. I just sat there in the basement like they all sat there in the basement. I'd even started to wrap up triangle sandwiches in tin foil – that's what capitalism does to you. When they rang the bell for the morning break, I took my headset off and walked out of the building – it only occurred to me when I was walking back along the motorway that I wasn't coming back. It felt good, walking against the traffic – the sun made the tarmac sparkle – for once it wasn't rush hour. The temp agency carried on paying me for another month, though I never told them I was leaving. Now and then it works in your favour – the total inefficiency of the system. I doubt anyone in the basement even noticed I was gone.

Let me get this over with so I can go to bed and try not to doomscroll. By the part I'm getting to, I'd put back out all of the photos of Mother – apart from one, which I told Dad he could have back when he'd shown a sustained improvement in his behaviour. I stopped thinking about A4 when I saw her drive off with the child one day and not come back. I'd done what I could to help her. The shoe shop kicked up a fuss about the heels – said they'd clearly been worn more than twice – but stores always back down if you threaten to shame them on social media. It was good I'd reserved the last photo as a final reward – it gradually dawned on me what to do. I knew S was still going around exploiting people – got a reply to the email I sent pretending to be Dad, from Dad's hidden account. I mimicked him – all sentimental – mimicked him well enough to get a disgustingly sentimental reply in next to no time. He said he was taking a break, for personal reasons – but he'd be in touch. I could see how things would develop with the slightest encouragement.

It was driving me crazy – thinking all the time about what that man did with other vulnerable people. Plundering their savings, getting them addicted to him, dependent – taking everything they had and leaving nothing for the younger generation, who in the meantime are slaving for the gig economy. I'm sure he had eloquent justifications for his abuse. He was pretty with words. I knew it first hand. He'd probably make you believe he was fucking Jesus – laying his hands on the needy. Which was why I contacted my old university acquaintance, who in the meantime had become a hot-shot lawyer. You probably know the kind of person. Nice enough to talk to – he never disagreed with a word you said. Came along to the rallies, said the right things when he stood for student elections, then as soon as he got elected there was suddenly all that talk about difficult compromises. He kept going on about how he was training to be a human-rights lawyer – only apparently that was too competitive or expensive. But he was still going to do charitable cases on the side – naturally – it wasn't like he was going to be one hundred per cent corporate. We'd lost touch, the way you do – a friend said he'd muted me. Didn't bother to unfriend – just muted me. Still, he agreed to meet. He must remember that chat group we were in – some of the things he said sound even worse with the passage of time. Or maybe he was curious about why I wanted to meet.

I was trying to spot the piercing where his nose ring used to be, but it was hard to find. Maybe the law firm pays to seal up all the holes. Clearly he'd become even more used to making difficult compromises in the years since I'd last seen him. The bar had seen to that. His voice was even more grown-up sounding. *Of course he could understand my being upset*, he said, *but the law didn't offer obvious recourse* – which I translated back into it turning a blind eye. *The judiciary had got their hands burned on recent high-profile cases – public prosecution would only press charges when there was a good chance of conviction.* He was sighing, like it was the two of us against them – but I don't think he grasped the seriousness of it. Every time I brought up the specific things S had done to my father, he'd just go back to generalities.

Absent a clear allegation of harm from a client, he said – frowning sympathetically – *it was a non-starter. Even with one it'd be touch and go, whether it ever made it to court.* Well, that made things easier. *Now we can go about getting a clear allegation of harm.* That's what I told him. My father just needed to put his name to a description of what had actually happened. The details were all fresh in my mind. I had to go through seven or eight drafts – the boxes they gave you to write in were ridiculously small. Dad's always been a slow reader, but that afternoon was bordering on the ridiculous. All the same, I saw how happy he was when I finally put the best photo back on the bookcase. I saw Mum's smile – back again – knew we were doing the right thing.

I'm not totally naive. I know the conviction rates. I have no faith whatsoever in the outcome. But it's not about the outcome. The punishment's in the process. It's like I said a moment ago – the system's totally inefficient, so you have to turn it against itself. You have to use its inefficiency – make him live in doubt, make him worry for where the next phone call is coming from. I know it's already started. I know because I carried on watching, waiting for the next bus that never came. It's not much. It's barely anything at all – when you said it against all the harm he perpetrated. What he must have done to countless others. But it's a start. That's why I'm telling you all this. I want it to be set down. So others can learn. So others can take heart. So others can fight in the way I've had to fight. It's not as if you're going to do all the work for me – no offence, I know this is for a degree, but that's not what I have in mind. What I'm telling you is really only a first draft. To try to get my thoughts in order. I'm going to write something much more ambitious. That's why I'm signing up for every peak slot – to give myself time to concentrate on it later. It's going to have my personal experiences, but mixed with more theoretical material. It's going to show the structures of power. But for now this will have to do.

Dad said the words we'd prepared, when I took him to the station. He kept it simple just like I told him. He did fairly well, if I must be honest. Even if I could tell his heart wasn't really in it, I doubt the police noticed. They're not the sharpest tools in the box. They're police. We'd done our homework – we explained how it wasn't the kind of abuse that left visible scars.

S walked differently – I can tell you that – from the moment he got the letter calling him in. To get to hear from my friend with inside contacts that they were pressing charges was more than I could hope for. For a split second I thought I might almost start trusting the system. It's a bit strange, really, when you come to think about how it is for our generation – those moments of sheer joy are so rare we don't know what to do with them when they come along. It didn't last, naturally. The pandemic delayed everything – so much the better. This drags it out. If he doesn't get off, he doesn't get off – if he gets off, he still doesn't get off. The front garden was overgrown by the time the wife came back. After a while I started to lose interest in her. I'm busy in the research phase – whenever I have a moment. Sometimes I worry about a car swerving into the bike lane and sending me flying – when I still have all these ideas in my head. I've said what I've wanted for the time being – at least there's that. Do you ever get that feeling – the feeling you're going to sleep well tonight? Dad's perked up at long last. Started sleeping well enough to be back snoring. Got his appetite back. Just last week I asked him if he could tell what was special about the greens. He shrugged. *That olive oil*, I said. *I found the bottle.* It was symbolic – a way to draw a line under it all.

B I

I last saw S in a service station Little Chef – of all places.
An old friend was putting him up temporarily – an artist,
so loose enough morals, is how he put it to me, joking
without laughing. She lived in the country. He could stay
at mine for as long as he needed, I told him – but crowds
made him nervous. He did want to see me, he said – he
really did. I felt it, fell for it, rushed, when he suggested
meeting at the service station, just off Junction 17, where
there was sure to be nobody. Relic of bygones, S said,
when we sat down on the red plastic chairs – they
wobbled beneath us, every screw loose or gone. The last
Little Chef closed shortly after we met – I read about it
the other day. We sat in silence till something caught his
eye. He gestured, with a wry smile, to a dismal-looking
hotel by the parking bay reserved for heavy vehicles. *Hotel
Frank.* The dusk was drawing in, the neon sign came on,
flickering. Dancing girls. Only three of the letters worked.
H, he said significantly, *O, F. HOF.* It took me a second.
Fire? I asked. *Hole of Fire*, S confirmed. I put my hand over
his – he didn't pull away. *It'll just be like before*, he said,
*when a new element transforms the world we made – which we
presumed would go on for ever. And just like before, we'll figure
out which organisms adapt to the new reality.*

He finally ran through all the details. Like he was reeling off a shopping list. Told me more than he had on the phone, but with much more control, so I came away feeling I'd been given less. The story was already growing a protective casing. Not a story that vindicated him – a story that punished him, in ways he could live with, in ways that made him the butt of a cosmic joke. *Don't be so hard on yourself, S*, I said. We both knew the form of the words was all that mattered. *I'm not being hard on myself*, he said. *I can barely see myself, looking down from this height.* His hand was still in my hand. I thought it might get clammy like mine – but it just stayed cold. I thought he might snatch it away – perhaps that would've been better. Sensation slowly drained out of my own hand. Like that day under the bedframe, shredding football magazines. Forgetting where my body ended and his began. How many times had we touched, in the intervening years? We always greeted one another with a hug. But we'd figured out a way to hug without touching – the way men do.

I noticed the waitress. We'd been there for twenty minutes – she must have finally accepted we weren't going away and came over to us. She'll have been made redundant not long afterwards. I wonder where she is now. A nice smile not quite buried by terrible lipstick. S gave me the fatal gift of being interested in everyone. *We only have the apple pie*, she said with a smile. Perhaps it wasn't a smile. She didn't seem able to change her expression. I used to like it when people mistook us for lovers. *Then we'll share an apple pie*, I said – S wasn't helping. He resumed, without missing a beat, as she walked off – ever more clipped. His lawyer reckoned he'd probably get off – in large part because his case revealed structural failings in the care system. If the press got hold of it, it would be terrible for all parties. I bit my tongue – when there was a lot I could have told him about the care system.

According to the lawyer, they'd probably find a way just to give him a ticking-off and hush it up. Lawyers were paid to do that, he said – keep up the clients' morale. All the same, there probably was a decent chance. That he'd get off. He said 'get off' as if it were the worst punishment imaginable. I looked down at the apple pie – to wait for it to cool down and to have something to look at. Its latticework. Everything's intricate if you look at it closely enough. *I'll form a moral judgement*, I thought, *when this apple pie has cooled down – in a million years*.

Stay with me, I'd told S on the phone. *Stay with me* – over and over. The stupid reiteration I'd always had on my lips – never been able to say it. Now, saying it, it turned out to mean something different. Fumbling for the keys, scrunching my neck so as to keep talking, while I turned the key in the ignition, my car too old for Bluetooth, my heart still racing from the minutes beforehand, when I'd phoned S, over and over, on his mobile phone, until the painful sound of the unanswered ringing gave way to something else – the high tone, straight to answerphone. Straight to S's pre-recorded voice, which joked and charmed while he was killing himself, I knew he was doing it, hanging his head in a noose, without a plea, without a complaint, without a note. I got out old address books and found a landline that surely must have been disconnected, like all the landlines in the world. It was my last idea before the police, and I imagined S wanted the police less than anything. It went straight to answerphone. This time I left a message, knowing he wouldn't hear it, so free at last to tell him to let me care for him. There was a click, and S was with me. The landline hadn't been disconnected. He'd heard me, from wherever he'd been slumped or collapsed. I berated him. He was sorry, he replied, he was sure I was phoning to tell him I wanted nothing more to do with him. *S*, I said, *you idiot*. I was crying with happiness. I drove with the phone wedged between my shoulder and ear. Nearly went into the back of someone when I merged from the slip road. Sat waiting in the car park, for him to come to me. And now the steam rose from the pulverized apples. *The very worst thing*, S said slowly, *about being charged for something you didn't do — walking free on all the things you did.*

I squeezed his hand. Asked cautiously how A4 had reacted — she was the one missing part of the story he'd just told. S had met my gaze until that point — almost as a kind of challenge. Now he dropped it. *S*, I said, *what did she say — surely she can help, in some way?* He was silent. The garbled message she'd left me — when I hadn't known she even had my number, which had made me so worried for S that I called his landline — suddenly made a different kind of sense. *Please*, I said, *please don't tell me she doesn't know.* Me and my stupid begging rhetorical questions. *S*, I said — for want of something to say. He spoke only when I'd given up hope — telling me she thought he was a common-or-garden adulterer. He enjoyed the phrase. Common-or-garden. Coughed it out, like a ball of phlegm. I waited for the tears that at any minute I thought would start to form at the edges of his eyes. Hysterical tears. Saw the clown dancing while we sat on other plastic chairs, decades ago, convened by our mothers.

S, I said, *you have to tell her. Whatever's happened between the two of you, she still cares for you. — You think it's better*, he asked — now he was suddenly eager to reply — *you think the* truth *is better?* Fixed me again with the challenge of his face. *S*, I told him, *it could hardly be worse.* He looked at me, calmly waiting for my evidence that it couldn't be worse. I was suddenly flustered. All I could do was repeat it couldn't be worse. The truth — of who he was. Maybe I should have said *what.What you are.* But that's how it came out. *The truth of who you are.*

He gazed at me placidly. Like he wasn't going to dig me out of the hole I'd dug. That I'd dug without knowing, to bury us both. And I finally grasped it, what I have no one to share with — apart from you. That the truth was the one thing that he'd never be able to offer, in his defence. It wasn't just the nature of that truth — his need to satisfy others. That was long since old news. It was something different. It was the fact he might be discharged. Sent away scot-free. That he might make his confession and be pardoned, walk away a free man. Walk away with his unbearable freedom. To never, never be punished. Not by the courts — not by us — not by the people who, even now, couldn't take their needy hand away from his cold hand. He could never expose himself to the possibility he'd be forgiven. Forgiveness would be the worst fate of all. By accepting it, he'd have to confess he was just like all the rest. That he too had a need. A need for care. I saw it all – the verdict was neither here nor there. I see it. His hand in mine. The hotel lettering flickering in the dusk. The Little Chef that no longer exists – the apple pie slowly cooling.

A4

We're out walking in the park. I must say it feels very naughty, like sneaking out from school. Yes – I'm talking to the secrets lady. That's what she calls you. The secrets lady – you live in the magic box. I'm trying to keep her away from smartphones as long as I possibly can. No easy task. She caught me recording a message the other day – I told her Mummy was filling the magic box with secrets. She has some she wants to give you. Hold on just a second – do you want to tell your secret to the magic lady? OK, OK. She's gone shy. Shy of the magic box. She had so much to tell you a moment ago! She asked if you had eyes and I said lovely eyes. If you get high-pitched gobbledygook about the evil potion later in the day, you'll know it's from her. She makes it from leaves and mud – she feels bad because she thinks she's turned the neighbour's cat evil. Maybe potions would be a blessed relief for you. After what you have to sit through.

Sometimes I wonder whether you could still hear me – in the spaces between pressing stop and record. One more secret for the magic box.

*

She's run off. There's a delicious chill in the air. Or maybe it's just me. Screw it – I want to tell someone, so I will. I've started seeing someone these past two weeks. I know we shouldn't – I'm sorry, I should feel guilty but I don't. He's stayed over twice. Both times he left his clothes scattered on the floor. I tried the tops on for size. They fit me better than they do him. He laughed – had to agree. Strange to talk about him. In all our time together, I never said a single word – not even to my closest friends – about my relationship with S. Which is why it all came tumbling out of me. S liked to pick out clothes for me. He had an eye for what looked good. As soon as he took it from the clothes rack, I felt sure the outfit was made for me. Never doubted it, for as long as I wore it. The clothes I wear now – and those I find on the floor – feel difficult. They fit well enough – but I always know I could be wearing other clothes. There's a distance between me and what I've put on. It doesn't feel bad. It feels good.

A3

I'm sorry I wasn't in touch sooner. I can't pretend it's
because I was busy – however busy I was. Telling you how
bad S was would have made me have to face up to it. Face
up to how bad it was. For two or three days it was very
bad. Even S had to admit it. I'd dug out one of those old
indestructible Nokias – put it on the plate for one of the
meals I left in the garden three times a day. I waited, on
tenterhooks, for hours. You forget how slow it was to text
on those phones. Sometimes I thought about recording
you a message. I had this stupid thought that whether he
lived or died, at the bottom of my garden, didn't matter,
to you – might even prove a distraction, from whatever
you're trying to get straight. I hope you got it straight –
and it turns out he's alive.

    It's bad, he texted at last. *Nobody has any real idea how to
treat this.* I felt like an idiot – paracetamol on the plate,
endless jugs of fresh water. For three or four days I was
convinced he was going to die – all because he wouldn't
tell me early enough he needed to be taken to the
hospital. Just like him. I know he's afraid of the outside. I
knew it when we walked together the other night. Feels a
lifetime ago. For the first time in my life, all I wanted was
to care for my brother. For the first time in my life I

thought my brother might need to be cared for by me. The children sensed it. They never said a word – children are supernatural. I had to get out of the house and so went round to Mum's. Finally insisted on clearing out some of her junk in the upstairs bedroom. I used to sleep there looking up at the stars on the mobile – now it's just filled with bright plastic boxes of random junk from our past, stacked on top of one another. Sometimes I wonder where Mum got them. For a disorganized person she must have had a moment of organization – deciding to buy random bright plastic boxes, to dump all the random stuff inside. They'll survive the apocalypse, those boxes. Social distancing gave me an excuse. If she was there with me, sorting through, we'd just have reminisced – then put it all back in a different random order.

I found things that could have belonged to S or me. Erasers, playing cards come loose from the deck, plastic figurines. All these tapes we used to record. The old stereo still worked. Both of us being disc jockeys – putting on silly voices, ad-libbing the stupidest things that came into our heads. That the decision had been taken, S shouted in a high-pitched radio presenter voice, *to start 1991 immediately – even though it's only September – because 1990 has been going so badly! And now to our special correspondent!* The special correspondent collapsed in giggles. The special correspondent was me. We tuned in across the bandwidths at random – shortwave and longwave were best – pressed record whenever we found something that didn't fit with whatever went before. *Mum!* we shouted. *Come and be interviewed! – Mum's tired*, she shouted back in her long-suffering voice. This is what I couldn't tell you earlier. When I didn't know whether he'd live or die. The things I want to tell you more than anything – the things that don't mean anything. That are allowed not to mean anything.

I put the cassettes on the plate – next to the stupid sandwiches. No idea whether there was a lead for the old cassette player we put in the garden shed. Listening to it wasn't the point. The next day he seemed a little better. To judge from his three-word text. The next a little better, and the following day too. The day after that, when I came to pick up the plate, I saw the bundle of paper, folded neatly, put under the plate, to stop it blowing away in the wind. Addressed to the boys. Dated yesterday. The title, written with a flourish. *Snail and Snake*. I'm going on in a way I normally never do, because I'm putting off reading it you. It's the only way I'll be able to read it – to say it out loud to you. I don't know why that is. Just give me a minute to find it.

Dear children. This is a story about Snake and Snail.

I'm sorry – I can't do it. Not right now. I hate the sound of my voice. After a while you forget you're speaking – but then it comes back to you. You must have all these voices in your head. They must start to sound like one another. S told me stories in the morning when we were young. We used to do musical chairs. Musical beds. I hated sleeping on my own – I'd have nightmares. Got into bed with my parents. My dad complained I kicked them in my sleep. He got into S's bed. He had the double bed from when our first grandma died. Dad left for work in the morning. Then I'd crawl into bed with S. It was still warm from Dad's body. So strange to think of this years on. At the time you never give it a second thought. I used to wonder what they ever talked about. S and Dad. I asked S to give me a story. He said he would if I gave him tic-tic. I can't remember what it even means. Must be short for 'tickle'. And so I stroked his back while he told me a new story. Then Dad was gone and there was no more tic-tic and no more stories. And S never asked me for anything again – until the plates of paracetamol.

C7

Well, dear girl, we have come to it at last – to my final chance to confess precisely what I had S do to me. I would

like to drag this out for ever, to stall for time, to
circumlocute for eternity, to soak in a hot tub of
synonyms, to play two-chord vamps which arpeggiate
beyond the horizon, die infinitesimally in a golden sea of
relative clauses, filibuster the deadline until there is
nothing to say, bar the blue sky of day – endless silence,
the sky blue of no words. Let me fetch myself a glass of
water or something stiffer.

It is a shame that my lung capacity no longer suffices.
Were you to permit paper and pen, I could go like the
early modern stylists whom I have so loved over these
lonely years, Lancelot Andrewes, Thomas Browne. The
syntax of early seventeenth-century prose has a supple
rigour that reminds me of the muscled lads I used to
know, too, too long ago. My heart raced when I read them
to S, until the thought of losing him or of him finding this
all so silly and antique made me close the book with a
gulp in my throat.

Yes, there is no getting around it. I will tell you my
riddle. My little koan, palimpsest, those mysterious
griffons in the margins of the incunabulum, trapped
behind shatterproof glass. You know what the
archaeologists nearly always find, when they finally fit a
code to those mysterious letterings? Fragments of wax
tablets say things like, *Lucius Caecilius Iucundus has just*

popped to the shops for a loaf of bread. Shaldrick is an old dog
with a flaccid member. He visits brothels just to impress the
other men, he will never get it up – so says Baldassare. They say,
in other words, that dusty bones were just like you and
me, so long as they had flesh upon them.

Well, then, yes – out with it. I will tell you all. Dear
Boy would approach me, from the side – it had to be the
right side, for some reason the left never worked, though
I am receptive to new ideas – and with his soft hand
ruffled my hair. I have alluded previously to the gesture.
Well, there was no more and no less to it than that. I have
been finding ten thousand ways around telling you – Dear
Boy simply ruffled what remains of an old man's hair.
Dear girl, forgive these trivial skittles.

A I

Thank you. For hearing me. For not telling me more than
I needed to know.

B I

I had a weird dream last night. Have yours gone strange? I
heard someone say the other day our dreams have been
synchronizing in lockdown. The only way for us to get

close to one another. Or maybe it's just our group unconscious being starved of material. I'll tell you – even though nobody likes to hear other people's dreams – just because I didn't want to sign off with Little Chef. *Sign off*. There I go – giving myself airs and graces.

Engineers had designed a chip – you implanted it in your head to relive memories. You saw them – felt them – exactly as they'd been when you lived them for the first time. The government had commissioned them for seniors – a cost-efficient way to help them cope with isolation. But the technology flopped. People found the accurate memories weren't as nice as they remembered them. They preferred to remember it all wrongly. So the government abandoned the project. Mothballed the remaining stock, which languished in warehouses.

Until another generation discovered them years later. Started using the chips differently, against the guidelines, which stated that users should sit in a quiet darkened space – a bit like what I've been doing with you. They started living memories as they went about their daily lives. Parallel streams. Past and present collapsed into one another. You think young people today are distracted – you haven't seen anything yet. It became a viral craze – to put together choice combinations of past and present. They called it *rhyming*. The manufacturer's share price rebounded. People wrote advice columns. *If you're having difficulties in the bedroom – watch the sex you used to have. With the same person – or with another!* Then there were more out-of-the-way combinations. People aimed for the perfect arrangement of moments – the way you'd arrange a salad. *Relive your first handstand – at the precise moment that you take a hairpin bend. Only be careful to keep hold of the steering wheel!*

Me? I was looking down on it all – the way you do, in dreams, not yet a person. But then out of nowhere I was in it. I was implanting the chip. I was sitting in a pub, with S, towards closing time. And I was watching the smile that wouldn't play on his lips – that wouldn't play in the present, but which I saw, on the other channel, in another pub, another closing time. There's no point in holding this message back. I gave myself away a long time ago.

A3

Dear children. This is a story about Snake and Snail. Snake is a snake and Snail is a snail. You might think these names indicate a certain lack of imagination on behalf of their parents – you'd be right. Not every little rascal can have such parents as nice and as clever as yours. You might have thought Snake and Snail would be friends. They did share certain things in common. They both took great pleasure in spelling the capital 'S' of their names – when Snake slithered and Snail slathered across the ground, they both left very similar trails. But it's true for animals – just like it's true for humans, who as we know from the animal game are the funniest animals of all – that individuals are prevented from discovering how much they have in common because of the silly groups and herds to which they belong. Groups, herds, cool kids, nerds – you know exactly what I mean. Well, animal species are similar – it's hard for even the most beautiful friendships to cross gaps. Two creatures from different species can be on the verge of a nice chat – before they realize they're supposed to be chasing or being chased.

But let me get down to the plot – your mother didn't give me much paper. Every good story should have a plot. (Though, really, your mother should have given me more paper. You can tell her that from me.) It was true that Snake and Snail also had some important differences. Snake's favourite colour was green – Snail's was brown. Snake got up late – Snail was more of an early riser. Snake liked sun – Snail liked damp. They had such different routines and such different favourite places that their paths rarely crossed. There was one more very important reason why they never became friends. Snake really liked to eat things – and Snail would be very easily eaten. His shell was a lovely pearl colour, but it had seen better days – its cracks were the perfect invitation for Snake's slithery tongue.

So their paths rarely crossed – until once upon a time. Yes, 'once upon a time' is supposed to come right at the start – but I'm a forgetful uncle, please forgive me. Late, they say, is better than never. That was in fact what Snail was saying to himself, as he slathered along. *Better late than never.* Because, you see, it had been one of those strange days, weather-wise – when it's sunny, then rainy, then cloudy, then sunny again. A good old-fashioned English day. Snail's alarm clock hadn't rung, because Snail's alarm clock was a friendly bird who only sang when the sun came out. (Incidentally, doorbells are all little birds trapped inside a small box that are made to chirrup when someone presses the buzzer. You should try to free them.) In any case, Snail was slathering along, thinking to himself, *I'm going to be late, I'm going to be late* – even though he had nowhere particular to get to. The sun shone very brightly all of a sudden, as if trying to make up for its own late start. It shone so brightly it woke Snake up, even though he was ordinarily a very late riser. He rolled around on his belly, which was very enjoyable, because unlike you and me his belly was on every side of his body.

After a while he thought, *Enough basking in the sun, time for some food*. Which was when their paths crossed.

Snail was reflected in Snake's green eyes. Snake was reflected in Snail's brown eyes. What they saw – reflected in each other's eyes – was very similar, but they both instinctively froze, because that's what being part of a species makes you do. Snail froze in terror. Snake froze because he saw prey. Only he wasn't really hungry. He'd actually been slowly digesting a delicious twelve-course meal while he basked in the sun. Snail, fortunately for him, knew nothing about the twelve-course meal – it would have given him a heart attack. He tried to tiptoe away – or whatever snails do without toes to tip on, but rather those slimy pads, which are actually quite nice to touch if you can put from your mind how slimy they are. *Stop right there!* shouted Snake. Well, it wasn't so much a shout as a sleepy hiss. *Where are you going in such a hurry?* And he rubbed his sleepy eyes with his tail, which is one of the prime advantages of having a tail.

That's it, thought Snail, *I'm done for.* He was retreating into that pearly shell of his that had seen better days – he knew it wouldn't save him. *Mmmmfffmmmm,* he said, by way of reply – before realizing his voice was echoing so much that Snake wouldn't be able to hear a word. So he pushed his antennae slowly out – just to take the air –

then slowly, very slowly, he pushed out his face. *Well, hello*, said Snake. *When the sun comes out, it's lovely — I'm so well sheltered under this tree. You should come and see.*

Now there was no way Snail was going to take Snake up on that offer. He'd read enough fairy tales to know the way these things turn out. *Actually*, he said, his antennae twitching. *Actually, I'm in a bit of a rush.* Snake laughed at that. A soft, hissing laugh. *Are you scared of Snake? If so, you might want to think about why you're judging him — without really knowing him. But can you explain*, he said to Snail, *on a day like today, why you need ever move at all?*

Snail thought hard about the question. So hard that he forgot he might be on the verge of being eaten. That's the thing about interesting questions — they take up all the space in your head. *I keep moving*, he said, *because wherever I go, I'm always at home — with the aid of my trusty pearly shell.* Then he had a question for Snake. By this point he'd forgotten all about retracting his head. *Don't you get bored sitting here all day, doing nothing, sunning yourself?* he asked.

But my home doesn't stay the same, replied Snake. *You don't need to travel to change, you know. That's where I'm special. I'm regularly shedding my skin — and every time it grows back, it's more and more beautiful. I can never predict which marbled patterns I'll make.* Snail saw the marbled patterns coiling around him. He panicked, began to run away as fast as he could. It wasn't very fast. He was a snail, after all, and some things can't be changed simply by wishing them so. Snake's laughter sounded like the rustling of leaves. *Don't worry*, Snake said, *you're not my type. I don't think I could digest your shell.*

In that case, said Snail, his panic beginning to subside, *can I show you something? I'm afraid you'll have to get out from under that tree, though.* Snake yawned dubiously. *Very well*, said Snake. *If you tell me what we can expect to find on the menu. I only get out of bed for dinner. — There's no dinner*, said Snail, who was beginning to relax enough to get a bit irritated at his new friend. *Was that what I just called him, in my head?* Snail thought. *My friend? — No dinner*, grumbled Snake. *What else is there in the world — apart from sleep, which I can perfectly well do here? — Follow me and you'll see*, said Snail, who took off as fast as he could — not terrifically fast — with Snake following behind him, making irritated noises and pretending he was struggling to keep up. Little children sometimes pretend that they can't keep up when they want to be carried. I'll let you into a secret. Sometimes adults do the same. *You're going too fast!* shouted Snake. *But I'm a snail!* yelled Snail.

After all the grumbling, they finally turned off the main path to a little road that ran along the side of a small brook. On the ground lay the sodden slimy leaves that Snail loved to glide over and under and on which he sometimes – if he was feeling peckish – had a munch. Droplets lay on the leaves and the flowers and the grass. The sunlight danced on the brook and on the puddles of water. It danced so much it forgot it was really supposed to stay in the sky. There were dragonflies – like those we saw by the pond last year – swooping overhead. *I love to come here on days like this*, said Snail. *After the rain, when all the little creatures, some littler even than me, come back out again. I watch the whole scene from the safety of my shell.*

Beautiful, said the Snake, grudgingly, *though I don't see much for dinner. – Please be quiet about dinner*, Snail was about to say – only then he saw a strange look in Snake's eyes. Snake's body was shaking. His forked tongue was hissing something too soft to hear. *It's starting*, he said – finally forcing out the words in a little voice that was the opposite of scary. *What's starting?* asked Snail, who was pretending not to have seen his friends the beetles, who do like to repeat the same gossip over and over again. *I'm shedding*, replied Snake. *I'm shedding. It's never happened like this. When I'm so far from home.*

Snake's skin started to expand and move. *I'm scared*, he said, in a tiny voice. *Don't worry*, said Snail, in the biggest voice he could manage. When he heard how big it sounded, he had the confidence to make it bigger. *I'm here with you. You're not in any danger here. I'll protect you. —* *Thank you*, said Snake. *Stay with me, please. I'm going to be quiet for a bit.*

He was quiet. His skin peeled clean off. This had only ever happened before in his special place – the place where he was protected, where he didn't need to show his vulnerability, where he could look out at the trees and the flowers, thinking how they changed too, but they always came back. And then he could zoom around on his slick new tummy. But this time everything felt strange and new. He was exposed to it all. He felt the breeze blowing on his fresh layer of skin – the sun bringing out his new mottled patterns. And he found, to his great surprise, that he liked feeling the world in this way – this unexpected way, this unexpected world. He moved closer to Snail. *Snail*, Snake said, *I'm back. — Who the hell are* you? replied Snail, before bursting into a laugh that sounded like rain plashing into a stream. *Sorry*, Snail said, *I know perfectly well who you are, you don't look* that *different.* But then a thought hit him. *Sometimes life is like that – you're joking one minute and thinking hard the next. Sometimes you're thinking because of the joking.* Snail was reflecting on how he, too, was the same – only different. He'd been so concerned for his new friend – just a moment ago – that he'd quite forgotten his usual routine. He'd quite forgotten to watch the beauty of the world from the safety of his shell. Like Snake, he was exposed – like Snake, he liked it. And so, this turns out to have been the story of how Snake and Snail showed one another the meaning of a home.

Appendices

The following three documents have been included as further evidence for consideration in relation to the audio transcript. For the provenance and nature of the third document, see the 'Ethical Considerations' subsection of supporting document 4.3, pp. 17–22.

Appendices

Care homes defend legal right for patients to access prostitutes

Investigations ongoing to establish whether care homes hired **SEX WORKERS** to offer 'special services' to disabled residents

Chris Shales for the Weekly Chronicle*
Published: 10:33 GMT, 23 March 2017; updated: 13:26 GMT, 28 March 2017

A whistle-blower, speaking exclusively and on condition of anonymity to the *Weekly Chronicle*, confirmed the practice was widespread.

---

*The editorial team of the *Weekly Chronicle* took down this article shortly after publication: an archived version remains accessible at https://web.archive.org/web/20160529673240/http://www.weeklychronicle.co.uk/escort-of-law/.

In the wake of the revelations, **TWO** separate county councils, located in the South-East of England, have launched separate investigations into the possible 'exploitation and abuse' of vulnerable people.

A fellow care worker, who also wished to remain anonymous, **DEFENDED** the practice: 'The fact is, sex workers are fully legal, and there is no way we can satisfy patients' needs in this area.

'Many of our patients suffer from dementia or other conditions that remove inhibitions, but not sex drive. Every care worker knows how hard it can be to deal with a patient who turns aggressive due to unexpressed needs.'

But not everyone agrees. Several local councillors are believed to have written with concerns to the Care Quality Commission, the independent regulator set up to monitor all health and social care services in England. These concerns have led to the current investigations.

'We called these sessions "special visits",' the whistle-blower elaborated to the *Weekly Chronicle*. Staff would apparently leave 'do not disturb' signs, to indicate an escort's visit. 'We borrowed them from the hotel next door. It made me sick to my stomach.'

The whistle-blower also expressed concerns about privacy and vetting. 'Whenever I asked questions, nobody seemed to know where these workers came from. They just showed up on the computer system. Management shrugged their shoulders and said they came through "third-party consultants".

'Quite frankly, it is outrageous that taxpayers' money is being spent to indulge the lewd fantasies of vulnerable people.'

Some residents are understood to have paid for the escorts themselves, through some combination of pensions, savings or benefits.

But in a further twist to the scandal, other sex workers are believed to have been hired through an 'experimental' treatment plan, which central government awarded to a number of county councils in partnership with ▮▮▮▮▮, a for-profit provider of care services.

▮▮▮▮▮ is already **REELING** from a series of scandals over the past few years, following a string of revelations of bullying, harassment and physical abuse. The company was **SLAMMED** by the Care Quality Commission in 2015 for 'serious failings of managerial oversight', yet had their registration extended for a further ten years.

According to the whistle-blower, three separate care homes participated in the pilot scheme, at a total cost of **£2.5 MILLION**. Sex workers would routinely visit the facilities, each of which provides accommodation for between 50 and 75 people with neurological problems, learning difficulties, and serious mental health conditions.

On one occasion graphic video content was shown to a selected group of seniors.

One prostitute said: 'I visit these homes more and more often. Staff turn a blind eye. To be perfectly honest, they beat my regular punters.'

A spokesman for the Care Quality Commission said: 'We are committed to overseeing the best-possible care for those at need. Third-party providers are an essential part of this mission. We cannot comment on any pending investigations.'

CPS

████████████████

Crown Prosecution Service
Rose Court
2 Southwark Bridge
London SE1 9HS

Telephone: ███████████
Facsimile: ███████████
Switchboard: 020 3357 0000

Our Reference: █████████

To: ████████████
████████████████
████████████████
████████████████

15 October 2020

Dear ██████████

Thank you for your letter of 12 October 2020. May I begin
this response by apologising for the reply to your original

letter of 17 September 2020. This was composed by a junior member of the Correspondence Unit, to whom your initial correspondence had been redirected in error. Given the severity both of the case concerned, and of the supporting documents attached to your letter, we should not have responded in what may have appeared a summary manner. The fact that the Crown Prosecution Service is currently facing an unprecedented volume of casework, at a time when its resources are tested as never before given the ongoing COVID-19 pandemic, in no way justifies these oversights.

I read both your original letter of 17 September, and your elaboration of 10 October, with great interest. Let me put on record my admiration for your attempts to explore the many circumstances concerning a complex case. Clearly a great amount of effort and consideration has gone into your research. I am nevertheless writing to confirm I have not read any of the transcript that you included with your letter of 17 September. I see no reason to doubt your claim that each of the interviewed parties would be happy for their testimonies to be used in a court of law. Nevertheless, the Crown Prosecution Service will not – indeed cannot – make use either of this transcript or of the interviews themselves, which you generously offer to make available. The public prosecutors have long been in the process of constructing their own case: there can be no 'parallel' investigation in this regard. The Crown Prosecution Service must always stand far removed from what might be construed – rightly or wrongly – as vigilantism. Despite your assurances, it is moreover impossible for the Crown Prosecution Service to verify that these interviews were conducted in a manner that meets legal thresholds of informed consent, and that they have not been manipulated in any way.

Finally, any prosecutor that were to consider the information that you have provided would be obliged, under the Criminal Procedure and Investigations Act of 1996, to share any relevant information in good time with the defence counsel of the concerned party. You are of course welcome to share any material that you may wish with the defence.

Having followed this legal case so closely, you do not require me to tell you that public comment or speculation may endanger a fair and independent trial. You are certainly aware that the first jury had to be discharged for prejudicial publicity on 4 December 2019, following the publication of several media reports concerning the case. Further comments posted on social media platforms were also found to have generated adverse publicity and to therefore be in contempt of court – a prosecutable offence. The ongoing disruptions of the COVID-19 pandemic have delayed our appointment of a new jury. May I take this opportunity to remind you how vitally important it is that each juror approach the *relevant* evidence without preconceptions.

Let me end by repeating my great respect for the work that you have undertaken. I am fully convinced by your stated claim to have explored 'the details and complexities of a case that produces extremes of public opinion'. This surely bodes well for the success of your present and future research projects, in which detail and complexity are rightfully rewarded. The Crown Prosecution Service, however, must remain committed to the establishing of guilt, and to the bringing of offenders to justice.

Yours sincerely,

██████████████

heroacle

hey guys, big news   8:32pm

heroacle

anyone . . .   8:42pm

heroacle

ffs I thought you loners were all
permanently online . . .   9:12pm

fryman9

😂   9:17pm

j2021ca

hey @heroacle   9:19pm

j2021ca

ffs I thought you loners were all
permanently online . . .   9:12pm

uh so we are . . . it's just there are so many
convos to follow   9:20pm

occupy3058261

uh so we are . . . it's just there are
so many convos to follow   9:20pm

hehe it's like being in the pub irl   9:21pm

fryman9

Remember pubs? 🍺 9:22pm

j2021ca

I vaguely remember tables 9:23pm

squarecircle33

BRING BACK ANALOGUE TABLES 9:23pm

heroacle

guys . . . nice that you're finally here,
but . . . 9:24pm

occupy3058261

right you had some big news . . . 9:25pm

fryman9

If it ever fucking begins 9:26pm

heroacle

It's about S's trial 9:27 pm

fryman9

fuck it **@heroacle** we said we were
going to keep our mouths shut
about that until it finally begins 9:27pm

squarecircle33

No we said that we were going to
stop speculating when we had
nothing to say 9:27pm

heroacle
Right   9:27pm

heroacle
well I have something to say   9:27pm

heroacle
Heard from my source today that
S is going to plead guilty   9:28pm

fryman9
you're kidding   9:29pm

squarecircle33
No way   9:29pm

occupy3058261
Verification?   9:30pm

heroacle
Verification?   9:30pm

What am I, the fucking New York
Times?   9:31pm

occupy3058261
Just that we've gotten our hopes
up before   9:31pm

heroacle
yeah well it's the same source
as before   9:32pm

heroacle

The junior law clerk   9:32pm

heroacle

He was right on literally everything
before now. The trial collapsing.
The stuff disappearing from the
media.   9:33pm

fryman9

But why the fuck would S do that   9:34pm

j2021ca

Why the fuck would he do that   9:34pm

squarecircle33

#greatmindsthinkalike   9:34pm

heroacle

Beats me   9:35pm

heroacle

All I know is that it's S's decision
and that his lawyer is fuming   9:35pm

heroacle

He did NOT advise this course
of action   9:36pm

fryman9

But it makes no sense.   9:37pm

squarecircle33

He would probably have got off 9:37pm

fryman9

Maybe Covid has some side
effects we don't know about 9:37pm

j2021ca

Honesty 9:37pm

occupy3058261

Conscience 9:37pm

fryman9

LMAO 9:37pm

squarecircle33

There's probably a more cynical
motivation 9:39pm

squarecircle33

Like he wants to take the punishment
so that he can write a prison memoir
about it 9:40pm

fryman9

My Struggle 9:40pm

j2021ca

😂 9:40pm

fryman9
Yeah that title's taken 9:40pm

heroacle
But that's not all . . . 9:41pm

heroacle
guys? 9:43pm

occupy3058261
@**heroacle** just say it, we're not
going to sit and beg 9:43pm

heroacle
On the very same day that the
CPS get notified about this 9:44pm

heroacle
The principal witness says they
won't testify 9:44pm

squarecircle33
wtf? 9:45pm

j2021ca
You mean ███████? 9:46pm

heroacle
yeah 9:46pm

fryman9

████████ is going to be maaaad   9:47pm

fryman9

I mean even madder than usual   9:47pm

j2021ca

But so . . .   9:48pm

j2021ca

What happens?   9:48pm

j2021ca

If he's pleaded guilty then we don't
need a witness right?   9:48pm

squarecircle33

Or if there isn't a witness then
there isn't anything to plead guilty to   9:49pm

heroacle

Right. That's the problem. Both
statements are correct   9:49pm

heroacle

My law clerk source tells me that
it's been total meltdown today   9:50pm

heroacle

They've got out all the precedents   9:50pm

heroacle

Trying to figure out what they can do 9:50pm

fryman9

So just to get this straight 9:51pm

fryman9

You're telling me that a man has pleaded guilty to a charge that no longer officially exists? 9:51pm

squarecircle33

Sort of sums up the world we're living in 9:52pm

occupy3058261

😵 9:52pm

j2021ca

Shoot me now 9:52pm

Acknowledgements

Thanks are due to my agent, Jess Lee, who early saw shape in a formless thing. To my editor, Bobby Mostyn-Owen, for their always incisive suggestions, and for the incitement to fight back against their always incisive suggestions.

To Kate Samano and Kate Parker, whose eye for small changes changed the big notes, time and time again. To the whole team at Doubleday whose names I never learned, but who made the whole process seem to move – by magic! – all by itself.

To Rahul and Deepti, for the delicious odour that wafted through a courtyard in lockdown (and everything that followed upon it). To Martin and Kiki: 'to his fool-cum-king she's his wisest queen'. To James, for The Peacock, two decades ago, and everything since. To Jenny, who helped me see how to make the book better, by saying nothing, only looking at me in a certain way.

To Katy, for being such a splendid clown. To David and Breeze, for good cheer that never grew cold. To Steve, whose voice only carried more clearly across the years and oceans between us.

To my parents, Helen and John, for encouraging me to keep an open mind and an open heart. To my sister, Alison, for the bank of memories into which I could plug myself, whenever I felt down (remember Merlin 'Thumper' Bigfoot?).

To Augustin.

Even now, so late in the day, speaking at long last as myself, with the unimpeachable sincerity of The Acknowledger, I hear another voice, singing, to the tune of the dwarves in *Snow White*:

> *Inés, Inés,*
> *Remarkable princess,*
> *With a triple chin,*
> *And a cheeky grin,*
> *Inés, Inés, Inés, Inés . . .*

This book, then, is dedicated to Inés, and to her mother.

Ewan Gass is a writer, critic and teacher based in Munich. He was shortlisted for the 2020 *White Review* Short Story Prize. Other short fiction has appeared in *3:AM* and *Granta*.